THE WOMAN BEHIND THE WATERFALL

Leonora Meriel is the author of *The Woman Behind the Waterfall* and *The Unity Game*. She lives in Barcelona, London and Kyiv. She has two children. Read more about Leonora Meriel and her work at: www.leonorameriel.com.

The Woman Behind the Waterfall

LEONORA MERIEL

GRANITE CLOUD

Published by Granite Cloud 2016

ISBN 978-1-911079-23-1

Cover design by Anna Green

GRANITE CLOUD

To my mother Diana

The Woman Behind the Waterfall

PART ONE

1

I open my eyes to see falling white flowers.

I am lying on my back, a young girl dreaming in the springtime of Ukraine, and the branches of the lilac tree above me are moving from side to side in a warm wind. *Syringa, buzok, lilac* in a trembling morning light.

The sunshine touches my face as it tumbles between the bright leaves. It moves from side to side with the wind and brushes gently over my skin, painting it golden, shadow, golden, shadow. A girl in a white dress, painted gold and warm and springlight. I open my eyes and close them. This spring, the nights and days are stretching themselves out in a half-heat sleep, the garden is full of high grass and early poppies, and the fragrance of the lilac draws out the sunshine hours in a heavy flowered dream. Barely open, barely closed.

There is another scent here, quite distinct from the white star lilac. The smell of the black earth. I turn my head to the side, so that the sunshine is brushing just one cheek golden, and my skin is close down, touching the soil. Above me, the wind moves the leaves before my eyes between spectrums of light. White to gold, gold to white. I slowly turn my springtime head. Golden to black. I close my eyes. The smell of the dark earth enters my senses and I breathe deeply.

It is *Ukraina*. It is home.

I live in Bukovina, in a village that lies between the black and golden flats of farmland and the wolved forest peaks of the Carpathian Mountains. I am seven years old. The house where Mama and I live is a faded brick red, and our windows are painted in a cracked white and bright turquoise blue. There is a wooden gate with a broken latch that opens onto the dusty village street, and a path through our garden leading to a narrow white-painted bench next to the kitchen door. Our land stretches in layers of high grass and scattered flowers down to the woods below.

I am sitting now on the wooden bench, the *lavochka*, and I swing my warm legs up and down. Next to me, the kitchen door is open. Across the garden is the lilac tree and I watch as tiny flowers are carried down in the breeze, drifting to the ground below, to the pressed dark earth where I love to lie, daydreaming, gazing up into a panoply of lilac stars.

This garden, this spring, this dazzling sunlight, the sound of a solitary bird singing, feels like a dream shimmering around me. The white lilac, my thin dress, the constant deep smell of Ukrainian earth; it could all be a dream were it not for a streak of dirt on my skin and the touch of cold water when I wash it off. Cold water splashed from a silver bucket on a spring day. A dog barking in the distance. A faint smudge of dirt and my skin rising against the droplets. I look up into the light. Streaks of memory now forming against a background of falling gold.

Sometimes I prefer to sit in the tree above. A bird. A leaf. A single star from a cluster of lilac. I catch a thread of song across the garden and release myself into it, shift the girl into a quiet background and enter the breath of music, which carries me into the bird.

And for a moment I am that music, shimmering against the air, and then I am creating the music. It is I who am singing. I am within the spirit of the bird. And I look around me at the springtime garden and I know why I am singing. The insistent green that is everywhere! The birds that are returning to familiar gardens! The flowers exploding into bloom with every new instant of sunshine!

I look down and see that the lilac cups are filled to the brim with night-time dewdrops and I stop singing and urgently dip my head down and push my beak into the yellow centre to drink the delicious liquid. The scent and the taste are sunshine flowers and I dip again and again and splash my wings into the dew so that my feathers are sprayed with the droplets.

The rush of so many sensations makes me suddenly dizzy and I clasp the branch with my claw feet and open my wings, letting the warm wind calm me, blow my feathers dry.

I jerk my head from side to side, dark eyes darting around, and below I glimpse the outline of a girl, a star in a black-earth sky. I see her, a flower from the tree, a gleam of sunlight, me – a bird! And then I look up from the middle of the branch of bright leaves into the whiteness all around me. The wind touches my damp feathers. The river is not far. I turn my head, checking the air above and the girl below turns her cheek to one side. I open my wings and rise up out of the tree, flapping hard, a song gathering itself inside me. I fly towards the river.

A voice calls out to me in the garden.

I am swinging my legs out high from the narrow bench, my hands holding the edge of the wooden plank. Swing leg, swing leg. My head is warm with golden light. I put my hand up and touch my hair. Tangled curls. *Black like the soil*, as Mama says. A smell all around of heavy sunshine.

"An-ge-la!"

My mother's voice is calling. Tiny flowers fall around my shoulders as the three sounds move slowly towards me from the kitchen window, where Mama stands looking out at me. The lilac drifts like snow as the droplets of her voice push through the morning's heat, and I swing my legs up and down on the bench, which is covered in cracked paint, whitewashed, nails banged unevenly into rough planks. I imagine the reverberation of each nail. *Bang!* A blow, a shudder of wood changed forever. *Bang, bang, bang.* Swing the other brown leg. Every time I swing my leg, the bench is changed forever. The motion of my swing, my drifting thoughts on this flaking seat, the lilac that has fallen and touched my skin.

Mother's face is framed in the window, her golden-brown hair gathered on top of her head and pinned loosely. Her face is round and wide and flat, pale and winter. My own face – spring lilac, brushed with sunshine. The window is painted in whitewash like the bench, faint cracks and flakes coming loose from the wood, fading, deteriorating, every moment, I think, our lives passing by and through, opening and closing, and all the while they are quietly falling apart, disappearing into the dust around us.

Mother, deteriorating, calls, "An-ge-la!"

I stand up from the bench with the droplets of her voice covering me, and skip to the kitchen door. I stand halfway in the doorway so that she can see me through the window frame into the garden, and at the same time, in the kitchen. She laughs, her eyes creasing, hair tumbling from its pins, and she holds out her hand to me.

"I'm making a cake," she says.

4

Mama, Mamochka, Mamusya, Matenka moiya!

Mother's face, pale and winter, flat and wide and the most beautiful thing in the world to me. Mother's warm body like bread from the oven. Like a blanket around me on a dark, snowy morning, the cold well water in the midsummer dust. Mama, you are every comfort to every sorrow! I want to disappear into the dough of your body, pushing myself back in, you would roll and knead me into yourself and I would be safe forever.

The spring breeze lifts my hair in the doorway. I want to fly!

Mother hands me a jar of dark honey. On the kitchen table is a chipped bowl and I take a spoon from the drawer and stand over it. The honey is hard and grainy, almost black, and it smells alive, like the earth. Alive with growth, with work, with buckwheat, feelers, pollen, the weight of petals, the beating of wings, and now this dark, solid sweetness. The spoon bends as I dig it into the mass, and when I pull it out it is misshapen. I taste the honey with the tip of my tongue. It is alive, black, soil.

Mother's hands are sprinkled with flour, which she is pouring through a sieve. On the windowsill is a glass jar of sour cream. She passes it to me and I spoon the cream into the bowl on top of the honey and Mother comes to the table and checks the bowl and pours in the flour and a cup of chopped walnuts.

"Mix it, Angela," says Mother, and she lights the stove and I push the wooden spoon down to the bottom of the bowl and carefully fold in the cream and flour and the thick honey, and the kitchen will be growing hotter, and the inside heat will soon fill the room, moving all around and towards the window to meet the golden heat outside. An infinitesimal pause between them, trembling in their separateness before they merge, the scent of the baking cake and the scent of the lilac; rising dark honey and fallen white petals. I move the spoon around the bowl.

Mother opens the window.

"Angela, bring the rainwater."

The cake is rising in the oven, and I run outside to fetch the shallow metal bucket, which is balanced on top of an old rabbit hutch next to the outhouse shed. I carry it carefully into the kitchen and put it down on the wooden table. Mother is waiting for me, holding the comb that we share from the bedroom next door. I peer into the water to check for leaves and insects, and I dip my finger into it to catch a floating petal and a few flecks of dirt.

"It is time to brush your hair," says Mother. She pulls the loose strands out of the comb and drops them into the bucket of potato skins and scraps of purple beetroot. Three of its teeth are missing. She dips her hand into the rainwater and sprinkles it onto my hair and then she dips the broken comb into it and starts to run it through the wispy ends.

"There," she says as she combs, drawing out the curls, easing the tangles with her fingers. "Now your hair will always be beautiful." She sprinkles the water again over my head and she bends down and kisses my hair and the rainwater touches her lips and I shiver, because a drop of water has fallen onto my neck, and because her touch on me is the closest, safest feeling in the world.

"Mama," I say. "Just like you, Mama." And she touches her own hair quickly with her left hand, and then bends down to me again.

When she has finished with the rainwater, my hair woven into a long black rope, I take the bucket back to the shed and put it

6

carefully on top of the hutch. I dip my fingertips into the water and taste it. Warmish and like old leaves. I can smell the honey cake rising in the oven, and my damp hair in the sunshine makes my head and neck tingle as I walk back to the kitchen. Mother is bent over, peering through the dark glass at the cake. She turns her head around to me.

"Go and play," she says. "I'll call you when it's ready. Pick some flowers to put on the table."

"Which flowers would you like?"

She stares at me for a moment, and then shakes her head.

"Any," she says, and then she straightens up from the stove and picks up the comb from the table and turns away from me into the bedroom, her printed housedress hanging loosely around her.

I go out of the kitchen and back into the garden and I walk slowly down the path, the tall grass on each side of me. The flowers call out to me and I answer them. I blink, and I am inside them. *Blink!* And I am an intricate construction of fibres held together by the pull of beauty, a strange gravity suspending colours and filaments and cambia through long, sunshine moments.

And who are you? The flowers ask, as I move through them, into them, beside them.

A soul, a spirit, I answer. *A flash of light moving through this body, burning through this single human life. I am time. I am myself. I am the river.*

And to my answer, they bow their heads, and the wind blows, and we sway, petals quivering, stems bristling in the wind. We, here, alive.

2

In the night-time, the stars and the moon shine down on our garden. The moon traces the curve of my body where I was lying on the grass, recognising the white star that was there. It pours its light down into the mould of my body, and I, asleep in a springtime bed, fill with moonlight.

The stars are more careful. They dance around the lilac flowers, touching each one, turning it and filling it with light. The white transforms to moonlit grey, the tiny flowers shiver with excitement.

Starlight from the will of stars long dead plays with the night-time flowers in the garden, while I sleep filled with moonlight, and while a bird closes its black eyes, head tucked under its wing. The tulips have folded up their heavy petals for what may be their last sleep. In the morning, the red fibres will release to the pull of the earth and fall to join the dark soil.

In the house, my body and Mother's body are sleeping. We, two women, different only by dreams and by choice. A choice to be separate, and a choice to be together, here, beneath a starlit sky, in this ancient black-earthed land.

In my sleep, my Nightspirit comes to me. She is my protector and my guide. She has been with me since the beginning of this dream, since the beginning of remembrance. She is with me in the night-time, shaping the images I see, and her shadow is with me in the day, helping me to transform, to drift into the notes of a passing song, to feel the pulse of the opening garden, to be carried – a star of white lilac – on the spring wind.

She touches me and I arise from my body in the sleeping bedroom, and we dance, our spirits weaving in and out of one another, our similar energies plaiting and unplaiting. We dance. Parting and joining, parting and joining. Up to the ceiling and down. Up to the ceiling and then up, up into the deepest night over the grey, ridged roof where a late bird is perched, watching our moving shadows, held in the vision of this rope of twisting light.

My Nightspirit wants to protect me. I am open now, a young girl, my spirit catches the joy and the sadness of every moment, and she wants to surround me only with joy. *There is darkness close*, she tells me. *I must find a way to protect you.*

There is happiness all around, I tell her. *It is in every flower. It is in every breath.*

The moonlight shimmers through the dim shadow of our house, and I urge her back down to the bedroom, carefully unweaving our silver rope.

I will find a way, she says.

From the rooftop, I can see the patterns of the sleeping village. My twig feet lightly clasp the curves of the iron roof. The final song has been sung and the night is quiet. Soon the owls will begin to fly, but for a last long moment I can perch up here in the night-time heat, feeling the pulse of my flock around me.

I see a rope of shadow rising from the house. It is like the other shadows but brighter, burning in a pale light. The strands weave around each other, in and out of one another, distinct, separate, and yet when they touch, it is as if there is only one. The feathers of my wings quiver with excitement. I would like to fly into them and become a part of this exchange, or fly straight through them and let the sway capture me for a moment, hold me for a moment, change me forever.

I try to move my feathers but I cannot. Something prevents me from approaching this night-time dance. It will be enough to bear witness. I already will be changed forever. Just as when I drank today from the lilac tree and watched the white star through the star-white flowers. Changed forever, and forever and forever, a forever that lasts always and only until the very next long and unbearably beautiful moment. The rope of light sinks back into the house, a single twisting movement of a single shadow.

For a time I cannot stir, held by what I have seen, but at last I am able to fly back to my nest. I settle, and turn my head round to rest and tuck my beak down into the softness of my back, surrounded by twigs, feathers, moss. I close my eyes. The night passes around me, merging my sleeping heart into its quiet pattern. *Beat, beat, beat.* Fast-beating heart slowing with sleep. *Beat… beat… beat…* The warm night calms the rhythm and I merge into the other sleeping hearts, until there is only one long beat. Freed from division, the love released flows clearly for a few precious dark and shadowy minutes. It is never long enough before the morning comes again.

The spring night is beating down and Mother Lyuda is sitting under the lilac tree in bloom with a jar of *samohon*, home-brewed vodka, and a kitchen tumbler. From a nearby pond, the mating toads are calling out their deep laughter, *cra-cra-cra-cra*, and the sound rises up over the silence of the sleeping village.

Lyuda pours the vodka sloppily from the jar, a splashed half glassful, and then pushes the lid back on. She leans her head against the tree trunk and runs her hand over the black earth. Her hair has come loose from its pins and is tumbled over her neck in pale tangles. There is a half-fallen tear in the corner of her eye and she pushes it away, leaving a grey stain across her cheek.

"I don't seem to mind so much tonight," she murmurs to herself, and she glances to the other side of the garden to check that her neighbor, Kolya, is not watching over the wooden fence. It is clear. She raises her hand and knocks back the vodka and then breathes out with a little moan, her eyes closed, while the liquid draws through her body, quieting her thoughts one by one.

"I don't seem to mind anything at all," she says.

The spring breeze touches the tree above her and a few of the silver flowers drift down. One lands on her dress and another on the ground beside her. She picks up the flower from her lap and holds it to her face. She breathes in the sweet scent and remembers another night in the same garden, white snow falling from a sky of sorrow, and a mother holding a baby.

Why did I not die that night? she thinks, shaking her head. *It would have been so easy. It would have been like breathing in and breathing out again. Just breathing in and then disappearing with that last breath, that simple movement of air.*

She crushes the flower with her fingertips and drops it onto the black soil. She pours another measure of *samohon* and then leans the bottle against the tree trunk. She knocks back the second glass.

The liquid moves steadily through her body, dissolving her thoughts and calming the tears, which are always there, a silent waterfall behind each and every breath. The world drifts out of reach, fading into a grey cloud of forgetting and Lyuda, with her eyes closed, smiles as she enters this familiar place, as she enters one by one the long seconds in which she can breathe without effort, without restraint. A few moments of rest.

Her eyes closed, she floats up into the grey cloud.

High up above everything, she feels complete calm, suspended here not in colour but in-between colour; not in darkness but in-between darkness; not in thought but in-between thought. She sees Angela before her, sleeping, and they smile at each other, and a peace is exchanged between them. She has a far-away feeling, as if Angela would like to tell her something, but she doesn't want to hear it. She doesn't want to move away from this place of no thought, beyond the movement of her breathing in and breathing out.

The heat and darkness are close around her, and when at last she opens her eyes, it seems to her that she is still high above everything, not touching the earth; or as if she and the earth are high above everything and the sky is down below; or as if she and the earth and the silver-flowered tree are high above everything and the night stars are below them and above them and entirely all around them.

"That is it," she whispers, looking in wonder at the world turning around her. "That is what it is. The stars are surrounding us."

She pushes herself up from the ground and leans against the curved tree trunk.

"There is nothing wrong and the stars are all around us," she says, and she bends down to pick up the bottle and the glass. Silver flowers drift into her hair.

"Angela," she murmurs, as she goes into the house.

She closes the kitchen door and draws the metal bolt across. She opens the cupboard and pushes the jar of *samohon* to the back and lays the glass on the sideboard. On the table is the honey cake. She reaches up to the window to pull the curtains across. The grey net is fraying on one side and she rubs the coarse material between her fingers. *They must have been white once,* she thinks, and tries to recall a time when they were anything but this dirty grey, but no memories come to her. Through the drawn net, the outline of the lilac is blurred, a solitary pale shape in a dark garden.

Lyuda turns off the lights and goes into the bedroom. She pauses in the doorway to listen for the sound of her daughter's breath rising and falling. Moving through the unlit room to Angela's bed, she reaches out to touch her forehead, and runs her fingertips over her cheek, brushing against the soft hairs like tiny feathers. The usual darkness swells inside her as she touches her daughter; a mixture of panic and despair, muted by the glasses of vodka. Lyuda shakes her head quickly and pushes it down.

She goes over to her own bed, pulls the stained housedress up over her head and drops it over the back of a chair. She tries to bring back the feeling from beneath the lilac tree. *What was it?* she thinks. *Stars, sky, something.* She lies down and pulls the faded sheet up over her and feels the sky of stars merging with her familiar shadows. An image of the lilac tree shimmering through the net curtains comes into her head. She sleeps.

3

I am a star in the heavens and we are all light. Around us is darkness and it is we who light the darkness, and bring light to those who are in the darkness. It is we who are the other to the darkness' totality. It is we who illuminate what is and what could be. We are the light at the beginning of all understanding.

From here we watch everything. All that has passed over the silver millennia and every thread that arises from the eternal, immaculate moment that is happening now. We see the endless flow of sparks pouring out from this moment; explosions of possibilities splintering into worlds and dreams. Single choices made; one spark chosen with which to create a reality in a single lifetime, and the Earth turns, turns on a calm axis. And all the other earths, created from nothing with a spark of splintered light, turn, turn on their axes. Single choices, fragments, strands of silver-coloured dreams.

We see the girl, whose spirit is a woven bridge reaching across these dreams. She is young enough to move wherever her will desires, but soon her mind will begin to close the doorways one by one and her own dream will narrow until there remains just one solitary tunnel, the possibilities lit by the belief of a single choice, a single strand of existence.

But for now, she is open as a wide river with all knowledge flowing through her. For now, we can pour ourselves into her and she will transfer our light to wherever it is needed. She will carry it in her body to the water, she will let it flow into the garden where it will fill every flower, every living thing, she will carry it in her shining eyes and release it to each person she touches, each person she looks upon. She carries it now, and we are filling her with it, streams of silver flowing into her gentle spirit. She is a bridge, but she has come from us, and what she carries is her own true light. Every moment before her dream begins to narrow is a gift, for every second is a chance to transfer our light into the darkness, where it is not. It is a chance to bring our knowledge to a closed place. It is a chance to flood the river.

I am aware that my beak is black. I can see it with darting eyes. I can see my wings are striped dark and ruddy brown and the underside is soft grey feathers and twig feet, but the rest of me I can only assume. There are many other birds here in my flock and my image of myself is as I see them – brown-striped backs and grey heads, a fanned tail. I feel this is how I am, but I will never know for sure.

When I awaken, I pull my beak from among warm feathers and look around. I poke my head out of the nest and check for danger. I smell the morning. My nest is beneath the blue-painted eaves of the house, tucked away like a few blown twigs, safe, far from cats, hidden from owls. There is no danger. Another brief night has passed. It is time to sing. I must find a mate. My nest is ready. I push out of the nest hole and stretch my wings on each side. I dart my eyes around looking for insects in the air but it is early. Later the garden will be full of them. It is a good season to feed.

I fly up from the nest and into the early garden, into the cool air. It is damp with dew. I will sing from the lilac. Perhaps it will be filled with water again and I can drink. I fly all around the garden, looking, looking, listening for the calls of the females, for the song that I will know is for me. Not yet. I land in a cluster of lilac and for a moment the smell rushes over me. Scent, white, dew, morning. I dip my head and drink and dip again into the dew. Satisfied, my feet curl around the branch through the flowers. My mate is nearby. I feel her. I sing.

I wake early in the morning and push my feet out of the bed onto the thin rug covering the wooden floor. It is still dark, and yet that rising dark, the promise of a grey, mystical light. Mother is breathing heavily in her sleep, and there is a bitter smell around her. At this hour everything is still quiet. I find my white dress and pull it over my head and I slip out of the bedroom and through the morning kitchen. The honey cake is on the table and I reach out a finger for a crumb as I pass by to the kitchen door. I swallow the sweet morsel, then slide back the bolt and slip my sandals onto my feet.

Outside, the garden is calm. The air is holding the folded heat close, not ready yet to release it to the flowers, to the buds, to the silent bulbs pushing through the soil. This is the moment when everything is held tightly together, everything is preparing. The world is poised in a quiet, breathing grey. This is the time that I love. I walk through the lifting air to the very bottom of the garden, past the outhouse and the rainwater bucket, past the lilac tree and through the long, wet grass down to the rough wooden fence, and there is a flat stone where I can sit, and from here I can look up into the opening morning and the waking garden, and I can know the very beginning of the day.

The blades of the grasses tremble; minute drops of dew shiver, silver, the petals of the night-closing flowers experience an unbearable urge to push out, out, out; the water seeped back into them through a waking stem. An infinitesimal change of paler light. The petals open. In my body, I feel every movement, the waking desire of life is within me, the light rising through my skin, myself transforming forever and forever with every distinct movement here, in this waking garden that will never be repeated, in this perfect and impossible combination of moments, in this one, single instant of rising grey.

A brown-striped sparrow pushes out of its nest under the eaves of the house, pauses, and then flies up into the garden and settles in the lilac branches. It is the first. It ducks its head down into the flowers to drink the lilac dew, and again, and then raises its head up and begins the first song.

The light is risen.

With my petals open and touched with birdsong, I get up from the flat stone and make my way towards the house, running my fingers through the wet grasses. The garden is filling with sound now, as more birds join the first in shrill sounds. A cockerel grates out its guttural cry. On the stone step outside the kitchen the bucket of well water is covered with a broken plate. I bend down and pick it up with the metal handle and carry it into the kitchen.

It is time to pour the water.

Lyuda breathes out the bitter vodka with her sleeping breath and turns her head, her mouth heavily open, her mind closed to the spring morning. She is in a far-gone place on a late summer's afternoon, and her cheek is resting lightly against Volodiya's shoulder, the forests and peaks of the Carpathian Mountains stretching out before them. A wind is blowing here, at the top of the hill, and Volodiya reaches his arm around the shoulder of his *divchyna*, his seventeen-year-old girl, and bends his head and kisses her on the neck, where the pale gold hairs rise to meet his lips.

"One day I'm going to build you a house right here," he whispers in her ear. "I'm going to build you a bedroom where you can see all this." He takes her right hand and holds it out to where he is pointing. He touches the gold ring that he has put on her finger, and then pulls her hand to his lips and holds it there. She feels his breath hot on her fingers, still warm on her neck, and she feels her heart beating with the excitement of being here with him, and that feeling of being both heavy and light at the same time, and the faint dizziness in her head that makes everything seem unreal. She believes his words, just as she believes everything that he says; believes in the ring she is wearing, even without a wedding; believes in the dreams he paints for her; believes in his love, his touch, his smell, his weight on top of her, his dark hair and rough skin.

"When?" she asks him. "When are you going to build me the house?" Volodiya leans forward and runs his hand down her bare leg. She feels her insides moving at his touch, a quick contracting in her stomach and the lightness again in her head. She wants him to kiss her on the mouth. She looks out at the hills stretching before them, scattered with houses, and the distant forests in endless waves of deeper and deeper green and she smells his hair as he leans over her and she imagines for a moment a room full of light where they are making love.

Volodiya moves his hand higher up her leg, up to the short skirt of her dress, and he reaches across and kisses her on the lips. He pushes her gently onto the grass and holds himself above her, looking down, and touches the golden hair spread out around her face.

"The first money I have," he says. "The very first money, I'll buy the land. I'll build you a house. And then we'll have a little girl and she'll be beautiful like you."

Lyuda closes her eyes, feeling his weight sinking onto her, and she pictures the house in cream and red brick, the wide steps leading up to it, rooms filled with sunshine and endless green through huge windows. She opens her eyes and looks straight up at him.

"Yes," she says. A swallow darts into the path of her vision and she traces it across the clear sky.

"Yes," she repeats, "I want it, Vova. That's what I want."

4

It is time to go to the market.

Mother is dressed and has wrapped a blue shawl around her head. She has changed out of her housedress and put on the long patterned skirt she wears for the village, and the white top that shows all her curves. She looks so beautiful and I slide my arms around her waist and I can feel her heart beating through the soft material.

"Come on, Angela. Put your shoes on," she says, and she unfastens my arms and pulls the shawl a little further over her forehead.

She pushes open the garden gate, lifting the broken latch, and we climb the slope to the village street. A goat is tethered to a fence a few houses down, and a *babulya*, an old woman, in a red headscarf, sits on a wooden bench, watching it. The goat bleats as we approach and stops eating to watch us, and I dance up to it, but the old woman says, "Don't touch, little rabbit. Don't bother him." I smile at her, and her eyes follow Mother along the road, and I run back to Mother and take her hand.

The market is beyond the post office, and beyond the school where I have finished my first year. We pass Sveta's house, and I can see Taras and Petro at the bottom of their garden, and I want to call out to them, but Mother is walking fast and I have to run to catch up with her. Sveta always asks me about Mother when I play with the boys, and she tells me how beautiful Mother was at school, and how they were friends, but when I ask Mother, she turns away, and tells me to fetch something from the bedroom, or the garden, or to change my dress.

"Lyudmilla Hrihorivna!"

"Lyudichka!"

The women on the market stalls call out to Mother as we approach. They wear headscarves, open sandals and gold earrings. They have gold teeth and dark, sunburned skin. They flick at the birds darting down to pick at their wares, and they beckon Mother to their stalls and say kind words to her, and blow kisses to me.

"How are you, Lyudmilla Hrihorivna? Your little one is growing! She is her mother's daughter."

"A kilo of apples," Mother says, and they weigh out a kilo and then add some more when I am looking, with a wink.

"This is for you, little swallow," they say.

I wander around the stalls while Mother is shopping. There are piles of prunes and nuts and dried apricots, apples and early cherries and tomatoes and small, knobbly cucumbers. There are heaps of black-skinned beetroot and carrots covered in soil, young white potatoes and big roughened ones. A stall of skinned rabbits and plucked chickens and long blocks of white, glistening *salo*, raw pig fat, which the men eat with vodka and garlic.

At each stall, the sellers hold something out to me – a couplet of fat cherries, a slice of apple, a dried persimmon from Kazakhstan – and I fill the pockets of my dress until there is no more room, and I say, "*Dyakuyu*. Thank you! Thank you!" And they wink and say, "Come again soon, little rabbit. Cheer up your mother. Beautiful girl!"

My feet crooked around a twig, I dart my eyes across the marketplace from the centre of bright green leaves. My glance takes in the piles of sweet fruits and nuts where my flock is feeding. I see a woman turning away and I fly down and grasp a black fruit in my beak just as her hand flashes towards me and I am up! up! in the air with my prize and I fly fast to my hidden branch, jerk my head back and swallow the fruit. Sweet black grape.

My wings are warm with sunlight. A good feeling. I have sung all morning. I am filled with food. Catching insects through the air and fat crumbs on the windowsill. The spring is here. A song is building in me. I feel my flock returning to the garden and I am drawn upwards, flapping fast in our single movement, and we fly towards the house, towards our home, the nests we have built in the trees and in the eaves of the roof, our feathers open and alive against the sunlit air.

We carry the bags of fruit along the dusty road back to the house.

"What was it like when you and Sveta were at school?" I ask. "Sveta says you were so beautiful. Were you always friends?"

Mother doesn't answer at first, but then she looks down at me and says, "Yes, little one. Yes, but we were older than you. It was before your grandmother died. Before you were born. And Taras and Petro."

"Why don't you see her now, Mama?" I ask, and immediately I feel the change, her body closing to me, and I think that she won't answer the question, but she starts to say something, and I take her hand to help her.

"We were so young," she is saying. "We didn't really know anything. We had these dreams, Angela. We had these plans. And then Sveta met Vasya. And..."

"And you met Father. You met *Tato.*"

She is closed. She tried, but I feel that she cannot say any more. We are at the top of the slope leading to the gate and to our house. Mother stops to take a stone from her shoe.

"Go on ahead," she says, but she doesn't look up, so I slide down the slope with my bags of fruit and I don't glance back. I know that the tears are coming up into her eyes. I know that she will fight them with that expression on her face, which looks like anger, but I don't know why she is angry, or at whom. I know that I am a part of those tears, I know that something is connected to me, and I want more than anything for Mother to be happy.

I leave the bags of fruit on the kitchen step and I run down into the garden. A bird is diving into the lilac blossom and I follow its path through the flower beds, looking for the nest.

When I come back up to the kitchen, I can see that Mama is crying. She is standing at the window and looking at a bird in the lilac tree, a sparrow, or one of the swallows. She wipes her hand across her eyes and her face is shining with tears. She doesn't know I can see her, coming up the garden path holding a stem of wild grass, and before, after I had eaten my dinner one night when she was washing the plates, and before, after she kissed me goodnight and I heard her in the kitchen, sitting on the wicker chair making little sounds. She doesn't know I can see her but I can, and it's always in the moments between, not when we are sitting at the table and eating soup, or playing in the garden, or reading together on the bench, but in the moments between them, when she slips away from me, not looking at me, forgetting that I am here, that I am in front of her.

I run my fingers up and down the stem of grass, plucking off the smooth, oval seeds, and now I have that feeling in my stomach again, as if I have done something wrong, and I feel scared that I have made all those tears, that I have made Mama cry, that it is all my fault.

I go back to the garden gate and open it and close it noisily, pulling the broken metal latch up and down so she will hear it. I drop the grass and scattered seeds. I call out "Mama, Mama, where are you?" and then I come towards the house, and she has gone from the window and comes round to the door to me, and she has the look that she has in the moments after she has been crying, the tight look, when she is breathing too hard and smiling without her eyes, and it looks to me as if her mind is going quickly from one to the other, from the tears to now and from now to the tears.

"Mama?" I say, and she breathes in and looks at me, and then at last she smiles with her eyes.

"*Dorohenka*, darling," she says.

"Come into the garden. I think I can see the nest where the little bird lives."

"Now?"

"Of course, now!"

I pull her hand and we go together down the path, through the long grasses and the scarlet tulips and poppies. I lead her to the bottom of the garden, where the raspberry bushes and the potato plants are, and then I say, "Pick me up so I can see, take me in *rooki*, in your arms," and she laughs when I say this because she knows how I love to be held in *rooki*, and she bends down and I take a jump like a little bird lifting up from a branch in a tree, and I am in her arms and she is holding me to her and I reach out my hand and point and say, "Look, *Mamochka*! Look through the branches over there. Can you see the nest? Just in the elbow, where the branches go away from each other?"

She looks and spots the nest and puts her face against my neck and against my hair, breathing onto me. "I see it," she says. "What a clever girl to have found it."

"Do you know how I did it?"

"Tell me," she says, and I say, "I followed the bird. I sat under the tree and watched it. It took the crumbs from the window and then flew over the garden and down to here and I couldn't see anything because the bird had disappeared and then it came out of somewhere and I looked closer and I saw it was a nest. Wasn't that clever?"

"That was very clever." She lowers me gently to the ground and she turns and starts to walk back to the house. "I have to get lunch ready."

"Mama?" I run up beside her.

"*Dorohenka?*"

"Are you sad?"

She stops and looks down at me and something passes over her face.

"What do you mean?"

We are at the kitchen door. Her foot is on the stone step.

"I thought you were crying."

Mother pauses for a moment and then goes up into the kitchen. She slips off her sandals and pushes her feet into her house shoes and sits down at the table. I come and stand in front of her. She holds out her arms to me and I feel that she has somehow become very serious.

"Sometimes I cry," she says at last. I move into her arms and she pulls me up onto her knee. "But people can cry when they are happy or sad."

"Why do you cry?" I ask. She puts her arms around me and holds me against her. She whispers into my hair.

"I don't know."

And I feel that she wants to start again, but is pushing it back, and her arms wrap tighter against me, and she whispers again.

"It is like I see you laughing when you are doing something in the garden." She pauses. "Or when you are in the sunlight…"

She has stopped talking, and I know that she is crying now. I try to turn around in her lap but she holds me where I am and the kitchen has become very quiet and I hear her breathing long, shaky breaths, but that is the only sound, and I think that if a drop of water fell now, that I would hear it.

And then I think that I might hear one of her tears falling onto the floor, or onto her dress, and I picture a single droplet falling slowly, slowly, and then she says, "That is how it is," and I have forgotten what she means. "Like when you are in sunlight and you laugh," she says, and then, "This is how it is. Sometimes I am not in the sunlight, and…"

I push myself off her lap. She lets me go and I turn to her, standing, and see her face turned down, eyes closed and cheeks covered in tears. They are not falling, they are gathering on her face, making it wetter and wetter. I suddenly feel that I shouldn't have asked. She didn't want me to see. I have made it worse. She reaches out her hand and opens her eyes and squeezes my hand. Then she shakes her head and smiles at me with a strange, crooked, downturned mouth through her wet face.

"Go and play, darling," she says. "I'll be fine in a minute." And she lets my hand go with a little push towards the door.

When I step outside, I look up to the nests under the eaves of the house and I see the red throat and pale breast of a swallow emerging from one of them. It flies over to a high branch of the lilac tree and starts to chirp and trill, and without thinking I laugh and blow a kiss to it, and I think that its dark blue feathers must be so lovely and warm in this springtime with the sunshine on them, and I stretch out my arms on each side, like wings, so that my arms are held in the sunshine, and I wave them up and down while Mother is crying. And she doesn't see me lifting into the air. She doesn't see me rising, rising and flying. She doesn't see me caught across the surface of the sun and the surface of the land, my warm blue feathers stirring the heavy spring air into a rising laughter.

In my sleep, the tendrils of a willow tree wind their way around my dreams. Through the serpentine motion of the strands, I see a river moving slowly, and a figure appearing on the distant bank, a face of wrinkled bark, a flash of blue.

My Nightspirit watches me, weaving the images into my sleeping thoughts.

I will protect you from the tears, she says. *You are too open, too full of light. The tears will go deep and you will not be able to return. You are too young.*

She watches me as I dream, creating a barrier of light around me so that Mother's sleeping darkness does not come too close.

Your grandmother will help you, she tells me. *She is waiting.*

5

It is morning.

While I lie star-shaped under an infinity of tiny flowers, Mama is far away in her thoughts. She watches me through the kitchen window; its cracked, wooden frame thrown open to the scent of lilac and the vision of me, white and sun-brushed, on the garden floor.

Her own face is framed by the flaking paint. Her cracked face gazing into the garden with tired eyes. Her long hair is pinned clumsily over her head; it half tumbles, half holds, light brown and when caught by the sun it turns golden. Her face is wide and flat, her eyes are brown and full of a thousand flecks of constant sadness. She looks out at me lying beneath the lilac, open and dreaming.

"Everything I have done is wrong," she murmurs.

"You have created me," I say. "You have created a white star."

Her body is soft, wrapped in a stained blue housedress with red flowers. Tumbled brown hair. The layers of flesh and fat rest on her body below the dress like a burden of unused dreams. She carries them heavily, always with her, always close. She reaches out for a dab of sour cream from the open jar next to the window. She puts her finger into the jar and brings the cream to her mouth. She sucks her finger. The dreams come closer. Her body softens.

"I regret everything," she says quietly.

The sunshine draws a long, golden brushstroke over my cheek, and then shimmers into a thousand separate dreams.

Each dream is a drop of sunlight, droplets of gold suspended around me in the heavy air. Each dream a perfect expression of a perfect life, held here by the beams of my heart, by my desire. The belief of a white star. The knowledge of the impossible. The droplets of light tremble, breathing in and out, waiting to be chosen. My heart pours out to them. I open my eyes a little and I exhale lightly, as if blowing away the seeds of a dandelion clock. The dreams disappear.

In the kitchen, images are appearing one after the other in Mama's head. Sunshine on a grassy hill. A hand moving up a smooth leg. A house overlooking endless woods. She wants to reach for the *samohon*, to stop them, but now the anger is rising through her body, blocking out everything but the remembrance of his hands on her, the shadow of the house that was promised, the ring on her finger. Her failure. Her mistakes. The pain that only she created. She wants to howl.

She looks around and sees the jar of sour cream on the window. Her head is alive with pain. She picks it up and lifts her arm, the images gathering into a swirl of blame within her vision. Her mistakes. Her mistakes. Her mistakes. She hurls the jar to the ground. It smashes over the paving stones, spewing white liquid. She steps back, panting. Broken glass is everywhere. Her heart is beating violently.

"I have ruined everything," she says, breathing, crying.

I hear a crash of glass breaking on stone and sit up, dizzy for a moment from the bright sunlight on my face. I put my hand up to shade my eyes and squint towards the kitchen window.

"Mama!"

I can see her head through the window frame, turned away from me, and I see her hair has come loose from its pins and hangs down her back. From her eyes, droplets of salt and water are falling. Each tear is a dream; a perfect spent droplet falling from the belief of nothing. Held by nothing. They fall onto the stone, onto the glass, into the cream. Onto her slippered feet.

"Mama!"

I stand up. The back of my white dress and the warm skin of my shoulders are covered with black soil. I run to the kitchen door and tiptoe over the broken glass to my mother. My feet are bare but she does not see.

She looks up at me and tries to compose herself. Her head is bent and she is breathing heavily in and out and the tears are covering her cheeks. She shuffles through the broken cream to the kitchen table and reaches for a tea towel and holds it up to her face. She pulls out one of the chairs and sits down on it. She opens her eyes and closes them.

"My darling," she says, struggling. "My little one."

Her eyes closed, she is seeing her own childhood, in this house, in this garden, in this kitchen.

Her mother, Zoryana, is standing at the kitchen window and Lyuda can see her from the flowerbeds, where she is playing.

She can see that something is wrong.

Zoryana is watching her daughter, Lyuda, playing in the tulips and her husband, Grisha, hammering nails into a new wooden bench. The kitchen window is painted fresh with whitewash and the smell of the paint and the sting in her eyes makes her think how little there is in her life that a new coat of paint can make this day stand out from all the others.

She watches Grisha finishing the bench, getting ready to paint it the same whitewash as the window frames. She doesn't think he has made the bench wide enough. Her body is starting to spread with age and she doesn't want her flesh to hang over the edges of the planks.

Lyuda is dancing among the high grasses and summer tulips and watching her father hammering in steady blows. Her bare feet are dirty from the black soil. She picks a red tulip and runs up to the kitchen window where her mother is standing, her eyes full of tears.

"Mama!"

She hands her the flower.

"For you *Mamochka*!" she says, holding it up. Zoryana reaches down to her daughter and takes the flower.

"Thank you little swallow, little *lastivka*."

And then Zoryana is crying. Where have her dreams gone? How is it that the excitement of her life has become a coat of paint on a kitchen window and a new bench? Where has her passion for Grisha gone?

It is the tang of the paint. The fresh, acrid smell, which is so different from her daily scents of cooking beetroot, and potatoes frying in sunflower oil, and meat, and overgrown grass, and lilac. It is this new scent that suddenly makes her aware that all those other smells – the soup, the oil, the garden – are her life, and nothing more. That the moment for dreams has passed; the moment for choices, the moment for romances, the moment for leaving, the moment for a wild spirit exploding against the background of a miraculous universe.

That is gone, and what is left is a path so ordinary that it seems almost pointless to tread it. The same path as her mother and her grandmother and her great-grandmother. The feeding, the cleaning, the working, the ageing, the birthing, the pains and then the passing. And right now, this smell of whitewash and a dancing daughter and her hand holding a red tulip and her husband hammering nails into a narrow bench.

Her tears fall onto the floor and onto the cloth of her apron. She pushes them down into the stone with her slippered feet.

Outside, a bird is singing. *Lastivka*.

In the evening, while Angela is sleeping, Lyuda steps outside the house holding a bottle, a glass and a chipped plate of food. She sits on the bench and sets down the plate next to her. The planks are too narrow for her body and she rests her feet heavily on the ground to balance herself. She takes a piece of dark rye bread from the plate and holds it up to her nose, breathing in deeply to take away the harsh smell of the vodka. She lifts the glass of *samohon* to her lips and knocks it back, feeling the fire in her throat and stomach, and then she takes a slice of the *salo*, the raw pig fat, and chews it slowly with a clove of garlic. When she has finished the fat, she reaches down and pours another glass of vodka. She takes a sip and shivers.

Why now? she thinks, looking around the garden at the overgrown grasses and the rotting wood of the fence. *Why am I falling apart now? It has been so long, and nothing has changed.*

Her mind drifts back over the past seven years, the years of Angela's life since Volodiya left, and she touches her finger where the ring was, rubbing it softly. She almost wants to go and look again in the garden, between the plants, on the soil, as she has so many times before, as if finding the ring might bring him back. She shakes her head. Stupid. Of course it won't.

And why now? An image appears in her head of a little girl and a red flower, and she wonders if it is Angela. She tries to picture the hair, to see if it is dark like her daughter's, like Volodiya's, or fair like her own, but she can't see. The image fades. *I have held on,* she thinks. *All this time I have held on. I haven't asked for help. I haven't let Angela see. And all this time the weight has never left me, pulling constantly down on my head, on my heart, on my stomach, day after day. As if my entire existence is a journey through a tunnel that I never chose to enter and which has only one possible way out. And the way out is calling me, every second of every day. It knows how much I desire to go there. To step out of the darkness. To end it so quickly. But I will not choose that. I will not leave Angela. Not like that.*

Lyuda picks up another piece of dark bread and holds it to her nose, breathes in the rye, and then knocks back the glass of *samohon*. She chokes from the force of it and waits impatiently for it to reach her thoughts. She tries to focus on one solitary image. Angela. Thin brown arms filled with flowers and a rope of plaited hair. She holds this image in her mind while the vodka closes down the colours and the memories around it.

It is done. She nods, unsmiling, her eyes are quieter, and she picks up a slice of *salo* and a small clove of garlic, and puts them into her mouth.

As Lyuda sleeps, the Nightspirit comes to her, a faint shadow of moving grey, and she calls up into her memory the eyes of her mother and the movement of a willow branch blowing across the water of a flowing river. Spoken words and memories and a blue dress swirling around a dancing woman. The blue of her mother's eyes and a scream of laughter diving into cold water. In her sleep, Lyuda reaches out her hand to her mother, and in her sleep her mother takes her hand and pushes something into it – a flash of red – and then disappears into the laughing current.

Lyuda smiles, pulling her dream up over her like a cool sheet, and the Nightspirit drifts quietly away into the waiting moonlight.

6

Mother stands on the kitchen step. I swing my brown legs on the whitewashed bench. Up down, forward back.

"Let's go to the river," she says.

Mother packs food and towels into a basket. She wraps rye bread in a cloth and puts in a knife with a silver blade. Sour pickles in a jar filled with brine and wet strands of dill. A jar of pickled apricots. Slices of *salo*, cloves of garlic and the last of the honey cake.

We walk together down the main street of the village, past the green well with its pointed wooden roof and past the houses, which look like ours with bright blue painted eaves and fat white geese waddling on the grass in front. Many of the gardens have cherry and apple trees in bloom, purple and white lilacs, vines growing over trellises and rows and rows of potato plants, cabbages, herbs.

Mother holds the basket of food and I hold her other hand. Her skin is dry and I can feel its cracked surface against my warm fingers. We pass Sveta's house, and I look over the fence into the garden of growing sunflowers, but she isn't there. I would like to ask something but I glance at Mother's face and it is closed. She is looking straight ahead and I have to run and skip to keep up with her.

A thought comes to me.

"Mama," I say. "If we're going to the river, can we go to where the willows are? You remember you told me how Grandmother used to take you there when you were little?"

34

Mother looks down at me, smiling. Her face has opened again. *Like the flowers*, I think. *Their petals opening and closing with the sunshine.*

"That's where we're going," she says.

A narrow path leads off into the woods from the dusty street and we walk down it. The air smells different here, and I brush my hand against the trunk of an oak tree as we pass, pink fingers across dark ridges. The path leads further into a glade of silver birch trees, and Mama stops.

"Look, Angela!"

One of the birch trunks has a funnel of thin metal protruding from near the base, and a glass jar below with some liquid in it. Mama goes to the tree, picks up the jar and dips her finger into the cloudy grey. She puts it into her mouth and then holds the jar out to me. I suck the droplets from my finger. They taste sweet and bitter, like sugared bark. I like it.

"We should do this next year," Mama says. "Before the end of the snow, we'll come and collect the sap. We can drink it for months. I can show you how to do it. Would you like that?"

"Yes, yes. I would!"

I stroke the slender trunk of the tree, smooth silver and rough crevices, and then I reach out my hand to the little bright leaves and touch them with my fingertips. I blow a kiss to the tree and take Mama's hand again, and we go on down the path.

We emerge from the glade and the ground is softer as we approach the water. I can see the willow trees from here, lining the riverbank on each side, and the river flowing calm and high between them.

"Where shall we sit?" asks Mother.

"Where did you sit with Grandmother? The place you told me about?"

Mother looks up and down the bank and then she points to one of the trees.

"I think it was over there. The trunk is curved. She'd sit under it and watch me swim."

I slip off my sandals and carry them in my hand as we walk through the thick grass to the tree.

"This is the place," she says.

She lays down the basket of food and sinks onto the grass. She leans back against the trunk.

"Can I swim, Mama?"

"If it's not too cold." She smiles at me, and it seems that her face is just a little softer here, as if something had made her happy inside.

I pull my dress over my head and drop it onto the grass. My body is brown like the bark of a tree, like the feathers of a bird; not pale like Mama, with skin like sour cream. My hair hangs down my back, almost to my waist, black, curled, brushed with rainwater.

Naked, tangled, full of dreams, I lift my arms high into the air and rise onto my tiptoes, stretching my body into the springtime sky. My wings flutter lightly. I breathe out.

I feel the strength of the river when I step into it, pulling me this way and that. My body so light and small in the mass of moving water. I could be carried away – down, down, below – but I go carefully forward until the water is up to my waist and I wait for one long moment and then I push myself out into the current with a little gasp at the coldness.

I am swimming, using all of my force, struggling against the current, and then I suddenly feel that it is easier, that something is helping me. I look up, and there is a flash of bright blue, a movement in the trees, and I look closer and see that my grandmother is standing on the riverbank. She is waiting for me.

"Come, Angela. Come, my little one. Up onto the grass."

I reach the far shore and I stand, balancing on the smooth stones and look up into blue eyes. Then I reach out my hand and put my fingers into hers, green-veined and ridged like ancient bark. A bright star touching gnarled wood.

She helps me up the bank and I glance back at Mother, who is biting into a dripping apricot; juice and sugar running down her chin to her stained dress.

"Sit down, my *harnenka*, my *dorohenka*, my beautiful, dear girl," says Grandmother.

Her voice is cracked, as if she hasn't spoken for a long time. Gnarled and ridged. She sits with her back against the willow tree and holds open her branches. I lie down on the warm grass so that the willow strands are hanging above me, and I lay my head in her lap.

"Little Angela, little *lastivka*," she says. "Let me tell you how it was."

The sun dances through the willow strands and a warm breeze blows the slender leaves and ripples the waters of the river and disturbs the soft hair around Mother's face, sitting in a dream on the far riverbank, remembering her own mother.

If only she were here with me, she thinks. *Nothing bad would have happened. I wouldn't be alone. There would be nothing wrong.*

She closes her eyes. She imagines her mother's voice speaking to her now, calm and sure. A flock of wild geese flies overhead, shifting in and out of a fluid arrow formation, like the movement of trembling water.

"Listen," my grandmother tells us.

"The moon hung low and golden over our village the night I was born," says Grandmother, her creaking voice rising over the soothing hiss of the river.

"Our house was there, just the same, two rooms filled with our generations. My mother, my grandmother. My mother gave birth to me in the bedroom in the middle of summer with a midwife. Hot water and blood, grey towels and screams, and

37

a new baby girl that was me. They called me Zoryana, the star. And outside the house, in the garden, my father and his friends were drunk on *samohon* and singing *Ochi Chorni*, Black Eyes, until my grandmother had to chase them from the garden with a stick, and he came back three days later, still drunk, to find that my eyes were bright blue."

Grandmother strokes my head with her veined hand. Her skin scrapes dry against my damp face. "Close your eyes, little one," she whispers. "Listen to the story."

"I lived my whole life in that house," she continues. "I played in the garden, just like you. We had chickens and white geese and rabbits and I looked after them. My *babulya*, my grandmother, kept a goat for milk." She smiles. "Then I got married, and we all lived together in the same house. There wasn't much room, but it was what we had. Sometimes I felt like running away. Sometimes I cried. Little Lyuda saw me crying sometimes. I wish she hadn't."

She gazes across the river to Mother, golden-brown hair curling softly around a sleeping face. The sun touches a streak of apricot juice around her mouth.

"Your Nightspirit has called me here to protect you," says Grandmother. "You are too open to your mother's tears. We need to find a way to bring her out of her sadness. Will you help me do that, little Angela?"

"Why is Mama sad?"

"She is trapped in her memories. All around her are shadows, and she cannot find her way out of them. Look."

Grandmother leans forward and takes a loose strand of my hair and wraps it around her fingers.

"There is a rope," she says. She holds out the strand of hair to me. "Just like this. It holds us all together. You, me, your mother, my mother. It is made up of feelings and thoughts. It is made up of all the love we have for one another."

She takes a strand of her own hair, tinged with green like the willow branches above, and she winds it around her fingers so that our hair is woven together.

"Your mother has forgotten this. When she is in her darkness, she thinks she is alone. But wherever she goes, she carries us with her. The footsteps of her life have been marked out by the shadows of ours."

Grandmother has stopped talking. I open my eyes to the sunlit willow above and Grandmother's tired face. She releases the strands of hair from her fingers.

"This is what I wanted to tell your mother," she says. "My sweet *dochenka*, my daughter. My little Lyuda."

"Why can't you tell her these things, Grandmother?"

"I cannot cross the river," she replies. "It is only you, my little one. I know what you can do. I know what you can be."

I feel a quick rush of excitement. A flash of the bird comes to me. I look into her eyes.

"Could you do it, too, Grandmother? When you were a girl?"

Grandmother nods, and puts a crooked finger to her lips. It is time to leave. I lift my head out of her lap and smile at my grandmother, and her blue eyes smile back at me.

"See you soon," I say, and I clamber down the riverbank, and into the water.

Mother wakes from her deep sleep, a half-eaten apricot in the skirt of her dress making a dark stain. She smiles, rubs her eyes with the back of her hand, and puts the apricot into her mouth.

"Your grandmother Zoryana once danced under these willows," she says, as I dry my feet on the long grass. "With your grandfather. On the night of *Ivan Kupala*, when the fires were burning in the village, and they could hear the music in the distance. She loved to tell me that story. She wore a blue dress and her feet were bare."

I rub myself with the towel from the basket and then I pull the dress over my damp body and start to dance around the tree. "Like this?" I ask, throwing the green tendrils up in the air, dancing through them with light feet.

Mother gets up heavily from the ground and wipes her apricot hands on the front of her dress.

"Just like that," she says, smiling. "Just like that."

In the evening, Lyuda stands above Angela, watching her sleep, the little face smiling and the black hair brushed with rainwater spread out over a white pillow.

How like her father she looks, she thinks. *She has Volodiya's skin and dark hair. Not like me or Mama. And yet he doesn't even know what she looks like. He doesn't know that he has this reflection, this child like a hidden river flowing beneath his life.*

She thinks about the willow trees this morning and remembers Angela dancing in the sunshine, throwing the green strands in the air, a white star dancing in sunlight. She reaches out her hand and strokes Angela's soft cheek, and her heart lifts. *I have her*, she thinks. *I have this white star.*

Grandmother, on the willowbank, hears the voice of the Nightspirit, and then she sees it; a soft grey shadow before her.

It must be soon, the Nightspirit says. *The girl is too open.*

"Is she strong enough?" Grandmother asks. "Can she help my daughter?"

I do not know, the Nightspirit replies. *There is not much time. Soon the tears will be woven too deep into the rope.*

"Then we must hurry," says Grandmother.

The Nightspirit fades into the shadows, and in the nearby forests of the Carpathian Mountains a wolf passes silently through the trees; silver fur and eyes blazing yellow.

Grandmother watches her daughter sitting with a glass of vodka, the white lilac tree above her a great lantern in the darkness, and she feels the heaviness of her failure moving through her roots.

In the house, Angela turns in her sleep, pushing the patched sheet off her springtime body. She is dreaming of her grandmother Zoryana, swimming in the river as a young girl, in love and full of desires filled and filled and filled. And her grandfather Grisha, pushing Zoryana's wet hair back from her face and kissing her, the river water flowing around their bodies under the summer willows.

Grandmother moves her spirit through the forest of stars above her. She weaves her way between shafts of starlight, trailing a faint shadow of willow leaves. The blackness between the stars is absolute, and it is difficult not to release herself into it. A quick sigh of relief, and rest.

"Not now, not yet," she murmurs, and moves on, weaving and twisting.

As she comes to each new star, she speaks to it, opening herself into its light and whispering her words into its being.

"Shine here," she says. "Shine here, onto this place. This is my daughter. This is my child, this is my own."

To the stars, she shows the river and the house. She shows them Lyuda in a blast of light, weeping. She shows them Angela, the star-flower, dancing. "I need you," she says to them. "I ask you for this favour."

The stars are moved by the tears, and one by one they bow to her, acquiescent. She weaves back through them, strands of silver in her wake. The blackness between the stars calls to her, but she resists. "Soon, soon, soon," she whispers. "You can wait for me," she says. "I will not be long."

7

Mother Lyuda is sitting on one side of the river and Grandmother Zoryana on the other.

Between them, the past flows, dancing light on silver water. Together they remember. Together they try to find shapes of a memory they can merge into one.

Lyuda pushes open the door of the kitchen and walks past her mother, her seventeen-year-old body aching from the touch of Volodiya. Zoryana stands at the window. She draws her eyes away from the garden where she was watching the shadow of Grisha, not long dead, hammering nails into a new white-painted bench. Her body feels cold and strange from the loss of his closeness.

She brings her gaze back to her daughter, forcing herself to return to the moment. She sees Lyuda's shining eyes and the flush in her cheeks, her body tense and close.

Zoryana snaps at her. "Where have you been?"

Her daughter turns towards her, one shoulder rising, her eyes clear in challenge.

"I've been with Volodiya."

Zoryana sniffs.

"Have you been drinking?"

"Of course I haven't."

Zoryana feels a twinge of anger and draws it around herself. She breathes in and feels it gathering inside her.

"I've told you not to see him outside the house."

"He met me after school."

43

Lyuda raises her chin. She feels her mother's anger and her body responds to it naturally.

"Then you should have brought him to the house."

"He walked me home."

"You should have brought him in."

"He didn't want to come in."

"Are you only doing what he wants?"

"I didn't want him to come in, either."

Zoryana wishes that Grisha was here with her. She wishes that Lyuda had not met Volodiya. She wishes there was something she could say that would make a difference to what was going to happen. She feels a wave of sadness and helplessness and she grasps on to the feeling, pushing it harder, working it up into anger. Working it into the strength to resist her daughter's force.

"Lyuda, darling, he's too old for you."

"He's not that old."

"He's too old for you. You're only seventeen."

"What difference does that make?"

"You should find a boy your age."

"I don't want a boy my age. I want Volodiya."

"Why do you think Volodiya wants to be with a schoolgirl?"

"I'm not a schoolgirl, I'm a beautiful woman."

Zoryana snorts. "You're seventeen. You're a schoolgirl."

"You don't understand anything, Mother. He loves me. He wants to marry me."

"Did he say that?"

Lyuda touches the ring on her finger. "Of course he said that."

"Lyuda darling, listen to me. Please listen to me. What's going to happen if you get pregnant and then he doesn't want to be with you? Doesn't want marry you? What would you do?"

"That's not going to happen. I'm not going to get pregnant, and if I did, then he'd stay with me."

"Ask him."

"What?"

"Ask him. Next time he's kissing you. Ask him what he'd do if you got pregnant. If he'd stay with you and marry you and support you."

"I can't ask him that."

"Lyuda darling, *lastivka*, please think about it. If you got pregnant you'd spend the next ten years of your life right here with the baby. You'd have a part-time job at the post office and you'd probably lose your figure. How are you going to get a husband like that? And with a child? Lyudichka, I've seen it so many times. Please understand."

"I understand everything."

"That's fine. Of course you do. But please listen to what I have to say."

"All you do is lecture me. I don't know why you don't want me to be happy."

"I want you to finish school and get a job and find someone who will give you a good life. You're so pretty. You can move to Ivano-Frankivsk or Lviv. You don't need to live here forever. You could sell the house."

"You think I'm such a stupid girl. I know exactly what I'm doing."

"Lyuda, darling, everything could change so quickly. You must be careful."

"This is all just words. You're saying words that don't make any sense. You don't know what you're talking about. I love Volodiya and he loves me. I know what I'm doing."

"But Lyuda, listen…"

The wind blows through the trees and I come walking lightly through the silver birch grove and along the riverbank, to

Mother. She is sitting under the willow tree, the sunlight playing on her golden hair. Her eyes are closed.

"Mama," I whisper, tiptoeing up. She smiles and opens her light brown eyes and holds out her hand.

"Darling, *dorohenka*."

She catches me in her arms and pulls me onto her lap. I love to be so close to her. I smell her soft, grassy scent and her hair and her flowered dress. I smell the skin of her face and neck when I lay my head against her shoulder.

"*Milenka, dorohenka*."

She wraps her arms around me and holds me to her.

Across the river, I can see Grandmother sitting, the arms of the willow tree wrapped around her. She is watching her daughter, and remembering.

"If she had listened," Grandmother whispers to me, "then we wouldn't have you. Little Angela. Little swallow. *Lastivka*."

They both look lovingly at me, Grandmother and Mother, and I am smiling because I am in the safest place in the world and the willow is dancing sunlight over my eyes, in Mother's arms.

I am winding water from the well into the metal bucket. The handle squeaks as I twist it round, using two hands to pull it up the dark shaft. In the winter, the handle gets stiff and I have to wear woollen gloves and struggle to pull it up, but now it is easier, just the squeaking and the weight, and I reach out and unhook the bucket, water spilling out from the top onto the ground, and onto my sandals and my feet.

I carry the bucket down the slope to the garden and push open the gate with my shoulder. I have left it unlatched. I swing the pail from side to side so that the water tips out over the top and it is a little less heavy. I put the pail down on the step and cover it with the chipped plate. The kitchen door is ajar.

I stand at the open door and imagine myself stepping up into the room, my feet dusty and sprinkled with well water. I imagine seeing Mama at the window, her face lit with happiness. She is wearing a new white dress and her hair is combed and falling around her shoulders in a golden waterfall.

"Angela!" she will say. "We are going to the café! We are going to Chernivtsi! We are going on an adventure!"

"Yes, Mama!" I will say. "Yes, yes, yes, yes, yes!"

A cat is sitting beneath the wooden bench, watching the garden with narrowed eyes. I am high up on a branch and I have a clear view of it between the lilac leaves. I fly down to the ground and then quickly up, pecking for an insect in the soil, which scuttles away.

I am distracted. The cat has noticed me. The cat's ears twitch – a touch of pink, eyes yellow – and it remains still, waiting to see what I will do.

I land on a branch above the bench and start to call out in a harsh, high voice. The cat twitches its whiskers in anger, raises its ears slightly, but still it does not move. I cry out again and another bird answers my call in short repetitive screeches. I continue to call out until the cat creeps from under the bench, pads to the door of the house and slinks into the kitchen. I give a single last rasping call, and then dive down into the garden for another insect. I snatch it in my beak and land on the ground to swallow it.

The cat, from the kitchen window, pounces.

I slip inside the bird just in time.

I was watching them from around the wall. The white and tabby cat, which comes to our garden for scraps and the bird – my bird! – which Mama leaves crumbs for on the windowsill. My bird, the body I love to fly in, the body in which I feel the springtime world touching my feathers. To be part of an unspoken flock, to carry pure desires, certainty of what to do in every moment. But my bird was not quick enough.

I feel that death is close, and I have a great desire to understand it. I sense that dying is merely the flow of spirit from one place to another, just as when as I flow from one body to another, but I have an urge to know what it is, to feel it, to understand the movement, the coming and the leaving.

I see the bird. It is almost too late.

Blink!

I am inside the familiar body. The heart is beating so fast and so high, I don't know if this tiny form can stand it. I know immediately that there is no time to look to the left or the right, but that I must fly up, up, up! The insect falls from my beak and I push into the air with a wild flapping. I sense the cat pulling back onto its haunches and pouncing towards me. Claws and narrowed eyes coming straight at me. I cannot see it, I am flying too hard, but I can sense the trajectory of the cat's body through the air, approaching me, and something in my own body tells me that I am not fast enough, that this is my death.

An intense calm comes over me, even as I am frantically flapping my wings in escape, and I enter a quiet tunnel which is this one moment, and here in this tunnel I feel the cat taking my life as it is about to, and I feel myself leaving, as I am about to, and I feel as if it couldn't possibly be any other way. The wild perfection of this makes me dizzy, and I feel a strange, deep gratitude to the cat for playing its part in this, for simply being itself in the long, miraculous moment of my death.

This tunnel which is my final second feels almost endless and yet I know that I can control it; that until I choose to release it and allow the next moment to go forwards then I can stay here, suspended, between this lunging cat with its jaws open, and my body which has prepared itself for death.

I have never known anything so quiet.

At last, it is time.

I slip out of the bird's body and back into my own. The bird releases the inevitable second, and the cat's claws enter its flesh, jaws moving to meet each other around the bird's body and together they complete the curve of the arc, which the cat began, returning together to the waiting soil. Victorious, dying, infinite.

I lean back against the wall while the bird dies. I am still in the power of that long, breathtaking moment. I know that the bird has gone and that the cat has caused no harm as it slinks away with its prey. I will find another bird to carry me up into the high white flowers. A fork-tailed swallow, a wide-winged stork, there is no difference for me. In each, I can feel the sunlight on my feathers as I dive from high through the morning air. The flock of birds I always feel close by, moving in one continuous thought, which I can enter and leave at any time. They fly as I fly in a constant movement with one another, a single movement with the world. Soaring, beating wings along the length of the springtime moments.

Mother is in the kitchen rolling out dough for cherry dumplings. Her face is tight, but as she moves the rolling pin, her eyes soften and harden, soften then harden. Next to her is a bowl of sour cherries.

"Angela, come here," she calls to me. "Come and take the *kistochki* out of these cherries."

I go to the corner and wipe the dirt from my fingers on a towel. I look at my hands, thinking for a moment that they might have blood on them. I look up at my reflection in the speckled mirror. My face has a strange smile.

"I died today," I mouth to my dark eyes. "I died with the bird. I moved with its spirit."

The thought fills me with a strange elation. I know now that death is the same as everything else. It is the flow of self. The flow of will. The movement of spirit to spirit. The constant changing and opening of everything around me.

I put the towel down and I go over to Mother and pick up the bowl of cherries. *Kistochki*. Little bones. Take out the bones. Are these cherries dying or are they already dead? I look up at Mother's face and it is hard again.

"Take them to the table," she says. "And hurry! I'm almost finished with the dough."

One by one, I open the cherries, take out the bones, and lay them in a little pile on the table.

That long moment. The tunnel. It is still here, inside of me. Happening. Transforming. Shifting.

"Angela!" Mama is staring at me. "Hurry up!"

She takes the few cherries that are ready and sprinkles them with grainy yellow sugar on a tin spoon. Then she scoops them into the middle of a small circle of dough and squeezes the edges together into a neat parcel. *Vareniki, pirohi*, cherry dumplings.

I slip my hand into the pocket of my dress and pull out a little brown feather and put it on the table.

I glance at Mother, and then I push aside the long, dreaming death inside me, and I concentrate on the bones.

My Nightspirit comes to me.

I lie on the bottom of the river, which is clear like a sheet of glass. Below me, pale spirits from that other river – the river below this river – rise up and bring me flowers. Women in ragged white with long trailing hair made from the riverbed strands. I hold out my hands.

Take them, my Nightspirit says.

I take the flowers and the women sink back into the depths.

The riverbed clouds over into silt and weeds and stones.

I rise to the surface.

8

Mother, dreaming, is walking along the willowbank. It is a hot spring day in the village and her feet are bare. A bird is singing in the branches of the tree, and Mother sits on the grass and leans her back into the curve of the trunk. Her golden-brown hair falls around her face. Her eyes are soft and scared and full of tears.

The river flows slowly, drawing the tendrils of the willows into its steady current.

She has come here to talk to her mother, on the other side of the river, and to me, floating on my back, covered in flowers.

"Why were you weeping?" Mother asks her mother. "I saw you in the kitchen when I gave you a red tulip and you took it from my hand. I was a little girl. Was it because of me?"

A slender coil of guilt weaves up through an invisible rope. The bird changes its song ever so slightly.

"No," says her mother. "It was my fault. I felt trapped. I was angry. I made so many mistakes."

"I thought I had done something wrong. I thought it was because of me."

"Nothing was because of you. The choices I made were wrong. Grisha was wrong. I was wrong. My life was wrong."

"But I was a part of that."

"They were my mistakes. They were my tears."

"I brought you a flower. I was dancing in the garden."

"I'm sorry, Lyuda. I'm sorry."

Mother's wide, pale face crumples a little. Her eyes are guilty and scared. For a moment, she is a girl again, one who does not know that the flower she has picked will forever be held in time, a small brown arm outstretched towards an open window.

She turns to me, lying on my back on the river's surface.

"All my mistakes are my own," she says.

A twist of sadness weaves deep into the coils of the rope. The bird ceases to sing. It rises in the air and flies from the tree.

I stretch out my arms in the water, covered in flowers. I wave them on each side of me, pushing the water away. The flowers are starting to rot on my body. I begin to sink beneath the surface.

"Mama!" I call out, but she is not there. I sink into the calm depths, down and down. There is no current in the river and as I descend, the rotted flowers float up to the top and lie still. Grandmother gets up from the grass and stands above me on the riverbank. She sees me lying in the perfectly clear water.

"It is all your fault," she says, and turns away.

Mother drops the jar of sour cream.

I lie in a pool of my grandmother's tears and look upwards. I see the sky through rotted flowers and somewhere, a bird is flying.

When I awake, it is night-time. I am looking up at the surface of the water and it is like a clear skin stretched across the top of the river. I wave my arms a little, and the water ripples all the way to the top. There are plants here on the bottom of the river and I am lying on smooth flat stones. It is dark, but the water is translucent and I can see everything. I like it here. It is peaceful. I am wide awake and aware of everything around me. A fish swims past. The water is moving steadily over me. It pulls at me, but my body rests calmly on the stones. I am unsure of my weight in this current. Perhaps it could carry me away, but for now I am still.

I sit up slowly, and find that the river is not so very deep. My head almost touches the surface. I push myself upwards out of the water and I stand. My white dress is clinging to me, so I pull it over my head and off my body. I lay it on the surface of the river and it floats away. My body is brown from the sunshine. The night is serene and the water is warm. It is wonderful, standing here alone in this night air. Flowers fall from somewhere onto my body. White and yellow daisies, red tulips, blue cornflowers, scarlet poppies. They drift into my hair and onto my arms and then into the clear water of the river.

The shadowy ropes of a willow tree are hanging nearby over the green bank. I climb up one of them, balancing on the slender oval leaves. I climb easily to the top of the strand, and then with a little jump I climb to a higher one. Soon, I am at the top of the tree, and I perch, and look down at the river flowing beneath me. It is so calm in the moonlight, like a stream of breath being exhaled across the sleeping land.

I exhale, and my dreams float out into the night air.

I jump, and my wings are flapping and I fly down to the surface of the river and dip my beak quickly into the water. It tastes of flowers and spring heat. I dip again, and then rise up over the river. It is a long way back to my nest. The girl will be sleeping in her bed. The woman will be sitting under the lilac tree. I am full of moonlight and flowers and spring night-time river. I fly across the fields towards the village, leaving the soft hiss of the flowing water behind me. If there is an owl watching then I may die. I fly. I reach my nest. I am safe. I dip my beak into soft feathers. Around me, the river closes.

Mother comes into the kitchen, smiling, and kisses me on the top of my head.

"You have brought the water from the well," she says. "What a good girl."

She picks up the jug of cold water and she pours some into the saucepan and strikes a match to light the stove.

I am filled with happiness at her words. She has been so sad lately. I push the chair back and come to her and I wrap my arms around her warm waist.

"*Mamochka,*" I say. "Don't be sad, don't ever be sad."

She holds me tightly to her body and then she crouches down and looks into my eyes. Her own eyes are filled with a strange light, and after a few moments it seems as if we are not looking at each other, but the light is getting stronger, and then it feels as if her eyes are somehow exploding into me, splintering into flecks and flecks of an indescribable feeling; an incredible love beyond sadness, beyond desire, beyond memory. She looks into my eyes and her mother's heart explodes into me. She holds my hands tight to keep me steady. I do not fall.

She blinks, and smiles gently. "My sweet little girl," she says.

I fall.

I am a girl filled with dreams. I sometimes imagine that I am in a dream right now, that there is another girl with tangled hair lying beneath a silver lilac, dreaming of me; dreaming that I am lying here now, creating worlds with my silver thoughts. I like to see how far back I can go without getting lost. I am a girl, dreaming of other girls, but I am the dream that another girl is dreaming, but she is also a dream, which someone else is dreaming. And she, and she, and she...

And if this was my dream, here and now, then I would keep the lilac tree just as it is. But I would make the bench a little wider. It isn't comfortable for Mama to sit on. And I would have more birds. I would have birds in all the trees. And it would always be springtime or summer, just like now. The flowers wouldn't fade and the snow wouldn't come to cover everything. I wouldn't have to go out in the cold to get water from the well in the mornings when I am half asleep. It would be like it is now.

But what about Mama? If this is my dream, then why is she so sad? I would not have made her so sad. Even when she smiles she seems to be crying. I bring her flowers from the garden, but I don't seem to be able to bring her happiness any more. We don't play together like we used to. When she makes soup it tastes of tears.

I wish I could go back to the dreamer and ask her to make Mama happy. Ask her to dream that something wonderful will happen to her, that *Tato* will come back, or that she will suddenly see how beautiful everything is, or that she will be happy when I am happy. I would ask the dreamer to do this.

The wind blows, and a few of the fading lilac flowers are carried across the garden and land on me. I love this. I try to guess where they are going to fall. I see them floating in the air and twirling down and I guess that this one will alight in my hair, and this one on my arm and this one next to me on the black earth.

Mother comes out of the house wearing her housedress and a dirty apron. Her hair is loose around her face and she looks so beautiful to me, so soft and gentle. She smiles down at me in my white dress and my long brown arms and legs.

"My little flower," she says. "My little swallow."

The river flows wide and slow. It is high spring. It is carrying the fallen flowers; some rotted, some still fresh. The river sighs. *Too many tears*, it thinks. *Too many tears*. It carries the flowers lovingly. They float back to the dreamer, who is lying on her back, a peaceful smile on her face. She sits up languorously and catches the flowers as they float past. She holds them in her hands, dripping green stalks and hanging petals. She holds her hands out in front of her, the flowers laid across them. She closes her eyes, and blows gently, and the flowers rise in the air for just a moment, and then disappear.

9

Mother stands at the sideboard below the window with a bowl of pale potatoes, which she is cleaning with a small knife. The strands of peel curl into the bowl as she releases them, and one or two are clinging to the skin of her hands. She looks down as she works, her eyes narrowed against the sunlight pouring through the window.

On the kitchen table is a heap of dried poppy husks and an empty bowl. I am to open them, one by one, and pour out the poppy seed, the *mak*. I sit at the table and take the first dry stem in my hands. I break the top from the curved pod and carefully pour out the tiny black seeds. I pick a piece of broken husk from the bowl and then tip it to the left and to the right, so that the seeds flow from one side to the other. I think of the new scarlet poppies growing in the garden, and how each of them started from one of these tiny black dots. Black into red. Red from black. My hair is black. My lips are red.

"Mama?"

She looks up and wipes the strands of potato skin from her hands without looking at them. "Yes? Are you finished with the *mak*?"

"Mama. Did *Tato* have black hair?"

She stares at me, and although her face doesn't change, her eyes widen and narrow and widen and narrow as if waves of something are passing through them.

"Why?" she says at last. "Why would you ask that?"

58

"I was thinking. I have black hair and the poppy seed is black, but you don't have black hair."

Mama stands, just looking at me. Her mouth is open a little. At last, she speaks.

"Yes," she says. She pauses and moves her tongue over her lips. "Yes. He had black hair, just like yours."

"What else? Do I look like him? What was he like?"

"Why do you want to know?" Mother puts down the potato she is holding. She wipes her hands on the front of her apron, leaving a long, brown stain over the cloth. She comes over to the table and sits down next to me. She looks into my eyes, and I think that I shouldn't have asked the question. She is breathing in and out very heavily.

"I've told you about him, my love."

"But I want to know more. What did he look like? What did he do?"

Mother reaches out and touches my hair. She takes a strand of it and untangles it carefully. She wraps it around her finger.

"He had hair like this," she says slowly. "And eyes like yours. Dark. Deep. Loving. Eyes."

"Mama?"

"Yes?"

"Where is *Tato*?"

She is curling and uncurling the strand of my hair around her finger. I can hear her breathing.

"He is somewhere," she says. She stops. Her face changes. Her features look like they are being pulled down by a heavy weight, one by one. Her forehead, her eyes, her cheeks, her mouth. She tries to pull them back and her face looks so strange. Down, up. Down, up. She swallows.

"I don't know where he is. He is somewhere, but I don't know where."

"Is he going to come back?"

"I don't..." she stops. "No. No, he is not going to come back. He is gone and he is not going to come back."

She is still touching my hair. She takes a deep breath.

"And we don't need him to come back. We are fine here together. We are fine, my darling. We are fine my little swallow, my *lastivka*."

"Mama?"

"*Milenka*."

"Why did *Tato* leave? Why isn't he going to come back?"

Mama carefully unwraps my hair from her fingers. She leans forward and kisses me on the forehead. She holds her lips on my skin and strokes the back of my head with her hand. Then she pulls away and looks into my face. Her eyes are full of tears. She tries to say something, but she can't. She is shaking her head.

At last, she says something, very quietly. I cannot hear what she says.

"Mama?"

"He didn't know…" she whispers. She picks up my hand and holds it to her cheek. I start to cry, too. I can't bear to see her like this, hurting.

"Mama?"

"He didn't know…" she says again. Her eyes and forehead are creased up, and she looks so very small and scared and old, and the skin of my hand is wet from the tears on her face.

"…how wonderful you would be." She breathes in deeply and holds the breath inside her.

She breathes out. "He didn't know how wonderful you would be."

She lets go of my hand, reaches across the table for a cloth, and wipes her face with it. I try to stop crying but I can't. It is so awful to see Mama cry. Our faces are mirrored now; wet faces, old and young. She crying for me and I for her. She wipes her tears again and then takes my head in her hands.

"But I know," she whispers. "I know how wonderful you are. I'm sorry. I'm sorry I made you cry. He doesn't matter."

"I'm sorry, Mama. I'm sorry he isn't coming back."

And I think, *he left because of me. All these tears are because of me. All Mama's tears and sadness are because I came, and then* Tato *left.*

I gather them up inside me. Fallen under the table, onto the floor, onto the chair. Each of Mother's fallen tears I collect carefully, and I take the ones from her old cheeks and then my own, and I store them inside of me in a secret place. My fault. My tears. My mother.

Mama gets up from the chair. She looks shaken. I am quiet now. I have hidden away what needed to be hidden. I will not ask again. Mother goes over to the sink and takes a cloth. She dips it into the water jug and comes over to me and carefully washes my face. Then she kisses my cheeks, my nose, my hair.

"How about that poppy seed?" she says. "I'm going to make pancakes for dinner with honey and *mak*. Would you like that?"

"Yes, *Mamochka,*" I say. "Yes, yes, yes, yes, yes."

When the pancakes are cleared away, Lyuda pours herself a glass of *samohon*, and steps out into the warm evening. Over the wooden fence, she can see Kolya working in his garden, digging with a spade. He has a basket next to him, which he is filling with vegetables. He looks up and raises his hand to her.

"Lyudmilla Hrihorivna," he calls. "How are you for *samohon*? Need any more? I have some fresh in the shed."

Lyuda raises her glass. "I've got some left."

"How about a rabbit? I've got traps in the woods. I can bring you a good fat one tomorrow. Something for your little girl."

She shakes her head. "Kolya, you know I won't."

Kolya straightens up and comes over to the fence.

"Your mother would have wanted you to have a rabbit," he says. "She'd have wanted me to keep an eye on you. We were friends, you know. I used to play in that garden with her, when I was your girl's age."

Kolya wipes his hands on his trousers. His ruddy face is covered in tiny purple veins and short, silver bristles.

"Anyway. I'm here if you need anything. A rabbit. *Samohon*. A new husband. Just say the word."

Lyuda gives out a little snort. "Kolya, you're too old for me. You're probably a hundred years old."

Kolya winks at her and nods. "At least I know a thing or two," he says. "Like how to keep a woman happy. Not run off like a lame dog. Like that fellow of yours. Good for nothing." He draws phlegm into his throat and spits on the ground and then wipes his mouth with the back of his hand, and turns back to his digging.

"You mind your own business, Kolya!" Lyuda takes a quick sip of the *samohon*, pushing her anger down, and turns away from him towards the lilac tree. She sinks beneath it, onto the earth pressed down by Angela, and takes another long sip.

Kolya was wrong. Volodiya wasn't a good for nothing. He was a man with dreams. Lyuda knows she shouldn't go back into the memories, but all of a sudden the images are lighting up in her head, one after the other. It is a long time since she has allowed herself to look at them. She pictures Angela in the sunshine beneath the willow branches and with a little sigh, she opens herself up and lets the memories come.

She is back when she first met him, when he had moved to the village for a job building houses in the surrounding hills. She had fallen in love and had let him take her everywhere in his old run-down car, a bright red Zhiguli. They had driven all over the *oblast*, the region, to waterfalls and woods, castles and lakes. They would pack a loaf of Borodinskiy bread and a *kovbaska* sausage to last them the day, and they would come home sunburned and happy and aching from making love on the forest floor, or beside a waterfall, or in his car.

And she had fought so hard with her mother over him. Her mother, who couldn't bear that he was so much older, that she hadn't finished school, that he was just passing through the region. They had screamed at each other day after day while her father had sat in the corner, crushed by the fury of his women, and not said a single word. And then her father had died, and she felt that her mother had somehow broken, had given up the fight. That Lyuda had won.

And then, on that hillside overlooking the mountains, he had put the ring on her finger – a band of gold – and he had kissed her. "I'm going to build you a house right here," he had said, and she believed him. She believed everything he told her. Even now.

Lyuda shakes her head and half laughs, half chokes. *Even now*, she thinks. *Even now I still believe him.* She has tears in her eyes again.

All he had wanted was to make something of himself, away from the *kolkhoz*, the collective farm, where his parents had spent their lives. He had an urgency to him, a burning determination to create a life for himself from his wits and hard work, which was all he had. That was why she believed him. Because all he had to rely on was himself, and he had dared to dream of making the life he wanted. And he had chosen her to share that dream with.

I didn't know a thing, she thinks. *I would have done anything for him. I was such a fool. And yet,* she pauses. *And yet I have this little girl who dances under the willow trees like a stream of sunlight.*

Lyuda looks up, and above her the lilac tree and beyond that the dark sky is so beautiful, full of stars, and she thinks that the tree is like her daughter; an impossible expression of light and beauty and radiance. She lifts the *samohon* to her lips and takes a sip. It burns through her, and she closes her eyes with a little grimace.

63

I wonder what I will tell Angela, she thinks. *I would like to tell her the truth. But I don't know what the truth is. I know that I did everything wrong, that I should have listened to Mother. I know that everything should have been different. I shouldn't have believed him. I shouldn't have let him go. But what can I tell her when everything was a mistake, and yet all those mistakes led to her?*

She shakes her head and knocks back the last of the vodka. She shivers. She shouldn't have thought of these things.

"It doesn't help to go back," she mutters. "It only brings more pain."

The night sky trembles around the garden, seeping down through the lilac, and fear creeps in shades of soft black over the soil towards her. It moves slowly and deliberately over Lyuda, covering her in a web of its darkness.

Lyuda breathes in deeply, sucking the fear down into her lungs and into her body.

She breathes out, a pale breath of hope which fades too easily into the quiet night.

She feels again the dizziness from the *samohon*, and from the heat, and from the village sounds around her. A dog is barking, the toads are singing, *cra-cra-cra-cra,* and an owl hoots in the distance.

Lyuda puts her head in her hands.

The sleeping bedroom is stiflingly hot and I have pushed the patched sheet off my body and onto the floor. Mama is breathing heavily in the bed next to me, her hair spread out over the pillow. My Nightspirit comes, and we rise together, and above the house the air is so light and fresh in the deep night-time and I let it flow through my spirit, lifting it.

You must return to the willowbank, my Nightspirit says. *Your mother is passing her tears on to you.*

"I don't want Mother to leave."

If she leaves then I will come to you. You will be protected.

"I wanted to make her happy. I thought I could. It is so difficult."

You can still help her. It is not finished yet.

"I will do anything."

She kisses me, and her kiss fills me with a blast of silver light. I will go to the willows.

She leaves, and I return to the bed where I am sleeping. I smile, and reach for the fallen sheet, deliciously cool.

10

I carry the metal bucket into the kitchen, holding it with both hands, and put it down on the stone floor. I fetch the cracked porcelain bowl we use for washing and a sliver of grey soap and a threadbare towel, and lay them on the kitchen table, next to the jar of flowers and the honey cake. Picking up the bucket, I carefully pour the clear water into the bowl until it is almost full.

I put the bucket down softly, so as not to wake Mother, and then I lean over and cup the water into my hands and splash it over my face. I rub the soap between my palms, then drop it on the table and turn my hands one over the other, the white lather rising, and bring the suds up to my face and rub them over my skin, closing my eyes tightly. I count to three in my head while I rub, one... two... I love the smell of the old soap and the smell of the water from the metal bucket – fresh, acrid, a touch of stone from the walls of the well, the waiting water – three... and I push my head down into the bowl and feel the lather sliding from my skin back into the liquid. I bring my head up and splash the water over it again and again until it is rinsed clear. I reach for the towel and bring it up to my face and hold it against my clean skin.

I drape the damp towel around my neck, pick up the bowl and carry it outside to the garden, pouring the dirty water into the corner by the wooden fence. Then I carry the bowl back into the house and set it down on the kitchen table. I pour fresh water into it for Mother. The bucket is almost empty. I take a tin

66

jug and pour out the remainder of the water and then pull the towel from around my neck and drape it over the top.

The bucket is empty now.

Mother enters the kitchen. Her eyes are swollen and narrowed from sleep. She is wearing a cotton housedress with patterned red and blue flowers. She takes a stained apron from the back of the chair and ties it around her waist. She sees the water jug and the empty bucket and says nothing. Her hair is uncombed, tumbled around her wide, pale face.

"Mama."

"Good morning, little one," she says.

"Mama, can I run to the willowbank? I won't be long."

She strikes a match for the gas and lights the circle of fire, turning the knob. She puts the small saucepan over the circle and pours the water into it to heat. She takes a glass from the cupboard and empties the remaining water and lifts it to her mouth and drinks.

"Yes," she says. "But breakfast will be ready soon."

I carry the empty bucket and lay it down on the garden step and I come back into the kitchen. I cross the room to Mother and rise on my toes and reach my arms around her neck to kiss her cheek, and I whisper, "Thank you, Mama." She turns her lips to my head and kisses my hair, the glass of water in her hand, her eyes swollen from the light.

"*Lastivka*. Little swallow," she says.

"You must break the rope."

Grandmother Zoryana reaches out a hand to me. My hair is wet from swimming and fat droplets of water are rolling down my skin. I put my hand into hers and her fingers feel like dried twigs.

"Grandmother, what is happening?"

Her blue eyes focus on my face.

"Your mother cannot free herself from her memories," she says, her voice creaking. "Her tears are touching you. Even I am being pulled back. You must break the rope."

I wind a strand of my hair around my fingers. A droplet of water runs down my shoulder.

"What will happen to Mama? If the rope is broken?"

"She will be able to see what would have happened. She will not be held in this one place, with the choices she blames herself for. It will free her from regret."

"What does that mean? Will she be happy? Will she forget all her memories?"

Grandmother tightens her grip on my hand. I am standing in front of her and I want her to let go, I want to swim back across the river. Grandmother is scaring me.

"She will be able to go to a different place."

"Will she come back?"

"The rope will grow again. Our thoughts and feelings will bring the strands back together. But your mother will be able to see. Just for a short time, she will be free of everything she thought was a mistake."

I do not understand what she is saying. I do not understand what has changed. Grandmother sees the fear in my face. She releases my hand and her eyes are suddenly kind.

"The rope contains all our memories, Angela. All our emotions. The feelings we had when we made our choices. It holds us to the single path, so that all the other possibilities are closed. If you break it, then time can breathe a little. The other paths can enter, just for a short while."

She reaches for a strand of willow, and holds it out to me.

"This is the path your mother chose," she says. "The path that led to here."

She reaches for another. "And this is the path that another choice would have brought." She takes a third and a fourth.

"And this is another and another. If you break the rope, then all these paths are possible again."

I understand.

"And what about me, Grandmother? What will happen to me? What will happen to you?"

Grandmother smiles. "You will be fine, little Angela. You are not held by any single path. You are a bridge between them all. That is how you can fly in a bird and flow as water."

"And you, Grandmother?"

"I do not know. The memories are stronger than I thought. I will be here, Angela. I will protect you until the rope grows back."

I turn away from Grandmother and look out at the river. I can hear a bird singing, I hear the hissing water, I feel the grasses pushing up through the soil. I feel the pull of all these lives, these spirits that I can flow into, as easily as imagining a dream. Everything is open to me and I know that the same stream moves through every path, that beats the wings of the bird up and down, that catches a falling flower and lets her dance in the air as she comes to ground, that pushes the sleeping petals open in the grey morning. All this is within me and moves in me and everything calls out to me to share myself, to flow with them, to share the knowledge of these different paths.

But Mama cannot do this. She cannot see the light moving in everything around her. And I have tried to show her but she cannot reach far enough. She tries, but she is pulled back into the tunnel of her own belief, and then I cannot get to her.

I turn back to Grandmother and stand tall, rising on my tiptoes. My brown wings flutter.

"I will break the rope."

Grandmother watches the bird rising and dipping over the surface of the water, and she breathes out deeply.

"She has agreed," she whispers to the Nightspirit, who is close by. "Now you must protect her."

Yes, the Nightspirit replies. She sees Grandmother struggling beneath the willows, caught in the darkness of her daughter's memories. She sees her eyes flashing in angry blue and then filling with tears.

I will always protect her, she says, and she leaves, a quiet drift of grey smoke.

Grandmother stands up from the willowbank and stares into the fast-flowing river. It looks cold and deep to her, as if it might wash away her anger. She gathers her memories around her and climbs down to the very edge of the water. She rises on her toes and dives into it.

In the garden, I am picking flowers. A flower for Mother, a flower for Grandmother, a flower for me. I hold them in my hands; white, red, white, red. I feel a pull of darkness through my body.

Grandmother is moving through the water. She is moving ancient tears. She is drawing memories into the wrong places. I can hear my Nightspirit calling to me and I see the flowers in my hands shriveling in the sunlight. White red white red.

Zoryana rises from the river into a summer garden. She is wearing a blue cotton dress with a wide belt and her fair hair is plaited down her back. There is a smell of fresh paint and Grisha is here, a hammer in his hands and a box of silver nails beside him on the ground. He winks at her and she smiles.

She goes into the kitchen. There is a bowl of soup on the stove and chopped vegetables and herbs spread out over the table. Beetroot, carrot, potato, parsley, dill, coriander, sorrel. She starts to pick them up in handfuls, dropping them into the soup. The broth changes colour as the vegetables touch the water; purple, orange, green. The smell of sorrel rises to her from the pot and she breathes in deeply, and then another smell drifts over to her – the tang of wet paint. She looks towards the window, gleaming with whitewash. Grisha has just finished working on it. She can hear him hammering outside, building the bench, which she has been asking him for, the bench just across from the lilac tree where she has dreamed of sitting on a summer evening.

Something in the tang of the paint starts to distress her, and she breathes heavily in and out, in and out, and the smell of the green sorrel, and a drop of soup bubbles up and splashes onto her dress. Why wasn't she wearing an apron? Why was she wearing her best dress in the house? She looks down at the wet droplet of soup and rubs at it. She doesn't have another dress like this; she only has housedresses. Why was she even wearing it? She goes to the window and looks out at Grisha who is on his knees, banging nails into a plank with the hammer. And the white paint on the window. She feels a wave of panic coming up around her. What if all this is a mistake? What if she doesn't want a life where all her dresses are housedresses? What if this is it? The painted window, the new bench, the blue dress. She puts her hands out and leans against the sink. She feels overwhelmingly sick, as if she wants to vomit out her life and her choices. Vomit them out and start again.

Run away! she thinks. *I could run away and marry someone else! Run away and have an affair! Live in another city. Have beautiful things. Never have children. Play music and dance, dance, dance!*

Her tears are falling onto the sink, and onto the paving stones of the kitchen floor. She feels dizzy and the stench of the paint is filling her mind as if someone is taking a great wet paintbrush and sweeping it back and forth inside her head, blocking out her self, her dreams, her desires, her wants, her everything, everything, everything!

"Mama?"

It is Lyuda at the kitchen window. Zoryana sees her from far away, from through white painted walls and tears and sickness. The child is holding out a flower to her through the window. She is standing on tiptoe, and she reaches her little pale hand up to her mother with eyes of sunlight, and she sees the tears falling from her mother's eyes, and the little girl feels a strange emotion surging through her.

"Mama, look! I've brought you a flower," she says, and Zoryana struggles to come back to her, to meet her. Through the whiteness, the dizziness, the wall of falling water. She reaches out her hand.

11

The coils of rope appear out of the darkness and twist upward between the night-time leaves of the willow trees. The rope is made of innumerable silver strings; individual strands of thought woven together into a single silver cord. This is the rope that holds together my grandmother, my mother, myself. These coils are the generations of women and the pain we share with one another, pouring up and down the fibres; through darkness, through death, through tears, through pain, blame, love, hurt and most of all, through a constant and constant repetition of the hours, the minutes, the passage of silver time. This is the rope with which we validate our womanhood. The rope we use as a guide to measure out our journeys. The cord that we wind around our bodies, binding our hearts inside and our choices outside, lashing them to the faults of our generations.

My Nightspirit comes to me.

It is time, she says. *Your grandmother is not able to help you. Your mother is lost in her darkness.*

"I am ready," I say.

In the silence of the night-time bedroom we dance, weaving in and out of each another, plaiting and unplaiting the threads of memory, passing between us knowledge, remembrance, a quiet, tender light.

I will break the rope. I do not know how I will do this but I know it is what I must do. The river is flooding with the tears of my generations.

"I will call down the stars," I say. "They are shining on me and they will help me now."

My Nightspirit draws herself around me in an embrace.

I will come if you need me, she says.

We unwind, like twisting smoke, and she leaves. My body, covered with a patched sheet, sleeps quietly.

It is night-time.

I awake from my sleep. Mother is lying in the bed beside me, her lips parted, breathing in and out her quiet sorrow. I rise from the bed in my nightgown, which hangs to my knees. My feet are bare. I push open the door of the bedroom and walk through the kitchen. The air in the house is heavy and the stones of the kitchen floor are cool beneath my feet. I draw back the bolt of the front door and pull it open, just wide enough for me to slip through into the garden.

On the step, the metal of the water bucket is gleaming in the moonlight. I lift the plate from the top and look down into its dark mirror. I dip my fingers into the water and send ripples across its surface. I touch my neck and my face with my fingertips and then cup my hand into the water and drink.

The night-time earth is dry; the lilac tree is a gentle grey. The garden is absolutely silent. Beneath the lilac, I lower myself into the mould of my body, pressed down from my hours of daylight dreaming. Beneath me, the soil pushes through thin cotton to my skin. I lay my arms out on each side of me, stretched into the form of a star.

I look up into the wild explosion of stars.

"I am ready," I say.

My spirit rises gently upwards into the sky. As it passes through the lilac tree, the grey flowers awaken and turn towards the starlight, growing brighter. The tree silently transforms itself into a burning white lantern in the garden, each of its flowers open and receptive to me, to my desires, to the mystery of its own expression. The starlight pours down through it and catches my rising spirit, bearing me up on a beam of silver light.

I close my eyes, and my body disappears into the light.

I speak to the stars.

"I am here to break the rope," I say.

"We are waiting for you," they reply, through the darkness.

Around me are stars, and the breath of the lilac that I carry within me, and a night-time universe.

I open my spirit and I concentrate on the star shape my body has created in the black soil below, and around this shape I draw a circle. Into the circle I pour silver lilac blossoms, which fill with light. I am now a silver star in a white circle. I merge my spirit into this form and then I start to draw the stars into me, into this glowing ring. One by one they come; at first carefully, and then suddenly, pouring their light into my form, filling me with themselves, the universe opening up its darkness to channel all the shafts of starlight into the single point of my body.

I summon before me the silver rope with which we are bound; Mother, Grandmother and myself. I picture vividly every separate thread woven from tears, pain and hurt. I see how it is wound around us three; invisible, pulsing, snaking. And with the starlight lifting me up, lifting me together with the vision of this silver rope, I create with my spirit a great sword with a silver shining blade and I lift this blade high above my head and I bring it down upon the rope. The rope shudders, and the outer threads writhe strangely in the deep night, cut off from the minds which created them, from the hearts which fed them. I lift the sword again, and cut again, and the sword goes deeper, slicing closer to the centre. The rope weaves itself tighter, creating new strength from the close-bound threads. I raise my arms one final time, and I ask once again for the stars to guide my stroke, to guide my will, and then I bring it down onto the last, writhing tendrils; those which would have held my mother in her grief, and my Grandmother, that would have wound their way around my heart for all my days, and the tendrils break apart, twisting madly, dancing wildly into the darkness with the last energy of their pain.

I watch, and they drift away, strand by strand, and are gone.

I release the sword, and the stars reach out and claim it back to themselves.

It is done. Before me I see my mother and my grandmother. The separate silver threads are unwinding, one by one, from around their limbs and hearts, shrivelling into a faint dust and falling to the ground at their feet. I hear a shout and I start to fade through the starlight.

It is done, I hear, falling. *It is done.*

I return to my body as the white circle disappears. I am dazed and profoundly calm. I sit up, and the black soil clings to the skin of my shoulders and arms. It is in my hair. I lean back against the trunk of the tree, and listen.

Mother awakes, her eyes flashing open and gasping, inexplicably desperate to touch her daughter. She reaches over and sees that the bed is empty. She calls out in a wild panic and runs into the kitchen calling my name. The garden door is open.

"Angela!"

I take a long, deep breath, and then I stand. My nightdress is covered with soil. Black earth falls from my hair.

Mother is standing in the doorway staring at me. Her eyes are wide open. Her head is pounding from vodka and her heart from panic. She can't seem to understand what she is seeing.

"Angela! Come in, quickly! What are you doing out there in the garden? Come in!"

I walk towards her slowly, the earth dry beneath my feet. I feel the deepest exhaustion, as if I could collapse right here on the ground. I am not sure that I can even make it to the kitchen door.

"Mama?"

I reach out my hand to her and she runs forward and picks me up in her arms. I start to cry as she carries me into the house and straight through the kitchen into the bedroom. I have never been so tired in my life. Mama lays me down on the bed and pulls the covers up over me. She wipes my eyes with the corner of the sheet.

"Angela, *milenka*, my darling," she is saying. "It must have been a dream. You must have been sleepwalking. Darling, stop crying. Close your eyes. Everything is alright. Go back to sleep. I'll sit here with you."

She is stroking my head and she leans down and holds me to her. I feel her body is different. Lighter, calmer, freer. I have done my task. I close my eyes.

My Nightspirit watches me.

She called down the stars, she whispers to herself. *She became a blade of silver starlight.*

Yes, I reply, my eyes shining.

Grandmother is on the willowbank when the rope is cut. She is pacing on the grass, caught in the sway of long-gone moments and half-forgotten anger. As the threads fall apart, Grandmother feels a coldness going through her, an emptiness, and the memories fall away, leaving her alone on the riverbank.

She looks around her, and sees no one. She feels for a thread of emotion and finds nothing to hold on to. She starts to panic, and she runs among the willow trees, thinking she has lost us, reaching out wildly to her daughter and granddaughter. She casts a strand of flame into the branches, and the tendrils light up, burning with the intensity of her fear.

"Lyuda!" she calls out. "Angela!" but getting no response, she grasps the burning strands of willow and holds them to her body, trying to create a new pain that will bring us back to her.

In the branches of the smouldering willow, my burned feathers shrivel and smoke. I must find a place to heal. I look around and my eyes rest upon the river. I open my wings and flap them a few quick times to see if I can fly. I rise up just a little from the burned branch and I am held in the air. It is possible. I focus my attention onto each of my feathers, pouring the remaining energy of my body into them, concentrating whatever life force I have left into the cells, the fibres, the barbs.

I am ready, and I rise, flapping my wings as fast as I can. I lift up from the branch and fly down over the blackened tree. The river is just there. My body is excruciatingly painful, searing pain through my feathers with every upward downward flap, and now I am falling. Let it be the water, let it be the river. Let it please.

I catch her.

Tumbling down towards me, burned and spent, a creature small and in pain, I catch her in my waters and I take her in. Her life force flows at once into mine and I gather the most generous powers within me and I pour them into her. Within me, she transforms, releases her pain and opens her broken cells to mine, which carry all the healing of the world. She gives herself to me entirely, frail pain and gentle song.

All healing is here in me.

I come to Grandmother, walking lightly, and I stand in front of her. A girl in white. Tangled, dark hair. She is sitting with the willow against her back on the green grass. Grey ash from the burned branches drifts around her.

"Grandmother."

She raises her head and looks at me. Through her eyes I can reach her. I open a tunnel of light.

"Grandmother, it is Angela. I am here." My words travel down the tunnel and she receives them, and tries to understand them.

I kneel in front of her and look up into her blue eyes. "I love you," I say to her, and a strand of silver winds its way towards her. "I love you," I say again, and another strand entwines itself with the first.

Grandmother looks at the silver wisps weaving together in a thin cord, and then she looks up into my face in wonder. New threads wrap around one another in winding coils.

"You have broken the rope," she says.

Grandmother swims in the river. She is naked, and her old body looks strange under the flowing water, almost insect-like, shrinking bones under flabbed skin. She swims from one side to the other, but she knows that she cannot emerge onto our bank, her time here is long gone.

I have broken the rope and all pain has disappeared. Grandmother remembers now that every moment of her life was a quiet perfection. She would like to go back to her youth, when she lay laughing under the sweeping branches, she green, they black in her eyes looking up into the sunshine. She danced in the arms of Grisha here under these willow branches. He held her around the waist, she in her blue cotton dress, and he whirled her around the willow trunk. And they lay laughing and flushed under the leaves and held each other.

"We swam," says Grandmother, swimming. "We swam, naked, in this river. Birds were singing. I dived underwater and all I could hear was the rush of the current flowing. When I came up, everything seemed so still after the rushing of the water, and the song of the birds came to me quite suddenly. The branches of the willows themselves seemed to be singing."

Grandmother turns around in the water. She has reached the far bank, where we all sit, listening, watching, waiting. Her granddaughters and great-granddaughters and great-great-granddaughters. Watching and listening, hands clasped in one another's. She smiles at us, knowing that we have always been here, and that she has always been here, and then she turns in the water and starts swimming back to the other side, where she must wait for now, for her daughter to make a choice.

"And then he came up behind me," she whispers to the river. "He held me while I listened to the birds singing, and he held my breasts under the water, and he stroked my green body, and we disappeared into the water," she whispers, disappearing into the water.

Lyuda sits at the kitchen table and looks straight through the glass jar of wild flowers. Through the white and yellow daisies, golden dandelions, tumbling poppies. She looks through them to the memory beyond and she breathes slowly. The spring air shifts when she breathes out. The air is heavy, and it sinks onto the petals of the cut flowers, resting on the ragged explosion of yellow, on the chapped petals of the daisy. Pollen rises from the gold, from the black of the poppy, weaves in time as it is held with an outward breath.

Lyuda breathes, and time hears her heart. It shifts. The flowers shift. In the garden, her daughter sits up with a start, her heart beating wildly.

Her mother has gone.

PART TWO

12

In Volodiya's house, the baby was always screaming.

And there was always a new baby.

Sometimes there was a respite, if his mother could organise the older girls to carry the children out to the yard, or down the lane to the fields. But apart from these brief moments, there was a constant noise of suffering or complaint or pain.

But that was better than the other noises. The late-night horrors when his father was home, drunk, and his mother was struggling in their bed in the corner with his father grunting like a hog over her and it sounded like Mother was suffocating. More pain.

And then there was the real pain. That was when he had to lie in his bed, not moving, while his father swore at his mother in a low, guttural voice. After that, there would be a silence, and he would clench his fists and wish, wish that the next part would not come. But it always did.

A thud. And the strange, bird-like whistle that his mother gave out when she was struck.

Another thud. And he would hear his mother fighting back, pushing against the heavy flesh.

And then a third thud, and he would hear the chairs moving, as she would try to get away, into the corners of the room.

The first three blows and sounds were so distinctive, he sometimes heard them in his head when they weren't happening. He would hear a bird chirping, and think that it was his mother, and that it was beginning. Or a tussle between boys, and think that it was his mother trying to push his father away. Or the scraping of a chair, and instantly he would see his mother trying to escape from the room. Although she never did escape.

He understood later that she didn't want to leave their father alone, drunk, in a house full of children.

After the first three blows, which followed the pattern, he would put his hands over his ears. It didn't last for long. He could still feel the thuds through the walls, and hear the whistle of the suppressed pain, but eventually it stopped. Sometimes, a baby would wake up in the middle and start to wail, and his father would finish with her early, and he would see his mother in the moonlight through the curtains, hurrying across the bedroom to the child, hunched over, and a face shaped differently to how it was during the day. She would pick the baby up and hold it to her body, which was in a strange position, twisted to one side, or uneven, and the baby in her arms would make them look even stranger, like some kind of deformed monster in the silver of the moonlight, and she would pace up and down the bedroom with it, not returning to the kitchen; this strange, night-time creature.

Those were the good times, when the baby cried, and often his father would fall asleep in the kitchen and he would hear the heavy, guttering breath and know that he could sleep. And eventually his mother would creep back into her bed, the baby calmed, and wait for morning.

It was never long before a new baby was howling.

When he was older, Volodiya tried to stop these night-time beatings.

When he thought that his father was angry, or he knew something had gone wrong on the farm, he would stay up late with his mother, resisting her demands for him to go to bed. They would hear the footsteps together and wait, and when he entered the kitchen, they would know, from the smile on his face, if it was to be a night of jokes and friendly advice and then the suffocating grunts, or a night of pain.

The first night he stayed up, it was a night of pain.

"Father."

Volodiya stood up from his chair when the kitchen door opened. His mother remained seated, in her usual place, so very still.

His father stopped in the doorway, his eyes moving from one face to the other, reading the situation, his smile held poised.

"Vova – come to your father."

Volodiya had felt his legs starting to shake when his father spoke, and a white sickness came into his head and stomach. He moved forward towards the door. His father waited, his bulk holding the space of the doorway, his face red.

"Come. Come here."

His father waited until Volodiya was standing directly in front of him, his head barely level with his chest. He reached out and grasped his son's shoulders with his huge hands, squeezing them, making him feel the vast strength behind them, reminding Volodiya of his own smallness, his inability to match his father.

And then he saw his father's arm moving back into a practised movement, and swinging round again in a familiar arc, and the hand was meeting with his head and all the white sickness came rushing in and then it merged with a darkness, and the two were together for a moment, the darkness and the whiteness, and then Volodiya remembered nothing else.

When he awoke, with his head pounding, he could hear a new sound. The guttural snoring from the kitchen, but then from his mother's bed: a repeated, jagged breath, as if there was not enough air to take in. He had wanted to go and see her, but then the whiteness came over him again, and he slept.

After that, he stayed in the bedroom while it happened. But he hated himself more and more for not being there, for not taking the blows. He grew taller, and started to feel strength gathering in his body, and he worked hard on the farm, determined to make his body huge like his father's, a body big enough to protect, to stop anything bad happening.

And he started to make promises to himself. Promises that he would repeat between the lessons at school, and after school helping with the farm work, and in bed at night. The words of his promises became like the hands of a clock for him, ticking behind every action, waiting for their next repetition, measuring out the moments until their fulfilment.

"I will have a big house," he promised himself, "with rooms and light and space for everyone."

And then: "I will have the most beautiful wife. I will buy her everything she could ever want. Every time I open the door of the house she will be happy. She will not know what it means to be in pain."

And then: "I will have money for everything. I will have money to travel to any country. I will buy a car. I will have endless food and drink for my family and for my friends. My house will be the biggest in the region."

He would repeat these pledges over and over, and as he got older, he began to understand how he might fulfil them. He started to earn some money on the farm, and he saved it up to buy an old Zhiguli from a friend of his father. It needed a lot of work, but it was his own car, and it was the very first of his dreams fulfilled.

13

He first saw her from the edge of the building site next to the school grounds. She was leaving the main schoolhouse, and the sun caught on a mass of her hair and it was dazzling in the light; a waterfall of gold shining through the greys and blacks of school clothes and village dust. He couldn't take his eyes off her. She was tall, and as he watched she moved forwards, and he saw that she was slender, and had a young woman's body in profile. The sun was shining so brightly that he couldn't see her face at first, but he had stopped his work to stare at her amongst the other students coming out of the school door and onto the main street.

Then she had turned to speak to a friend – a dark-haired girl with a shorter, stouter figure – and she was laughing, and her pale, lovely face was lit up in the midst of her mass of shining hair. It was the most beautiful thing he had ever seen.

He watched the girls until they had turned the corner off the dusty road, and then he brought his hand up to his eyes to shade them, feeling blinded by what he had seen.

He closed his eyes and images of black and white were swimming in his vision, and it was several minutes before he could see again properly and return to the building work, smoothing wet mortar and laying the bricks of a new wall.

That night, in the rundown apartment he was sharing with three other men, he lay on his mattress and thought of her. She was so young, and so beautiful. She would be the perfect woman to build his dream with. They could create a life happier than any other. They could build a house on a hill together. In time, they could have a family.

He decided to meet her.

"Excuse me."

The two girls looked round.

"I'm sorry to interrupt you, but I'm trying to find Moon Hill. I've heard it has the most beautiful views around here, and I don't know which direction it is."

The girls were studying him. He was staring directly into the eyes of the one with the golden hair. They were light brown, flecked with green and gold. They were looking directly into his. He drew his gaze over the rest of her face. She was smiling.

"Who told you it has the most beautiful views?" the one with the golden hair asked. Her voice was low and full of laughter. Not a girl's voice.

"I work at the school. I'm building the new classrooms. The men from the construction site told me."

"Did they?"

"It's a sunny afternoon. There's no more work today. I decided to explore the area. They told me to find this hill."

"What about your friends?" It was the dark-haired girl.

"All the men from the site have gone drinking. I don't have any friends yet. I've only been here a week or two."

The girls were both watching him. The brown and golden eyes held in his own made his stomach move in a strange way. He turned to the dark-haired girl and smiled.

"Do you know where it is?"

"We can take you there!" The golden-haired girl touched her friend's shoulder. "Can't we, Sveta? It isn't far. Come on!"

She was laughing and her friend was laughing and it was so easy. The two girls were walking up the village street, arm in arm, and he found himself hurrying to keep up with them.

It was the beginning of a dream.

From the top of the hill, they could see for miles around. The Carpathian Mountains rose up in the distance, wooded peaks with strands of cloud drifting among them; and before that, rolls of the deepest green and then stretches of yellow corn and black soil. The land he had grown up with had been flat, ploughed farmland as far as could be seen, broken up with pig farms and storage sheds. It was good, fertile land, but it was not beautiful like this. It was not the Carpathians.

The wind was strong at the top, and the girls were laughing and shouting to each other. They asked him questions – where he was from, why he was here, what he thought about this and that – and he answered them calmly, catching the golden-brown eyes when he could, and each time feeling that whiteness moving in him as their eyes met; her attention entirely on him for just that quick moment, her body and her voice so close.

"We can show you other things," Sveta said, when they had climbed down the hill and were approaching the village. "There are lots of places nearby. Castles, waterfalls, forests."

"And next time, Vasya can come, can't he?" the golden-haired girl turned to Sveta.

Sveta giggled. "Yes. We can take his car. You can make a friend."

"You can find me at the site next to the school," said Volodiya. "I'm there every day. Thank you for showing me the hill."

"We've got to go now," said Sveta. "Goodbye, Vova!"

"See you soon," he said to Sveta. He turned to the other girl, hoping to catch her face again, and there it was, waiting for his words.

"You never told me your name," he said.

The girl smiled. Her cheeks were flushed and she held his gaze.

"It's Lyudmilla. Lyudmilla Hrihorivna."

He nodded. "It's a pleasure to meet you, Lyudmilla Hrihorivna. I'll look out for you tomorrow. Maybe come to find me when your day finishes?"

"We'll see. Goodbye, Volodiya."

She turned, and Volodiya watched the two girls until they disappeared into their houses further down the street, and then he began his journey back to his shared room at the edge of the village, his mind full of gold and laughter and sunshine.

"Lyuda, this is for you."

His hand was resting on her knee and the Carpathian Mountains were stretching out before them. The wind was blowing her hair into a net of gold.

She turned to him and saw that he was holding out his hand, and in the curve of his palm there was a gold ring.

"Vova, what is this?"

He leaned forward until his lips met hers and he held her face against his.

"Lyuda, I want to live with you here. I want us to be together. I want us to live here in a house and I will give you everything you could ever want."

"Right here?"

"Yes. Right here. I'm going to build you a house where we can see all of this. The first money I have, I'll buy the land,

and then we'll build it. And we'll live together and we'll have a family."

"I've got to finish school first."

"Of course you do. But I want you to have this waiting for you."

He opened his palm again with the ring. "Give me your hand, Lyudichka."

Her fingers were shaking. She held out her hand to him.

"There."

Volodiya clasped her fingers in his, and pushed the ring easily onto her right hand. He held it there for a few moments longer, and then he brought it up to his mouth, to kiss.

"I'm going to give you everything you ever wanted, Lyudichka."

Lyuda brought the hand up in front of her face. It looked different. It looked like the hand of someone older. Her body felt light and strange. Volodiya was running his hand up her leg, pushing her short skirt higher. The sun was in her eyes and she was feeling dizzy, and he had wanted to make love to her for weeks now, but she had held out. She had listened to all her friends at school advising her not to do it, telling her to keep him waiting.

But now something was different. Now, it was as if the desire in her body was flowing evenly with the desire in her mind, as if everything was coming together. There was nothing more to hold out for. He was here, and his hand was moving over her waist inside her skirt, and down.

And then his body was moving on top of hers – gently, for his size, for his weight – and the dizziness in her head was getting stronger, and her body seemed to be deciding everything for her, and she lifted her hand, feeling the gold on her finger, and she put it behind his head, stroking the short brush of his hair.

Her eyes met his. Dark, deep, loving eyes.

"Yes Vova," she said. "Yes, yes, yes, yes, yes!"

14

"Vova, I'm going to have a baby."

She was stroking his head, just as she always did after they made love, running her hands over his hair, smoothing his forehead, touching the skin of his cheeks. He liked to feel her fingers on him as he drifted off, knowing her face would be there to meet him when he opened his eyes again, and her body, naked beside him, her breasts and her small waist and her smooth back and arms.

Her words were soft, and it took some seconds for their meaning to reach him through the daze, through her gentle touch. A baby.

He opened his eyes. A baby.

He shook his head and pushed himself up in the bed.

"Lyuda?"

She had moved back a few inches on the mattress, and was watching his reaction. She pulled the sheet up to cover her breasts. She was studying his face.

"How do you know?"

"I've been throwing up for three days now. My whole body is sore. I can feel it."

"You could just be ill?"

"Vova, I'm sure. It's a baby."

There was a pause.

"It's our baby, Vova."

He closed his eyes. It was too soon. He didn't have enough money. She hadn't finished school yet. It was too soon. He thought they had been careful, but then it had been going on for weeks now, the lovemaking, and he knew that things could happen. It was too soon.

He reached out under the sheet and found her hand, resting on her stomach. He pulled it out, feeling for the ring on her finger.

"What do you want to do?" he asked.

It was Volodiya who drove her to the maternity hospital, when the time came. Her mother was still in the forty-day mourning period for her father, and refused to leave the house. There was more room there since Grisha had died, and yet everything seemed smaller somehow. Her mother had started wearing headscarves, even in the house, as if she was practicing to be an old woman, and her black clothes had shrunk her body, as Lyuda's figure grew larger with every month, her pale face filling out and her golden hair lustrous and thick like a sheaf of harvest corn.

Volodiya moved into the house after Grisha's death, and they shared the small bedroom to the side of the back room, where Lyuda's mother slept. The house was hot and small and Zoryana barely spoke to him, laying out the food for each meal with a sullen face, and sniping at Lyuda for every detail.

He kissed Lyuda at the entrance to the hospital, holding a small bag with her slippers and nightgown and soap and money to give to the nurses.

"I'll see you soon, Lyudichka. Everything will be fine. Sveta will be with you. I'll come as soon as they let me in."

She waited for him to say more, or for something to happen, for a moment of sunlit hilltop romance, his arm around her waist, her heart beating with excitement. But it never came.

Another wave of the spreading pain entered her body, and she drew her face into a tight grimace.

When it had finished, she opened her eyes and he was walking towards the car.

She could feel the baby inside her, kicking against her womb, ready to come out. She turned and pushed open the door of the hospital.

Three days later, he came to pick her up.

Lyuda looked bloated and shaken, holding a small baby wrapped in hospital cloths.

"Lyudichka!"

He hugged her and kissed her face, while she stood stiffly, the baby in her arms. He led her to the car and opened the door. As he drove, she looked out of the window.

"I've got to work tomorrow," he said. "I'm being moved to a new site. I've got a chance to be the next foreman so it's a good opportunity."

"Can't you stay a few days?" she asked, in a small voice.

"It's a great opportunity, Lyudichka," he said again. "I want to build that beautiful house for us. We need money for that. I need to take the work where I can get it."

"How far is it?"

"It's an hour's drive away. I'll be back in the evening. I can take some bread and sausage for breakfast if you're sleeping."

"Aren't you going to help me with the baby?"

She was looking out of the window.

"You've got your mother there. You can manage between you. I might not have to work at the weekends."

She was silent, and he felt angry that she didn't understand. He didn't want to live in that small, dark house with her mother who hated him. He had to save their money. He had to make enough money for something bigger, something better. For their life full of happiness and sunshine.

He glanced over at her. He could see the side of her cheek, turned away from him, as she stared. A thin streak of water was glistening on it.

The baby started to cry.

When Lyuda came down the garden path, closing the gate behind her, the rain was pouring down.

She pushed open the door of the house. She had come from a check-up at the hospital, an hour on the village bus each way over bumpy roads, and now the rain was soaking through everything. The baby was hidden inside her coat, for warmth. She closed the door behind her and stood, the rain dripping from her hair and clothes onto the kitchen floor.

"Mama?" she called out. "Mama, the soup's not on. It's almost six."

She nudged off her wet boots and left them on the mat, going through to the bedroom. The soup should have been cooking by now.

Her mother was lying on the bed, her body unnaturally still, her face deep in a headscarf.

"Mama?"

Lyuda stood in the doorway looking at the figure on the bed. "Mama?"

Suddenly, she felt it. She knew that if she reached out and touched her mother's hand, that it would be cold. Her coat was dripping rainwater and the warm baby was wriggling in her arms.

"Mama?"

Lyuda called out one last time, but she knew that it wouldn't help. She balanced the baby over one side of her body and reached out to touch her mother's wrist. It was cold. She leaned forward and pushed back the dark headscarf, and her mother's eyes were open, and empty. Her fingers brushed against her mother's cheek and it was cold.

"Oh my god."

She stared at her mother's face, unable to move, willing it not to be true. A blankness came over her, as if her body was refusing to choose a reaction to what she was seeing. As if it knew that the longer she didn't move, the longer it could hold off the pain that was waiting to flow into her.

The baby wriggled and made a small sound. At last, Lyuda shifted, and looked down at its face; tiny eyelids folded over sleeping eyes, the mouth moving in little smiles. The sight of its face released something in her mind, and the first wave of fear went through her. Her father was gone. Her mother was gone. There was nobody to help her.

She thought of all the work her mother had done. She thought about the work that needed to be done. The soup to make for dinner. The pile of clothes to be washed. The constant buckets of water from the well. The cutlets for Volodiya's supper. The shopping from the market.

"I can't do it," she whispered. "Mama, I can't do it without you."

Then there would be the funeral to arrange. And Volodiya spending more and more time at the building site, sometimes not coming back for days. And every night the baby crying and waking her from her short sleep, and then having to get up again, and then again to make breakfast for Volodiya, when her head was banging and she felt like crying. She couldn't even imagine how she looked to him anymore.

She sat down on the edge of the bed, the baby in her arms, and she began to rock her body back and forth. Tears ran down her face the more she rocked, and she held the sleeping baby tight against her. She looked at her mother through the falling water and felt the panic rising in her body.

"Mama," she whispered. "What am I going to do?"

"My poor Lyudichka. My poor Lyudichka. I'm so sorry."

Volodiya held her as she cried, struggling to block out the noise of the baby, which was crying in the other room. Lyuda was shaking, her face bloated from all the tears, and she rocked herself in his arms. He tried to think about her, even though he had come home from a long day of work, hungry, and there was nothing to eat, no soup, no cutlets, no potato, no vegetables.

"What am I going to do?" she was saying. "What am I going to do?"

He held her close as she cried, and felt her body against his, thicker and heavier since the baby, and her clothes stained with milk and splashes of cooking. The shapeless housedresses she now wore, and the slippers. The look of exhaustion, always there. She didn't smile much any more. He couldn't remember when she had last put on a lovely dress. He couldn't remember the last time they had made love.

"It's going to be alright," he said. "It's going to be alright."

15

"Lyuda. The soup isn't hot enough."

The winter had come. Outside the window, the white flakes were pounding on the glass in a gale, piling up a bank of snow that he would have to clear to get to work in the morning.

"Lyuda?"

She was sitting opposite him. Her eyes met his. The look on her face was pure hatred. The baby was on her lap and her golden-brown eyes were full of such anger and disgust that he felt something inside him twist. She had been at home all day, in the warm house, just watching the baby. Her dress was dirty. The supper was terrible. The bread was stale. He pulled the lid off the vodka, half-filled a glass, set the bottle down. He knocked it back. He waited.

"Lyuda? The soup is cold!"

She stood up, and carried the baby through to the bedroom behind the kitchen. When she came back, she went to the stove and struck a match to light the hob. Every movement of her body was an expression of her hatred for him. Every movement of her body filled him with anger. The feeling twisted again. It reached out to his hands, wrapped in tight fists on his knees. He pushed it back.

Lyuda came round to his side of the table and picked up his bowl of soup. She took it to the stove and poured it into the saucepan. She stirred it with a tin spoon, scraping the metal round and round. The baby began to cry in a high rasping whine.

The noises seared into his head, each separate sound creating a layer of anger and rising panic. These were the noises of his childhood. The screaming babies, the scraping of metal on pans, the growling aggression of a male voice. Even the howl of the snow outside the window. These were the noises that he had escaped from, and now they were all around him.

It was worse when Lyuda started to complain, accusing him of something new every day, of something wrong, of everything that had been promised. How he wasn't supporting her, how alone she felt, how she cried when he didn't come home for two or three days. And then, at night, after all the accusations, she would lie close to him and expect comfort, and she would cry. But by that time it was all he could do not to get up and leave the bed, and he would turn his back to her, trying to block out her sobbing and ragged, jerking breaths. It was a relief when the baby needed feeding and she would get up at last.

He squeezed his fists tighter.

The soup was ready and he watched her pour it into his bowl – a drop splashing onto her dress – and carry it to the table. The baby was crying louder now, but she wasn't doing anything about it.

"Lyuda. The baby is crying."

He poured another glass of vodka and knocked it back. She fetched the baby and sat down opposite him.

"Shhhhh," she said. "Sssshhhhhhh."

He turned to his soup. Steaming red borsch with lumps of meat and potato and beetroot. He took a spoonful and a piece of rye bread and chewed it heavily, blocking out her voice and the baby's cries and the snow pounding against the window and the wind whistling through the cracks. The baby started to scream. She should take it to the other room. She should be able to control it.

"Lyuda…"

He felt the rage coming up in him again, and he glanced over to her. He met her eyes and there it was again. The disgust.

The hatred. Everything he had ever done wrong. Everything she wanted to tell him. He squeezed his fists.

Something had to change.

He got up, leaving his soup, and lifted his winter coat from the hook next to the door. He pulled on his boots and took his thick gloves, and a fur hat to cover his ears.

When he opened the door, the snow smashed into his face in a blast of wind, freezing his skin. He slammed the door behind him. He picked up the shovel that was leaning semi-frozen against the wall and began to dig the snow from the kitchen step, clearing away the soft fall before it settled into solid layers. He finished the step and then moved down the garden path, pushing the snow to each side to make an avenue towards the garden gate. The wind was flying around him and his cheeks turned a bright red with the cold.

He reached up to the icicles above the window and broke them with the shovel. He couldn't reach the ones on the roof. He worked the path all the way to the gate and then opened the gate and cleared the slope to the village street. Soon, the trucks would arrive to salt the roads. He had sacks of salt stored in the old chicken shed in case the trucks couldn't get through, or the garden turned to ice.

He thought about his job, about the construction work that was slowing for the winter, about the contract he had been offered in another region, on the other side of the country. It would be more money, it would bring him closer to everything he wanted. And Lyuda. All her stupid mistakes. Ruining the happiness they could have had. It wasn't so difficult. He worked all day at the construction site, it wasn't so much to come home to a hot dinner and a baby that wasn't crying. She wasn't out in the fields all day, working on the farm with four children and a savage husband to look forward to every night. He knew what it meant to have a hard life.

And now he was feeling this urge, every time she looked at him in that way. He remembered the way his father had dealt with his frustration, and he sensed how easy it would be for his body to follow the movements it knew so well. He had been pushing it down, but he felt it inside him, waiting, and at some point, if something didn't change, it was going to come out.

He had never wanted her to get pregnant. He had never wanted his dreams to twist into such distortions of happiness. He had never wanted anything but an easy, carefree life for her. The rage came up in him again, and he felt it overtaking him. He raised the shovel high and brought it down on the garden gate as hard as he could. The gate smashed, breaking from its hinges and swinging away from the path; the latch, the metal broken. Then, after the rage, he felt a rush of something else. An awful sadness, as if something inside *him* had broken. His strength, his will, the love that he had felt for her, the dream that he believed he could build for them both, his determination to struggle against the life he had always known, the life that was ready to pull him back at any moment. He felt a choking sensation surging up inside him. He didn't let it out. He coughed and pushed it back. He looked at the gate and at the shovel in his hands.

There was no big house. There was no beautiful wife. There was no peace and sweetness. There was no money. There was him and his anger and the vodka and his fists.

His promises watched him, waiting for him to make a decision. Waiting for him to accept the noise, the unhappiness, the pain, the anger, the drink, the struggle, the violence. Waiting for him to say yes to all the misery and affirm the one betrayal that would lead to all the others. The choice that would break every dream, every belief, everything he had always worked for.

"No," he said aloud. "No. This will never be my life. Never."

He walked forward in the snow, his fists clenched into huge mallets. The snow was hurling against his skin and the wind was blasting his body, and in his heart and in his head, he made what he knew was the most terrible decision of his life.

"What about me?" screamed Lyuda, when he said the words to her, and the baby started to cry. "What am I supposed to do? What about my life? What about the baby?"

He stood near the door, his face hardened. He looked at the woman in front of him and he tried not to see the girl she had been.

"Goodbye, Lyuda," he said.

He picked up his bag. He opened the door. The wind blew. Lyuda howled.

He walked out of the door.

Lyuda put her hands up to her head. The baby was crying.

"What am I going to do?" she whispered.

Volodiya walked out into the snow and pulled his fur hat down over his head, and the ear flaps over his ears, where he could still hear Lyuda's screams. He slung his bag up over his shoulder and went through the smashed gate, hitching it back up onto the broken latch behind him. He didn't see the last glimpse of Lyuda, pulling open the kitchen window and hurling the ring out into the swirling snow behind him, her tears already turning to a quick ice.

He climbed the slope and walked in the falling snow to the bus stop. The bus arrived, its windows grey and condensed with the heat of passengers, and he climbed on. There were no seats and it was packed with villagers and bags, heavy coats steaming and hats and the smell of sweat and smoke and vodka. And the bus moved off, carrying him, his life, his bag, and his memories of a place where he would be left a shadow, held forever alive by the energy of a single, desperate howl.

The snow fell, and the tracks of his steps disappeared into the whiteness.

Lyuda, quietly crying, was feeding their baby.

16

The darkness is crushing me. I open my eyes and feel it pushing down into every cell of my body. Dark, down, everywhere. My lungs feel too heavy to breathe, my heart too laden to beat, my body too weighted to move at all. Part of it must be exhaustion. I barely sleep with the baby sucking and crying. When she sleeps for a few hours I have to cook something so I have strength to feed her.

It seems there is no end to this winter. For days now it has snowed and snowed and snowed. The few hours of light show only falling snowflakes through the windows and the glint of icicles hanging from the eaves, before darkening again. In the garden, everything is white except for the trunks of the trees and a few twigs that have shaken off the snow. There are still birds. I cannot understand how they can live in this cold. Where do they go? Where do they sleep? How are they not frozen? Where do they find food?

The questions pass through my head without any desire to know the answers. Questions, questions, questions. How did I get into this situation? How is it possible that I am here? How is it possible that I am a mother and that my mother is gone and that I am on my own? How is it possible that I look like this, filthy in a filthy dress? My hair is filthy. My body is covered in dried milk. My face looks like it is a hundred years old. How long have I looked like this? A month? A week? What does it matter? Nothing matters. I am in this house surrounded by snow and darkness and silence. I am in this house on my own, and it doesn't make any difference what age I am, if I am eighteen or nineteen, or if I look hideous, or if I am alive or dead. If there is nobody to matter to, then nothing matters. Nothing at all.

Angela is sleeping. I must heat some water soon to bathe her. I must go out to the well and pull more water. People are passing in and out of the house like ghosts. Some of them bring food. Some of them pump water and bring me buckets. I wonder what would happen if they stopped coming. If one day they didn't come. I wonder. They look at me and say some words to me and it seems as if I have stopped understanding the meaning of words. It is like a dark dream, but I am in this dream alone.

I think about going outside the house. Just stepping out and lying in the snow. I would take off my dress so that I was naked. I would lie there, under the lilac tree, and the movement of my body would make some of the snow heaped up on the twigs drop down onto me. It would land on my skin and it would feel so cold. And it might settle on my hair or my face. How delicious it would be just to lie there, naked, and to know, beyond any possible doubt, that everything was going to be alright.

It wouldn't take long. Just a few minutes of cold, and then a few more minutes and I wouldn't feel any cold. I would feel deliciously warm, and I would know that I was starting to leave. And I would have a smile on my face as if I was sitting in front of a warm fire with my grandfather and he was telling me a story and we were drinking sweet black tea with slices of lemon. Except he wouldn't be drinking tea. He would have a glass of vodka and I would have a cup of the hot, sugary tea, and he once told me about how when it is very cold and you don't have enough clothing, then you feel very warm, and that is when you know you are going to die. He had been in the army. He had seen men die like that. Warm and smiling, with their blood frozen. And Grandfather would be with me, he would be with me through all of it. Just me, this untouched snow, my naked body stretched out, and Grandfather there waiting for me, saying, "It is nearly done, you are nearly there, little Lyuda, little Granddaughter, little swallow."

Mother's dead face in the coffin. Father's face, dead, and Grandfather. I would go where they have all gone. And the baby? I don't know. I don't care. There is nobody to take her. There is nobody to take me. She must go somewhere. I don't know. I don't know. I don't know.

The darkness closes in on me until I can't move anything. I can't move my thoughts. They pass through my head one after the other and they grow heavier and heavier. All I want is to stop them. To stop the thoughts. To stop anything coming into my head. Going out of my head. To stop everything. All thought. All movement. All everything. If the blackness wants to take me, then let it take me entirely. I cannot remain in this unbearable state. If it wants me, then let me go to it, let me disappear. But I cannot live like this. I must do something. I must run out into the snow and disappear into it. I must find some medicine, which will end everything. I cannot stand it anymore. I cannot.

Angela cries.

Lyuda gets up.

She moves slowly across the room. Her back is hunched over.

She looks down at her dress.

She wants to cry but she has no tears.

Angela is lying in the basket suspended above the stove.

Lyuda takes her out of the basket. She holds her, wrapped in a grey blanket.

"Little one, little one," she says.

"Shhhhh," she says. "Little one," she says.

She rocks the baby in her arms. The baby's eyes are open, looking into the face of pulled despair.

Mama, Mamochka, Mamusya, Matenka moiya!

The baby is quiet. Lyuda sits down, holding her.

She looks over to the window and the white, white, white outside, and the perfect silence in the house, the baby in her arms held against her warm breast.

"It is so beautiful," she whispers. "Angela, it is so beautiful. Angela, it will be spring," she says. "It will be. Angela."

She shakes her head from side to side. The baby closes its eyes. Mother is so very warm. She is saying something. Something nice.

The baby sleeps.

Lyuda lays her back into the basket and tucks the blanket around her, then turns away from her and her face crushes into an appalling grimace of despair. She clenches her fists, digging her nails into the skin of her hands, her breath held, everything frozen into a twisting misery.

And then, slowly, she releases her face, her hands.

She breathes.

Lyuda lies on the bed. She is curled into a ball, her body crushed in on itself. She is crying. Her housedress is hitched up and her legs, bruised and covered in stubbed, pale hairs, are pulled up to her chin. Her hair is draped over half her face and down her back, unbrushed, tangled, dirty.

The baby lies on the bed opposite her, propped up in a nest of pillows. She has a wooden spoon and a pocket mirror with a red velvet back which she grips in each tiny fist, and strikes at the pillows. Her eyes are bright and laughing, and they move from her mother, to the spoon, to the pillows, and to her mother again.

Lyuda opens and closes her eyes as she cries. She knows the baby is watching, but she cannot move. Curled up, she lets the grief flood over her. *It is a course*, she thinks. *There are tears that must come, and I must let them come.* She lets the thoughts of her life move through her mind. Volodiya, Mother, Father, Angela, scenes, moments, memories, tears to be cried for each of them. *They must flow*, she thinks. *However many tears to be shed for each of them, they must flow.*

The baby sees her falling tears and she laughs. She holds the pocket mirror in her fist and moves her arm, catching first a reflection of her own face, and then a reflection of her mother's, and then a reflection of tears. *A river*, her spirit calls out. *It is the reflection of a river.*

The river of tears flows out of the reflection and into its mother, that great long snake winding between the willow trees. Grandmother watches it rising – the river growing higher on the banks, tears and tears and tears.

Not a single drop, she says, *that is lost.*

Lyuda stands, the baby in her arms, and stares out at the endless descent of snow, which is all that is visible through the grey window.

The kitchen is stiflingly warm and her dirty housedress is thin, her legs bare, her feet in fraying slippers. The baby stirs and she glances down, but her face does not move. The baby is asleep.

Outside, the snow falls calmly like a slow and separate waterfall. She is behind the waterfall now, in that silent, nowhere place where the noise and the silence are the same. Where the existence and the non-existence are the same. Where the being and the not-being are the same.

This child is holding me here, behind the waterfall, she thinks. *She is holding me between the darkness, where I desire to go, and the sunlight beyond these tears, which I can barely remember. I could disappear,* she thinks, *like one of the snowflakes coming in through the window. Just go out into the cold, and disappear. And there would be nothing more natural, there would be nothing that could be less noticed than this tiny act of completeness, than this fact of having lived, and having died. Of having tried, and having failed. The snowflake does not struggle,* she thinks. *When the circumstances change, it changes. It disappears in a single moment and for all time.*

I have this baby, she thinks.

And if I didn't?

She carries the baby across the room to the cradle, warm from the heat of the stove. She places her into it gently and covers her with a blanket. The baby's cheeks are a delicate red and she has fine black hair on her head.

Lyuda returns to the window and takes off her slippers. She climbs up onto the cupboards and onto the sill beside the window. She pulls her knees up under her chin and wraps her arms around them. The windowsill is icy cold under her bare feet, and a faint draft blows against her legs and hips. The skin on her arms tenses, rising in tiny mountains against the cold. Her hair is fastened to the top of her head in a bun, and she reaches up and takes the metal pins out one by one, and lets her long hair tumble around her shoulders and down her back. She presses her forehead against the cold glass, and her breath clouds it over. She wipes the glass with her hair and peers out through the pattern of watery slashes she has made. Through them, the garden is entirely white with heavy, piled snow. *The snow would reach up to my waist,* she thinks. *I could walk through the garden and it would be like swimming in a frozen river. I could take off my dress and the snow would carry my body through the garden. A last, solitary walk. And I would just disappear into it. I would leave this life just as I came, holding onto nothing.*

The baby. I have a baby.

She turns her head and pushes her naked cheek to the glass, wiping the slashes and the last of the water from the window. Then she reaches with one hand for the latch of the window and pushes it open an inch. A rush of icy wind blows through the open gap and over her. She shivers. *The cold is so comforting,* she thinks. *It is so clear, so final. It does not come in waves. It comes, it creates its own world, and it transforms everything to its will.*

Her body starts to shiver with the touch of the snow, and she pulls her legs tighter towards her, knees pressing against her breasts, and she leans her head back against the window frame and closes her eyes. She sees the garden before her, and she is filled with a sudden happiness.

A moment shifts. She opens her eyes wide, in unexpected joy.

"It is not snow!" she cries out through the glass. "It is moonlight on white flowers!"

She pushes open the window with a strong thrust and falls out into the garden in a rush of warmth. Beneath her is a sea of white forest flowers in bloom, lush and thick, like moss. She drops sideways into them, landing softly and then she turns onto her back with her body laid out. She looks up into the face of a full, white moon and its light covers her body entirely. She looks down and sees that she is clothed all in white. She touches her hair, which is woven with strands of fern and summer leaves, golden curls draped over her shoulders. She is so warm she could even take off her dress, and just lie in this bath of silver light.

She pushes the dress back from her smooth shoulders and turns her head into the blossoms, drifting into their delicious summer scent.

"Summer moonlight," she says aloud. "For you, I might live!" She breathes in deeply. "And the scent of moonlit flowers. It is almost a reason. It is almost a silver thread I could hold onto."

Her pale, beautiful shoulders are cushioned in the flowers, and she reaches out a hand in front of her, watching it turn silver as it crosses the great face of the moon. Her body is growing lighter as the moonlight pours down into it, as if she is beginning to transform into the moonlight itself. She starts to laugh at the delicious feeling, a laugh of complete joy.

"Take me," she murmurs to the moon, between her laughter. "Take me! It is the loveliest feeling. I am dissolving into flowers." She reaches a hand out into the blooms and she can feel the tiny cups of the individual blossoms with her fingers. She breathes deeply. Lily of the valley. Faint snowdrops. A touch of lilac.

She hears a strange, rasping sound from somewhere close, and she looks around, surprised. The noise is entirely out of place. It comes again, louder, and the flowers and the moonlight start to fade away. Her golden hair starts shrivelling into dust.

"No!" she cries out. "No! It is something! At last, it is something."

Her hand, reaching for a silver thread of moonlight, clasps on nothing, and her eyes open and her head falls forward against the icy window glass and she gasps in a freezing breath, and for a moment she cannot see where she is, her body is so cold, and the white through the window and the noise! The noise!

"Oh my god," she says, and her hands are trembling. "Oh my god, I didn't die. I didn't die. I didn't die."

She pushes her legs back out over the cupboards and half-slips onto the kitchen floor. She slams the window shut.

Her body is shaking. She starts to cry. She pushes the slippers onto her feet and she stumbles across the room. She takes the screaming baby in her arms and holds its warm body to her own. The baby wails and Lyuda's tears drop into her hair and onto the baby's face and onto the blanket and onto the floor, like melted snowflakes.

She carries the baby into the bedroom and she climbs into the bed where her mother used to sleep. She holds the baby to her breast and starts to feed her.

Lyuda's crying slowly calms, and she wipes her tears away with the sheet, and quietens herself as the baby sucks. Slowly, she warms up. Slowly, she is calmed. Slowly, a single winter day passes.

17

From a place of the deepest peace, Grandmother hears a voice calling to her.

She does not want to respond to the voice, as it seems to be calling to someone who she no longer is; someone she has left behind. But the voice is insistent, and with the voice comes a path of silver, which she is able to follow.

She travels along the path, and images start to appear around her, connected to the summoning, and she finds a remembrance returning as the images take shape.

A face, a door, a curve of road...

At last, she understands that she is looking at the village where she once lived, but now she is seeing it in waves of colour, with all the elements merged together in the waves – trees and wind, blown leaves and water, the bricks of houses and the laughter of playing children, the entire village flowing in one living tapestry of constant movement.

She feels the earlier peace leaving her, as the familiar scenes ignite an excitement, a curiosity for the dramas weaving through every breath of village life, the variations exploding from one moment to the next, the irresistible expressions of love held poised in each flowing wave.

"Who has called me here?"

Grandmother looks around for the summoning voice, and she sees a spirit of pale grey hovering nearby.

I have come to call you back.

"Who are you?"

I am a protector. I am asking for your help.

The village around her comes closer, and now Grandmother can see a girl with knotted black hair lying star-shaped beneath a lilac tree. She can see her daughter, a circle of darkness expanding around her; and her granddaughter, drawing in her mother's grief. Grandmother feels the threads of forgotten emotion drawing tight within her, and she sighs. Beyond the joy, there was always the sadness.

"Do I have a choice?" she asks.

The Nightspirit draws a final image before Grandmother: a girl dancing in a sunlit garden.

There is always a choice.

Grandmother pauses, looking down on the village, at the thread waves of the tapestry weaving in and out of one another, in endless patterns. The emotion is moving steadily through her, the images of her daughter and granddaughter growing stronger, and she feels something pulling her; a sensation of being drawn towards them by something she cannot see, but something that is a part of her. She knows that she must go.

"How do I return?" she asks, at last.

Find a memory, the Nightspirit says. *Follow the feelings within that memory. They will carry you where you need to go.*

The Nightspirit departs, and Grandmother begins to draw back the memories of her life. She sees herself with Grisha, and a powerful relief comes over her.

"I was not so alone," she says softly, and Grisha laughs and reaches out his hand to her.

"You were never alone, my love," he says. "My beautiful Zoryana! My girl in a blue dress. Do you remember swimming in the river? When the music from *Ivan Kupala* was playing and we could hear it on the willowbank and we danced? Do you remember?"

"Oh yes, I remember. I remember! The blue dress. And you held me..."

115

"Follow it, Zoryana. Follow the music, follow the memory. The child needs you."

"I am going Grisha. I will return. Be close to me."

"I am always close to you. Go now."

Grandmother focuses on the memory. From far away she sees the village, nestled in a landscape of endless green forests and black fields. She draws closer and sees the river, like a coil of silver silk stretched out over the countryside, and it calls to her. She can hear the music now; accordions and violins, a chorus of singers and clapping hands. She sees the festival fires further down the river, young girls jumping over the flames, wishing for husbands. She sees their childish desires floating up into the starry night like tiny white feathers. Like tender, luminous dreams.

The music carries her closer to the riverbank, where she sees a girl dancing around the willow trees with a young man. She sees the fair-haired girl stepping naked out of a blue dress and diving into the silver water, and the young man diving in after her, and as she sees this, her spirit, carried on the music, touches the highest branches of the willow tree and her light merges into the light of the tree and the grass and the black soil and the droplets of moving, living water.

She releases herself into it all.

I am perched on the thin bough when I see it. I am calling out my mating cry and the river is echoing it back to me and the willows are full of swallows and dipping birds. The air is trembling with song and the river is answering all of them, one by one, and all at once.

And then something in the air changes. One of the willow trees across the water seems to be growing larger. There is no wind here so I know that the air isn't moving it, but I can see the tree growing wider and somehow brighter, as if it is casting a green shadow upwards and all around it, and it is moving; shimmering like clear water when it is flowing over shallow rocks. And I want to perch here and watch what is happening, but at the same time I feel an irresistible urge to fly up into the air and sing the most beautiful song I have ever sung in my life.

I flap up to a higher branch and I change my cry to one I have never sung before, and I am watching the two trees, the two fountains of green, and there is light all around both of them and I feel something bursting from inside of me and the river is singing louder than ever and I am singing with every drop of strength that I have and I can sense and hear that all of the birds in the other trees are doing the same.

I know that we are all watching what is happening across the water and feeling this unbearable joy, and at some point our song has become one song; all of us birds, the river, the trees, the air, the waves of heat, everything. And it seems that at this moment, the two trees are merging into one, and now there is only this green fountain of light, and light is pouring out from all of the branches into the river, and I feel that I have to start flapping my wings and take off into the air to sing out, and I do this! I lift up from the branch and fly up and out into the air and I fly and fly down to the river and up again and the air is entirely filled with singing birds.

Grandmother, hearing her song of welcome, lights up the branches of the willow and pours her spirit down through the green strands into the river and into the air and into the earth.

"Thank you," she tells them. "I have been here before. I have come back to help my child. I have come to help the white star."

117

We return to the branches through the heavy air, one by one. The river grows quiet and flows on, flows on. Our songs are finished and my strength is faded. I will rest. I glance up and down the river and hop along the bough. I find a crook of branch, hidden with tender leaves, and close my eyes.

The river flows.

When the day has faded, Grandmother sits on the willowbank. She is resting.

"There is much work ahead," she says to the river. "My daughter has gone too far, too deep."

The river flows, acquiescent. It knows the tears of Zoryana, and of Lyuda, and of Angela. It carries them all onwards and merges them into its clear waters.

"I must break the rope," says Grandmother. "I will show her there is nothing to regret. I will break the rope and all paths will be open. She will go to another place."

She closes her eyes. The river flows, and she listens to the rustling of the leaves around her, and the singing of the river birds, and she waits for Angela.

18

When I open my eyes, I feel that something is different. I am not in my nest. My head is not tucked beneath my feathers. I am lying on black earth and the scent is overpowering. It is the smell of growth, a sense of urging greenness, pushing buds. I smell worms in the soil. I hop up onto my feet. I am undamaged. I am well. I am strong. My strength has returned. I lift my wings and they carry me up. I return to the ground. Everything is in order. I glance around me looking for worms. Something is different.

I fly up from the soil and into the lilac tree. The girl is not lying beneath it as she often is, fallen white flower buried in sunshine. My nest is not in the tree. I perch on the branch where it should be, but it is not there. This is the place; the curve of branch where I have laid twigs and moss and leaves and pushed them close and tight with my beak. I rise from the tree and circle it, looking for what is different. I fly down to the bottom of the garden and up again. It is all the same. Back to the lilac tree and the nook is still there. My nest is not.

I dive down to the house where the window is open and perch on the sill. Inside, a woman is sitting at a table looking through a jar of gold and white flowers. A warm feeling comes over me. Time is breathing softly. I will be safe, I feel. All will be well.

Lyuda pulls her gaze from the scarlet rags of the poppies and shakes her head to clear it. The room is cool and she feels strangely light, as if air has been gently blown through the cells of her body.

She stands up and moves to the open window, where a bird is perched. There is a jar of sour cream on the windowsill, and Lyuda reaches out and takes it in her hand. Her fingertips tingle as they touch the cold glass. She dips one finger deep into the whiteness and raises it to her lips. She licks the length of it with the tip of her tongue, and then she puts her entire finger into her mouth and sucks the cream from it.

Cool, light, air.

Little sparrow, she thinks, looking at the bird. *Life is good.*

Slowly, I adjust to a new pattern on this side of the spring wind.

I look for twigs and feathers and I begin to rebuild my nest. There are plenty to find in this garden and the air is full of insects to eat. It is easier than it used to be. The trees are wilder and the grass is overgrown with flowers.

I see the woman standing on the step. She is familiar now. A girl is coming down the garden path. I fly with a twig in my beak to where I am building my new nest and I push it into the correct place. It will take a long time. I fly down, eyes searching for soft leaves and moss.

I cannot sing here. I have tried, but the urge has gone. My flock is not here. There is no mate to call out to. I want to return to my other nest, where the smell of the dark earth is not so strong. There is a scent here that is in everything around me –

pushing, green, soil, change. I will let this change take me where it must, but I want to go back to my nest. I want to sing again.

Lyuda, standing at the window, shakes her head again and looks around. She puts down the jar of sour cream. *How tidy the kitchen is*, she thinks. She glances down at her hands, clasped in front of her. They feel so soft. She rubs them together slowly, one over the other. Delicate, supple hands. There is a ring on one of her fingers, woven gold with an amber bead set in it. She lifts her hand up to her face and looks at the ring. It doesn't mean anything to her, although she feels that it should. She is aware of a delicious smell coming from somewhere. She wonders if she has smelled it before. It is some kind of perfume: exotic, sensual, arousing.

She walks around the kitchen. Something is different, she is sure, but she will find out what it is later. She goes out onto the kitchen step. *There.* The water bucket is sitting exactly where it should be, covered with a chipped plate. Angela must have put it there. Lyuda pauses for a moment. *Who is Angela?* The name just came into her head from somewhere. She breathes in, and then shrugs slightly.

"I must have put the bucket there," she says out loud.

She looks up into the tree for the bird that was on the windowsill. She catches a glimpse of it perched in the crook of one of the branches. It has something in its beak. *It's making a nest*, she thinks.

A noise makes her turn around. It is the garden gate being opened. A girl walks through it with a smile on her face. She closes it behind her. The girl has long, black hair and small gold earrings in her ears. She is wearing a white dress. She waves at Lyuda, and Lyuda raises her hand and waves back at her.

The girl calls out. "Is it okay? Can I play here today? Mama said I could come."

"Yes Marusya," says Lyuda.

Maria, Marychka, Marusya, Marusichka.

Lyuda pauses, and frowns. *Where did that name come from?*

She feels a strong desire to touch the girl. Her heart starts beating hard in her chest.

"Come here," she says and she opens her arms to the child, who runs into her embrace. Lyuda holds her for just a moment and then bends down and kisses the top of her head. Her hair smells of earth and flowers. The girl pulls away and skips back a step, her open face sun-brown and smiling.

"Can I have a box?" she asks.

"A box?"

"You said I could pick the wild strawberries. Remember? I told you. They're growing at the bottom of the garden. They're ripe already."

Lyuda answers slowly. "Yes, yes, of course." She pulls her focus to the idea of a box. *Where would it be? In the kitchen. In the cupboard. A girl. A box. Strawberries.* She steps into the kitchen and she closes her eyes for a moment, then goes to one of the cupboards and opens it. There is a small wooden box. A thread of pleasure goes through her. She knew! She reaches into the cupboard and takes it out. She turns round to Maria, who has come into the kitchen behind her.

"Here you go," she says. She holds it out to her, and for a moment, both of their hands are touching the box. Their smiling eyes meet, deep brown looking up into green and gold. Lyuda feels a stab of sadness moving through her and she twitches unexpectedly. A crease of pain touches her face, and she pushes it quickly away. She tries to smile.

The girl takes the box.

"*Dyakuyu*," she says. "Thank you."

"Eat as many as you like," says Lyuda. "But leave room for lunch."

"I know, I know," says Maria. She pushes her long hair away from her shoulders and her face and she starts to go down the garden path, hopping first on one leg and then on the other, the box waving in the air in an outstretched hand.

Halfway down the garden, she turns around, balanced on one leg, and smiles at Lyuda, and her small, happy face seems like the most beautiful thing she has ever seen, full of light and sweetness. Lyuda feels a pain going through her heart again.

"Remind me," she calls out to the girl. "How long have you been coming here?"

Maria's smile doesn't change. She hops onto her left foot and stands, balancing and smiling.

"Forever!" she calls back. "That's what Mama says!" and she swings around and hops down the path to the strawberries.

"Yes, of course," says Lyuda, and she turns away from the girl and goes back into the house. The scent is there again, luxurious, exotic, sensual. She glances around the kitchen once more, and then she goes through the doorway into the bedroom, where Volodiya is waiting for her.

19

When Lyuda awakens, she can feel the warmth around her body before she opens her eyes. *It can't be true*, she thinks to herself. *I can't open my eyes. I can't ever let this feeling go.* She turns slightly in the bed, and he shifts, and it is true.

She has awoken and she is in his arms.

She feels an intense joy, and he pulls her closer to him and kisses her hair and makes a low, sleeping noise. Her hair is spread out over the pillows and his heavy arms are holding her naked within their heat, her face pressed against the width of his chest. A wild tingling is running through her body, as if her cells have awakened for the first time.

At last, she opens her eyes and moves her head to look up, and it is his face sleeping there, his arms holding her. *It is possible*, she thinks, and a river of love so strong flows through her that it feels as if she might be swept away in its current.

Everything is possible.

She turns again, in his arms, and drifts into sleep.

Lyuda pauses in the middle of the sunlit kitchen and looks around. *This is how it is*, she thinks. *This is how it is meant to be.* Volodiya is in the garden, washing himself under the wooden shower he has built behind the outhouse. She can hear the splashing through the open window and the chirping of the morning birds. She pulls her green silk dressing gown around her body and shivers. Her feet are bare and everything feels close, sensual, delicious. Volodiya will be leaving for work soon and she wants to get his breakfast ready. She strokes her stomach over the embroidered silk and then she reaches over for the bowl of potatoes and starts to peel them with a small knife.

He comes in from the garden while the oil is heating in the pan. His hair is wet and a grey towel is hanging around his neck, with another tied around his hips. He walks over to the stove and wraps his arms around her from behind, pulling the silk against his damp body. "I'm starving," he says. Lyuda turns around in his arms and reaches her face up to kiss him, and he kisses her mouth, his arms around her waist, and she can smell his wet hair, and the water from his body soaks through the silk onto her skin.

There is a noise on the windowsill and they both glance over to see a bird perched there. For a moment it looks as if it is going to fly into the room.

"There'll be a stork landing there soon," Volodiya says, moving his hand around to rest on her stomach. He kisses her forehead and then lets her go, a smile on his face.

"Yes, yes," she says, looking at the little bird. "Soon."

He walks into the bedroom and Lyuda breathes in deeply and closes her eyes. *This is how it is meant to be.* The touch of water from Volodiya's body on her skin. She turns and picks up the slices of potato and drops them into the sizzling oil of the pan.

She sits opposite him at the table while he eats, holding a porcelain cup of sugared coffee. The radio is playing *shanson*

music; male voices growling over a background of violins and accordions. He looks up at her from his plate of fried potatoes and liver.

"The house will be ready soon," he says. "Why don't you come and look at it tonight?"

"Are you working there today?"

"Some of the other sites need checking. There's a new foreman starting in Khmelivka today, but I'll be back by evening. My driver, Zhenia, can take us up there."

"I'd like that."

"You're going to love it." He turns back to his plate and picks up a piece of black bread. He takes a bite and looks straight at her.

"And then we're going to start a family," he says. "As soon as we've moved in."

Lyuda smiles, and then unexpectedly, she shivers. She pushes back her chair and gets up and goes round the table to him. He slips his hand inside her robe and rests it on her bare stomach. She bends down and kisses him on the top of his head, breathing in the smell of his clean hair and body. "Lots of children," she whispers to him, and then she straightens up and slips out of his arms, picks up her coffee cup and goes to the window. She sees Maria already in the garden, playing in the morning sunshine.

I'll make her some breakfast, thinks Lyuda. *I'll make her some* romashka*, some camomile tea.*

She takes a sip of the coffee. The girl is dancing, standing on one foot and pushing herself round with the other, leaning forward into an arabesque. Her black hair is plaited into a simple rope and her white dress makes her look like one of the fresh morning flowers, lit by the sunlight.

Volodiya scrapes his chair back and Lyuda turns away from the garden. She goes to pick up the plates from the table as Volodiya is pulling on his boots. She lays them on the sideboard and goes to him and he kisses her on the mouth. "See you this evening," he says, and he puts his hand on her stomach once again before pushing open the door and stepping into the garden.

Lyuda watches Volodiya walking up the garden path and out of the gate. She leaves the plates stacked in a pile to wash later and she goes through into the bedroom. The sheets are lying on the floor and yesterday's clothes are scattered over the bed and chair. The morning sun streams through the window and Lyuda goes over to the bed and lies down on it, pulling the pillows under her head.

The sunshine draws a wide stripe over her body, lighting up the green silk of her robe and warming her legs, her stomach, her breasts. Through the window, she can see people moving on the village street, just visible behind their garden fence and a row of tall hollyhocks.

A yellow butterfly lands on a hollyhock. A stork flies overhead to its nest on top of a telegraph pole.

She slips off her silk robe and lies naked on the bed in the sunshine. She looks down at her body, admiring its slender shape, pale and smooth. She strokes her stomach and imagines a baby inside her, growing bigger and bigger, and she imagines her body spreading out, hips and breasts and legs. She puts her hand over her middle and strokes it, and the sunshine lights up the soft hairs into pale gold. *It would all be worth it,* she thinks, *for a daughter.*

She gives a little shiver of pleasure and then slides off the bed. She goes over to the wardrobe and opens it, staring at the rows of dresses and blouses and skirts hanging in colours like a summer garden. She reaches to the bottom for a pair of gold sandals, and steps into them, holding onto the door. She looks at herself, naked, her body lean and long in the high-heeled shoes, her hair falling around her shoulders and back. She chooses a red dress, and pulls it down over the curves of her figure. She shakes her head at the reflection and smiles, and for a moment her eyes turn hard and cold. She gathers her hair with two hands and holds it over her head, making her even taller, the golden mass framing her face, her eyes, her lips. She nods.

A woman's voice calls out from the front room. "Lyudichka! Are you there?"

Lyuda releases her hair and it tumbles down her back like a waterfall of gold. She goes to the door of the room.

"In here! Come through, Sveta. I'm just getting dressed."

She waits in the doorway as her friend takes off her shoes and comes across the kitchen in a pair of Lyuda's slippers. She stands in the doorway, staring.

"*Bozhe miy,* my god, Lyudichka! What a dress! Where the hell did you get the figure to wear something like that? I think you do it just to make me feel bad."

The women laugh. Sveta walks across the bedroom to the open wardrobe. She kisses Lyuda on each cheek. "*Bozhe miy,* Lyuda! You've become a complete princess! No wonder, with Vova doing so well. But just look at you, *dorohenka*! You look beautiful!"

Lyuda steps back from the wardrobe. "You looked like this before you had three children. By the way, you know that Maria's here, in the garden? I saw her this morning. Anyway, you still look beautiful."

"Rubbish!" Sveta rifles through the clothes. She pulls out another red dress, long and narrow with a low-cut neck. She holds it up. "Wear this one for the party. If I could wear it, I'd steal it off you, but I'd look like a *pampushka* in it. Like a fat garlic roll."

Lyuda looks at the scarlet dress and draws her fingertips over the silken material.

"Yes, I think it would look good. And I could wear it with the gold sandals."

She reaches for Sveta's hand. "Come on into the kitchen, I'll make you some coffee."

Lyuda looks for cups and saucers as Sveta sits at the table and reaches across to a bowl of strawberries. She chooses the ripest one and puts it into her mouth.

"I still don't know how you got so lucky," she says. "You married someone years older than you who's now building houses all over Ukraine, and I married an idiot from school who can't keep a job and spends all day making homebrew in the shed. I'm working a full-time job and my *babulya* is looking after the children and what do I even need him for? He's a waste of time, that's what."

She takes another strawberry. Lyuda puts a pot of sugar on the table. The kettle has boiled.

"And look at you, Lyudichka! Everyone said you were a fool marrying Vova, and now you're about to move into the biggest house in the region and you get to dress up like a princess and you spend more money in a day than I earn in a week. How the hell did that happen?"

Lyuda brings the coffee and a bottle of cognac to the table and sits down next to her. She pours the cognac over the coffee and adds spoons of sugar. She puts her hand on Sveta's, and her soft fingers with smooth red nails cover her friend's rough skin.

"Are you alright Svetichka? What is it? Has Vasya done something? Tell me."

Sveta laughs. She picks up her coffee and takes a sip. "No, nothing like that! No, everything's fine, *dorohenka*. Everything's fine. I'm just jealous of all your things. You've done so well and I'm so happy for you."

She squeezes Lyuda's hand, and then glances down and sees how dirty her short fingernails are. She pulls her hand away.

"Actually, I came to see if you wanted me to come to the clinic with you tomorrow. I know you were planning to go alone, but I thought you might have changed your mind."

Lyuda crosses her legs and pushes her hair back from her shoulders. "No. I want to go on my own. But thank you for asking. You're a sweetheart."

"Then you'll have to come and see me straight after."

"I will. I'll come straight to your house."

"Promise?"

"Promise."

Sveta finishes her coffee. She reaches for a last strawberry and puts it in her mouth. There is a red stain on her cheek from the juice and she wipes her mouth with the back of her hand. She glances around the kitchen and then back to Lyuda, and her gaze rests on Lyuda's red dress and for just a moment her eyes narrow and her face goes still, then quickly returns to normal. She stands up.

"See you soon my *harnenka*," she says. "You do look incredible in that dress. Lucky girl!"

"You're the lucky one with those beautiful children," Lyuda says, and they smile at each other.

Sveta goes out into the garden and calls for her daughter. "Marychka! Marychka! Come on. Time to help me with lunch."

Maria comes skipping up the garden path, her long, plaited hair swinging from side to side. "Coming, Mamochka!" She smiles at Lyuda, and slips her hand into her mother's.

"See you soon!" she says to Lyuda.

"See you soon, Marusenka! See you tomorrow, Sveta."

Lyuda watches them from the doorway as they walk hand in hand up the path, Maria still dancing beside her mother, and then she shivers and turns back into the darker space of the kitchen, and she sits down again at the table, watching Maria's shadow lean forward into a perfect arabesque, in the falling sunshine.

20

The bus comes to a shuddering halt outside the grey, concrete hospital block, and Lyuda steps up onto it and drops her token into the slot. She can feel the driver looking down at her tight dress, at her legs, and she walks past him without a word and makes her way down the narrow aisle to the back of the bus, through the stale summer heat, past outstretched feet and sweat and the smell of unwashed hair and blue-and-red checked bags crammed with fruit and vegetables from village gardens.

She pushes past a young man in a short-sleeved nylon shirt and sits down, leaning her head against the scratched glass of the window. The hot plastic of the seat sticks to her bare legs, and as the bus jolts along, the arms of the young man push into hers, his damp hairs rubbing against her skin.

Lyuda stares out of the window, her body turned away from the man, and she watches the villages passing by, the winding roads leading back to her village, to the house on the hill. Back to him.

She thinks about her visit to the hospital, and the doctors. Her first appointment had been some weeks ago, but today was her final check-up. It was always painful lying on that high, flat bed, legs suspended in cold metal stirrups. The white rubber gloves, the soreness. She sat and waited. Sat on the hard bed until he came back into the room in his white coat holding some files and not looking at her, just looking at the papers as if it were nothing to do with him, what he was about to tell her, as if those sheets of paper alone were responsible for everything.

There had been no sheets of paper in the other clinic, seven years before, when Mother had taken her to have the abortion. No papers; just money exchanged and her child gone, the future of her body decided. No white coats and no papers. Just cold eyes and women and blood and her child gone.

Out of the bus window, Lyuda watches the village they are driving through. It looks similar to her village. White houses with bright blue windows and long gardens full of vegetables, fruit trees and flowers. Black soil. Fat white geese pecking and goats tied to fences. Narrow, winding roads between the villages, up-and-down hills, miles of fields and forests in the distance stretching out towards the Carpathian Mountains and the borders of countries where Volodiya has been and where she once wanted to go. Romania, Moldova, Poland, Slovakia, Hungary.

And now she can't have children. He read it from the piece of paper without looking up at her. The tests all confirmed the same thing. Her blood. The examination. The papers. His words.

She feels her head aching and she breathes in the stale air of the bus. The small window above them is open but only hot air is blowing through it. The young man next to her gets up and moves down the aisle towards the front, his shirt stuck to his back with sweat. Lyuda wipes her arm where his hairs have been rubbing against her and she shudders. *Horrible*, she thinks. *How can he dress like that? Cheap, horrible clothes.* She leans her head against the window and watches him step down from the bus – sweaty shirt and plastic sunglasses, a blue-and-red checked carrier bag in his hand – and set off down the road. She feels strangely angry at him, at his ordinary life. *He can probably have as many children as he wants*, she thinks. *He'll probably marry some stupid village girl who wears ugly housedresses and they'll have a family and he'll have everything he ever wanted. And I have everything I ever wanted, and I've ruined it all.* She watches the young man as the bus moves away, wiping his forehead with his arm, and then she closes her eyes, trying to ignore the surges of anger and the images of the doctors in her head.

By the time the bus reaches her village, it is almost empty. She steps down onto the road, feeling the driver's eyes following her from behind, and she leans against the wall of the bus stop. Her insides are aching after the hospital and she feels nauseous from the heavy smells and the heat of the bus. She crouches down, suddenly sweating violently, and manages to pull her hair behind her neck before she vomits onto the concrete.

She stays there, panting, crouched above the circle of vomit. She wonders if anyone is watching. She took the bus today, instead of their car, so that Volodiya wouldn't know where she had gone. And now, if someone sees her like this at the bus stop, he'll hear about it. She'll have to make something up.

The sweating has passed. She stands up slowly and wipes her mouth with the back of her hand. She thinks she can make it home. She sets off down the street, finally glancing around to see if someone is watching from behind a garden fence or from one of the windows. She doesn't see anyone.

She reaches the garden gate and stumbles down the little slope from the road and pushes it open. Volodiya will be home in a few hours to drive her up to the new house. She looks down into the garden but doesn't see Maria there. *Sveta must have called her home*, she thinks. Inside the kitchen, she slips off her sandals and stands barefoot on the cool paving stones. She feels momentarily confused. She isn't sure what she is meant to be doing now. The sunlight is streaming in through the white-painted window and she turns away so that it isn't shining into her eyes. She wonders if she is going to cry or not. She still feels nauseous and unsteady. The kitchen seems quiet as she stands there; the window is open but she can't hear any birds singing.

She turns around and starts to open and close the doors of the cupboards. The shelves are filled with jars of food, boxes of grains, cups, plates, glasses. She opens the liquor cupboard and stops. She pulls out the bottle of cognac and two bottles of red

Crimean champagne and a bottle of vodka and puts them on the sideboard. She breaks the seal on the vodka and takes a narrow shot glass and pours the clear liquid to the very top. She picks it up and knocks it straight back with her eyes closed. Then she opens them and pours another. She closes her eyes and holds up the glass until it is touching her lips. She thinks about Volodiya, she pictures his eyes narrowing and hardening the way they do when he doesn't get what he wants. She feels his hands on her stomach. She pours the vodka down her throat.

She feels hot inside now and a little numbed. She likes the feeling. She looks around the sunlit kitchen. The image of Maria comes into her head and she has an idea. *I'll make her a cake,* she thinks. *I'll surprise her when she comes to play tomorrow.*

But she doesn't move.

Instead, she takes the bottle and the shot glass and goes into the bedroom. She draws the curtains so that no light is coming into the room and she pulls her tight dress up over her head and drops it onto the chair so that she is naked apart from a red silk thong. She slips on her silk robe, pours the shot glass full of vodka and sits down on the bed, her knees pulled up under her chin, pushing against her flat stomach. Her insides are still sore from the hospital, and she remembers how much she had hurt all those years ago, when Mama had taken her to the clinic on the bus and then back home while she was still bleeding, and she had been crying on the bus, and Mama had stroked her hair, and that had been summertime, too.

And now I will have no daughter, she thinks, and she remembers Maria in the garden and she thinks of herself as a little girl helping her mother to make a cake in the kitchen, stirring the mixture in the bowl with the wooden spoon, and she takes a sip of the vodka and she says out loud, "I will have no daughter," and she pauses, hearing how the words sound in the dark room, through the vodka, and through the pain of her body.

She opens her robe and looks down at her stomach and she lays her hand flat onto it.

Everything finishes here, she thinks. *Everything Mother taught me. The river.*

She puts the glass to her lips and knocks back the vodka, and then she lays her other hand on her stomach and she feels Volodiya's hands as they held her to him this morning, and every morning. Desiring her, desiring a life with her, his strong hands covering the place where his child once was.

She breathes in vodka and darkness and broken glass.

"I have stopped the river," she whispers.

21

Lyuda reaches up into the lilac tree and snaps off six branches for her mother's grave.

It is a short walk to the cemetery, along the main street and then up the dusty hill, passing houses and families that Lyuda has known all of her life. Children and parents, grandparents dead and replaced by grandchildren and great-grandchildren. She walks, holding the sweet-scented lilac in a jar of water and she thinks about her mother, her face, her voice, what she might be telling her now, after everything that has happened.

The grass grows high and wild in the cemetery, with poppies scattered between the placements. Her mother's grave is marked with a smooth, black stone, an image of Zoryana's smiling face carved into the surface. It is an image from a photograph, taken just after she was married. Beside it is an identical stone with her father's face and name. She glances around the graveyard, a garden of smooth black stones and smiling faces.

Lyuda sets down the jar of lilac in front of the grave and arranges the stems. Then she lowers herself onto the grass next to her mother and looks out over the cemetery and the hills in the distance. She can see one or two figures far off among the array of stones, but apart from this, she is alone. She narrows her eyes against the fading sun and she can see the hill where their new house is being built, the massive structure in cream and red brick outlined against the sky. She can see tiny figures of workmen moving around it and a car parked next to it. *Volodiya will be there now*, she thinks. *He'll be checking the works. He always goes in the afternoons.* She tries to make out the features of the people moving around the house, but it is too far away.

She feels a surge of love, thinking about Volodiya. How wonderful he was when Mother had died and it was the two of them in the house together. How hard he had worked to become one of the biggest building contractors in the region, and now he was building them a house on top of the hill, just as he had promised all those years ago. *He has given me everything I ever wanted*, she thinks. *And now I can't give him what he wants.*

An image of Maria comes to her, holding one leg out behind her in an arabesque. *It was just yesterday morning, in the garden. That seems so long ago now. How could it possibly have been just yesterday?* Her heart gives a strange ache when she thinks of Maria. She remembers when she was a baby and Sveta would drop her off at the house while Volodiya was working. She would look after her while Sveta was teaching at the school. She would carry her through the flowers in the garden and talk to her and hold her, show her the world moving around her and then she would sing the folk songs she knew from her *babulya*.

Lyuda picks one of the lilac stems out of the jar and holds it to her face. *I still have her*, she thinks, her head filling with the sweet scent. *Maybe I can't have a daughter, but I still have Marychka.*

A wind blows through the cemetery and Lyuda thinks back to the room at the hospital clinic, and the abortion. The blood, the pain, how she had cried, how she hadn't wanted to do it, how Mother had talked her into it, persuaded her that her life would be ruined if she didn't. She smells again the stench of disinfectant from that bare room and sees the eyes of the nurses. No white coats. No papers. Just the emptiness when they were done and she was left bleeding and her baby gone.

"And now what?" she whispers to her mother, shaking her head. "I have everything. And I have nothing."

From the willowbank, Grandmother stretches her river across the long reality and she touches Lyuda. "It is all the same," she

137

whispers, but to Lyuda her words sound like the movement of the wind through the long grass and through the poppies.

Lyuda puts the sprig of lilac back into the jar and stands up. She walks through the cemetery to the dusty path and starts off towards the village. Across the hills, the long shadow of the new house stretches down over the slope in the fading sun.

The gate to the house is painted blue, with white tips on the pointed ends of the wooden planks, and when she pushes it open, she sees the familiar garden full of yellow sunflowers, their golden-green, pollenous faces turned westwards towards the setting sun. Lyuda goes down the path through the blaze of yellow to her friend's door. She hopes that Maria is there, but she can't see her. *I wonder why she doesn't prefer to play in her own garden,* she thinks. *Sveta's is prettier than ours and we don't have any sunflowers at all.* She knocks on the door and pushes it open. "Sve-tich-ka," she calls. "It's Lyuda. Are you there?"

"Yes, hold on!" Sveta calls out. Lyuda steps into the blue-painted hallway and takes off her shoes. She looks around for slippers and sees a pair of Sveta's and puts them on. She peers into the living room. Brown-and-red carpets hang from each of the three walls, and another covers the red floorboards. There is a neatly made bed under each of the windows and in the middle of the room is a table where Maria is sitting, drawing a picture with coloured pencils. Her black hair is loose down her back and she is wearing a white embroidered blouse and a red skirt. Lyuda's heart jumps when she sees her.

"Marychka," she says, and the girl looks up and smiles, her dark eyes full of sweetness. Lyuda suddenly wants desperately to take the little girl in her arms and to hold her. She feels tears coming up in her eyes as they hadn't today at the clinic, and as they hadn't at her mother's grave, and she gives a half-gasp and pulls herself back and out of the room. Sveta comes into the entrance hall from the kitchen, wiping her hands on a dirty apron. She looks tired, her face is sweating and wisps of hair are hanging out of her plait.

"Lyudichka," she says, and she leans forward to kiss her on the cheek.

Lyuda struggles to clear the distress from her face and she swallows.

"Sveta, I'm sorry to just come round. I really needed someone to talk to."

"Don't be silly, *dorohenka*. I told you to come."

Sveta wipes her hands on her apron again and then glances down at herself. "Look at me, I look terrible!" She starts to laugh and turns around. "Untie me," she says, and as Lyuda unties the apron, she waves at Maria.

"Marusya, go and colour outside. Or go into the back and look after your brother. He's making such a mess in there."

"Yes Mama," says Maria, and she gets up from the table and gathers her colouring pencils and leaves the room. Sveta pulls the apron over her head and holds out her hands to Lyuda. "Come on, sit down. Tell me everything. No, wait. I'm going to make some tea. I've got cake. You'll tell me everything in a minute!"

She goes back into the kitchen, rubbing the sweat from her face with the apron, and Lyuda goes around the table and sits down in the chair where Maria had been sitting. The girl's drawing is still lying on the table and she picks it up. It is a picture of a lilac tree and a bird with a sun shining on them. Without thinking, she folds the drawing in half, and then in half again, and slips it into her pocket.

Sveta comes back, tucking wisps of hair behind her ears.

"Maria will bring the tea in. Now, tell me everything."

She draws up a chair and sits opposite Lyuda, and the two women look at each other. Sveta holds out her hands across the table and Lyuda takes them, and she says, "I can't have children. After the abortion, I can't have children."

Her hands go limp in Sveta's and Sveta squeezes them.

"Oh, my god! Oh, my poor Lyudichka."

The kitchen door opens and Maria comes in carrying two cups of tea on saucers. There is a thin slice of lemon in each cup. "Here, Mama," she says, putting them on the table. "I put sugar in them already." Lyuda watches her. "Thank you Marychka," she says, and the girl smiles, and Lyuda follows her with her eyes as she goes out of the room.

Sveta lets go of her hands and picks up her cup.

"I can't believe it," she says in a low voice, when Maria has gone. "How could that happen? There weren't any complications. I remember the whole thing."

Lyuda shakes her head. "I don't know," she says. "I haven't even cried. I can't tell Volodiya. We're meant to move into the house in a few weeks. And then what? Then what's going to happen?"

"Oh, my *dorohenka*," says Sveta, "My poor girl. How could this have happened? What did the doctor say?"

"I hardly remember. He came in with all these papers and started reading them to me. He said there was no chance of children."

"And you haven't cried once?"

"I went to Mama's grave. I took her some lilacs."

"She loved those flowers."

"I know she loved them. But I didn't cry. I can't even tell you how much Volodiya wants a child."

"You never told him about the abortion?"

"Of course not. He would have been happy to have a child even back then."

"You don't know that for sure."

"I suppose not."

Lyuda picks up her cup and she sees that her hands are trembling. She pictures Maria in the kitchen, spooning sugar into the cup and then stirring it, cutting the lemon into thin slices. Again, she wants to hold her, to embrace her; she wants to smell her and feel the child's warmth and sweetness against her body. She would smell of lilacs. She would smell of sunshine. Of the soil. Of sunflowers. She would smell of the river.

Lyuda shakes her head. "It's like some kind of awful ending. I don't even know how I should react."

"You don't have to react." Sveta takes a sip of the tea and holds her cup and saucer up near her mouth, looking at Lyuda. "Nothing's really changed. You've still got everything you ever wanted. Look at you! When's that house going to be ready?"

"The house is enormous! It's a house he built for children, not for me."

Sveta laughs. "Lyudichka, don't be so silly! He built it for himself. He just wanted to have the biggest house. So don't make up some nonsense about it being for you or the children. Now what do they say about Ukrainian men?"

The two women speak together, laughing. "For every two Ukrainians, there are three tsars."

"Maybe you're right." Lyuda puts down her cup as the door opens and Maria comes in with slices of cake on small plates. She has white paper napkins tucked under her arm. She puts them both on the table and Sveta passes one to Lyuda.

"Thank you, *sonechko,* my sunshine," Lyuda says, and Maria smiles at her. Lyuda reaches out to touch the girl's black hair, and just catches the ends of it with her fingers as Maria leaves the room.

"You know," she says, and she looks up at her friend. "It sounds strange, but I sometimes wonder, what if she was my daughter, not yours, you know? I mean, what if she was my daughter, and she lived with me, and you had Taras and Petro, but she was mine. Is that strange? You know, I feel this love for her..."

The two women are looking into each other's eyes as Lyuda speaks, and although she cannot stop saying the words, she sees

Sveta's eyes change, and change again. Sveta is shaking her head. She pushes her hair back from her face.

"Lyudichka, you're upset about the clinic. You're going to be fine. Anyway, it's a ton of work with three of them. You have no idea. Look at me! And look at you! How much did that dress cost anyway? More than all of mine put together."

She rubs her hand over her forehead, and the door opens and Maria comes up to the table and puts her small hands on it.

"What is it, Maria?" Sveta asks. Her voice is a little sharp.

Maria is looking around the table. "Did I leave my drawing here?"

Sveta looks impatient and frowns at her. "Maria, run along now. Mama is talking to Lyuda."

"I just thought I left it on the table." She is looking down at the table, and then she looks up at Lyuda, and Lyuda suddenly goes red. She puts her hand into her pocket and brings out the folded drawing. Sveta is staring at her.

"Marychka, it was such a pretty drawing, I wanted to take it home. I hope you don't mind, I thought it was finished."

"I was going to colour it," Maria answers sweetly, "but you can have it if you like."

"Finish colouring it," says Sveta. "Here!" She reaches out her hand and takes the drawing from Lyuda and hands it to her daughter. "Off you go and finish it."

Maria looks from her mother to Lyuda, and she can see that something is wrong. "Okay," she says. She is holding the creased drawing and she turns and goes out of the room.

Sveta watches her go and then turns back to Lyuda.

"What was that about? You took her drawing? What's wrong with you?"

Lyuda goes red again. She shakes her head, and then she puts her hands over her face.

"Sveta, I'm so sorry. I don't know what's going on. You know I love Marychka. It was just..." She puts her hands into her hair, pushing back her fringe. "She drew the tree in the garden." She stops. She sees Sveta looking at her and she knows she should stop, but she doesn't.

"It's what I told you before. I like to imagine she's my daughter."

She pauses. Neither of the women is moving. The cake sits on the table. Two plates, two forks, white paper napkins.

"If I had a daughter, I mean, if I could have a daughter, I'd want her to be just like Maria. I've always loved her. You know that."

Sveta coughs. There is a sound of a shoe by the door, as if someone is moving away from it. Lyuda picks up her cup and drinks the last drops of the sweet lemon tea, imagining Maria pouring it from the teapot. She pictures the drawing again, of the lilac tree and the bird.

"Look," she says. "I'm sorry. I'm having an awful day. I came round to talk and I've made a fool of myself. I'll come again tomorrow and bring some strawberry jam and we'll get Zhenia to drive us up to the house so you can come and see what Volodiya has built for himself. I'm sorry, Sveta."

She pushes her chair back and gets up. Sveta gets up, too. She licks her lips and smiles.

"Come here," she says, holding out her arms.

The two friends hug each other and Lyuda reaches to take her hands, but Sveta moves away from her and picks up her apron from the back of the chair. "Back to work," she says.

"I'll see you soon," says Lyuda. "You'll still come to the party at the new house?"

"Yes, yes. I'll come. Lyuda, don't worry about all these things. Everything will be fine. You've got everything you need. Really, you have."

"Thanks, *dorohenka*. Thank you. I'll see you soon."

The afternoon is fading as Lyuda walks up the path through the garden, and the sunflowers are turning their heads back down, towards the earth. She pushes open the blue gate, and it feels as if there is something final to her movement. Something momentous. She shakes herself. She thinks of the drawing again, and she slips her hand inside her pocket where it had been, as if it might still be there.

On the village street, in the fading light, she can already see the car waiting outside her house with the engine running, ready to take her to Volodiya, and her new home.

22

Father Yuvenaly takes a bottle of holy oil from his bag, and a gold incense shaker and a box of incense, and he puts them onto the glass-topped table in the middle of the kitchen. In the centre of the table is the *karavai*, a wide loaf of dark rye bread, set onto an embroidered tablecloth. Next, the priest takes out a thin silver paintbrush, a short horsehair brush, a large silver cross, a prayer book and a bottle of holy water and he sets them on the table next to the incense holder. Last of all, he takes out three thin yellow candles and he sticks them into the middle of the *karavai*.

He turns to Volodiya and Lyuda, who are standing next to the table watching him.

"Volodimir Volodimirovich," he says. "I will get dressed and then we will start the blessing."

He leaves the room, and Volodiya slides his arm around Lyuda's waist and leads her out onto the wide front steps of the house, from where they can see the hills and forests of Bukovina stretching out around them. Volodiya turns and kisses her cheek. He holds his mouth to her ear.

"Didn't I build you the best house in Ukraine?" he whispers. Lyuda turns her face to him, smiling. "Vova, it's perfect. You did. You built it."

"Volodimir Volodimirovich, I am ready to start."

Father Yuvenaly is standing in the doorway, dressed in a simple black cassock with a gold cross hanging from a chain, and a tall square hat on his head.

"Then let's go," says Volodiya.

They follow the priest back into the kitchen, where he lights the three candles in the *karavai*, and then takes four small pictures of the cross.

"We start with the east," he says, and they go along the hallway and into the main room: a vast, open chamber with high ceilings, entirely flooded with light.

Lyuda starts to laugh as they walk through the doorway. "Oh, Vova! It's bigger than our entire house. Just this one room."

The two outward-facing walls have huge windows, which are flung open, and sunshine is streaming through. Lyuda goes over to one of them and shades her hand against the bright sun, and the view of Bukovina stretches out before her. Green hillsides reaching towards the mountains in the distance, dark and wooded. Glimpses of villages and houses scattered over the hills and nestled into the valleys, twisting roads and wide fields of black earth and golden corn beneath a bright blue sky.

Father Yuvenaly fixes the picture of the cross on the centre of the wall, and then goes through the house placing a cross to face each direction: east, west, north, south. He returns to the kitchen to pour some of the holy water into a bowl, and he takes the horsehair brush and splatters the walls of each room with the water, as Volodiya and Lyuda follow behind him. When all the walls are wet, he takes the long, silver paintbrush and the bottle of holy oil and, singing in a deep voice, he returns to the main room.

He reaches up to the wall with the silver paintbrush and draws over the sign of the cross with the holy oil. Then he turns to Lyuda and draws the sign of the cross on her forehead with his fingertips. The oil and the priest's fingers are warm on her skin. A wild hope unexpectedly enters her heart. What if something could help her? What if something could change her impossible situation?

"Help me! Help me!" she wants to cry out. Suddenly, she wants to tell Volodiya everything that has happened. She wants to change everything. She wants to live in this beautiful house and have a daughter and have children with the man she loves. She wants her mother to be there. She wants to do everything differently. She wants, she wants, she wants.

All the decisions in her life seem momentarily to float before her. Wisps of dreams and desires; some chosen, some released to drift away into remembrance. And it seems as if she could reach out and choose again, select another path for her life, and she sees a moment, a choice, when a child was there inside her womb, and she stretches towards it, choosing again, choosing differently, choosing the path that she believes will lead to all happiness.

"Lyuda!"

A voice calls her back. It is Volodiya.

"Lyuda, I'm just stepping outside. The men are coming for the party."

There is the sound of a car driving up the narrow road, and then doors opening and the grunts and clinks of crates being unloaded onto the patio.

A tear drops from her eye and she wipes it from her face. No. She shakes her head in anger. This is her reality. This is the choice she has made. This is all there will ever be. She breathes in deeply and fights to close her heart to the wild longing that is echoing there.

She hears the car driving away and Volodiya comes back into the house. Father Yuvenaly has finished the blessing, and he ushers them both outside.

"Now I have some prayers for you," he says. "Come and stand together, just here."

They stand next to each other at the bottom of the steps, on the cream-coloured paving stones, and Volodiya puts his arm around his wife. The priest holds his hands above their heads and recites a low prayer.

147

"Now, join with me," he says, and he starts to sing. "*Mnohaya lita, mnohaya lita*. Many years, many years, for Ukraine, for honour and glory, for the people. *Mnohaya, mnohaya lita*."

They sing the familiar song with him, Lyuda's voice rising sweetly up above the two deeper voices, the countryside spread out all around them beneath a cloudless sky.

"May this house bring you love, kindness, and many children," he says, and he makes the sign of the cross over them a final time.

Lyuda calls from the bedroom, "Vova, are you ready? You want to see?"

"Come on in," he says, and Lyuda steps through the bedroom door into the kitchen, where Volodiya is sitting with his feet up on a chair, a bowl of sunflower seeds in front of him.

She is wearing the long, red dress, which covers her slender form from low neck to ankles like flowing water. On her feet are the high-heeled gold sandals and around her throat is a heavy necklace of amber beads, with hanging amber earrings. Her golden hair falls loose down her back, stopping just above her waist, and her light-brown eyes are almost covered by a fringe of gold.

"Twirl around," Volodiya says, and Lyuda can hear the pleasure in his voice as she goes to the middle of the room and turns around so that he can see her body moving in the dress, and see her hair and how beautiful she looks.

"Now, come here," he says, and she goes over to where he is sitting, and he pulls her up onto his lap, and moves his hands over her breasts and then down to rest on her flat stomach.

"You won't be able to wear that dress for much longer," he says, pushing back her golden hair and kissing her neck.

148

The car stops just outside the house and Volodiya gets out and then reaches down to help Lyuda. She can only walk slowly in her dress, and she has smoothed her hair down again, after the bedroom. Volodiya is dressed in jeans and a black shirt, his dark hair combed back and his shirt open at the neck.

On the cream-coloured paving stones, long tables are set out, covered in plates of food and bottles of alcohol. Volodiya pours a glass of red Crimean champagne for Lyuda and opens a beer for himself, and they stand on the porch steps waiting for the first guests to arrive, the waiters hovering below them near the vodka crates.

The setting sun is lighting up the surrounding countryside in a vermillion glow, and it gives the distant woods the appearance of a fire burning through them. Lyuda can feel her body aching inside after making love, and she looks at the woods and imagines wolves moving through the trees. She imagines them running in the burning red light. She imagines herself standing on these steps, pregnant with a child, with a daughter who would grow up knowing the beauty of the woods, of the wild countryside.

"It's going to be like another wedding," Volodiya is saying. "It's going to be like the big wedding we never had. I've invited everyone."

Lyuda sees again the day of their wedding, a summer day like this one. She had bought a new dress. *So cheap*, she thinks now. *But I thought it was stunning. And we went out to the restaurant in the evening with Sveta and Vasya and Mama and drank sweet red champagne and ate pancakes with caviar. And Mama died a few months later and Vova was wonderful, comforting me, holding me when I needed to cry. I was so in love with him then.*

She looks up at him, his black hair brushed back from his face, his dark eyes full of satisfaction, his hand resting lightly around her waist. *Just as I love him now*, she thinks, and for some

149

reason, Sveta's laughter comes back into her mind. "For every two Ukrainians…"

She turns to face him. "Vova, you've built the best house in Bukovina. And I've got the best husband in all of Ukraine."

Volodiya nods at her, and his smile is the smile of a man who has everything. "Look," he says. "They're coming."

By the time the moon has risen, Lyuda can barely hear herself think. The Bukovina musicians Volodiya has hired are playing wild country songs on the accordion, violin and drums, and it seems like there are a thousand guests in and around the house; dancing, laughing, talking, knocking back shot after shot of vodka, shouting toasts at the top of their voices. Lyuda's school friends are all here, and she has seen the surprise and jealousy on their faces as they explore the huge house, talk to Volodiya, look at her expensive dress and jewellery. There are children running around among the adults, and Lyuda looks for Maria but can't see her anywhere. She hasn't seen Sveta or Vasya tonight either.

The thought of Maria brings her back to the hospital visit, and she suddenly feels desperately alone. The moon is high now, and she can see Volodiya in the middle of a group of friends, his shot glass raised for a toast. She walks around the side of the house away from him, pushing through the drunken crowd, and stops to slip off her gold sandals. She reaches under the table to take a bottle of vodka from one of the crates and walks unsteadily to the back of the house, and then further up the hill towards the dark woods.

When she is high enough up the slope, she sits on the dry grass and breaks the seal on the vodka. She raises the bottle to her lips and takes a long mouthful, shuddering as it burns into her throat. Below, the house is lit up against the countryside with bright lights and music.

She knows what is waiting for her there, in the huge house – the emptiness – and a wave of despair goes through her as she thinks of the tenderness of her own childhood, the safety and joy of her mother's body, the fighting as she got older, and at last, before she died, when Lyuda was a married woman, the sharing, when for just a few months they didn't fight but helped each other, loved each other, took pleasure in being women together.

"I wanted a daughter so much," she whispers. "I wanted to be able to give her what I have, to show her what I know."

She looks down again at the house and she can feel the years ahead of her, echoing back their loneliness and regret. "I have stopped the river," she says again.

Lyuda puts her head in her hands and leans forward against her knees. From down below there is a bang, and fireworks explode into the sky. Lyuda watches them rise and fade, and she imagines a daughter, Maria, sitting beside her, watching them. "Look!" she would say. "Look how beautiful they are. My favourites are the gold ones." And Maria would say, "Mama, I love the red ones!" Or the silver ones, or the ones that make green fire dragons. Or perhaps she would like the white sparklers. She would draw the letters of her name in the air, one by one. M, A, R, I, A.

Lyuda wipes away a tear with her fingertip and then lifts the bottle and takes another long sip of the vodka. She shudders. She turns to the place where she had imagined her daughter sitting, and she smiles. "I still love you," she whispers to the space. "Even if you are not really here."

She pushes herself up from the grass and carefully wipes her eyes and cheeks where tears have fallen. She picks up the vodka and starts off down the hill. The musicians are striking up again after the fireworks and she can make out Volodiya. He is looking around, perhaps for her, and he is laughing. He looks so handsome in his black shirt and his black hair and her heart jumps a little, watching him. She wipes her eyes again as she comes round the side of the house, and she finds her sandals under the table and slips them on.

She moves through the crowd to where Volodiya is standing, and she lays her hand on his arm. He turns towards her and kisses her on the lips and smiles, looking into her eyes. "Isn't she beautiful?" he says to his friends. "You're drunk, Vova," one of them replies. "She's not beautiful, she's stunning!"

"Ha! You're right," shouts Volodiya, pushing his friend in the chest playfully. He wraps his arm round Lyuda's waist, and she leans her head against his shoulder, and takes the shot glass being held out to her.

It is enough, she thinks. *It is enough.*

23

Lyuda, in a simple summer dress, walks down the village street and turns into the woods leading to the river. It is early morning, and the silver birch grove is quiet and luminous. Her sandals on the path make a soft padding sound, and a solitary bird is singing in one of the trees. The tiny leaves of the silver birch are unfolded and bright green around her. The air feels heavy for the early morning, as if she is walking through a mist, pushing her face and body further and further in. She comes through the silver birch copse and out onto the riverbank to the low-hanging willows.

She remembers the stories her mother used to tell her about dancing here on this riverbank on the night of *Ivan Kupala*, with the music and fires in the distance. Dancing in a blue dress with Father, and then swimming together in the river. *I wonder if that was when she got pregnant with me?* Lyuda suddenly thinks. *They weren't married at the time. She was very young. I wonder if that was why she made me have the abortion. So that I wouldn't do what she did. And does that mean that what she did was a mistake? That having me was a mistake for her?*

She stares down into the river. So many questions. The water is flowing fast, unusually high for early summer. She takes off her sandals and climbs down the bank and dips her foot into the water. It isn't as cold as she had thought and its touch on her skin is calming. She climbs up the bank again and walks barefoot to the widest of the willow trees, to the one where her mother said she had danced.

She lays the palm of her hand on the rough bark and runs it lightly down the trunk. She leans forward and holds her cheek against it. She thinks about the child she might have had by now, the one who would be Maria's age. She pictures a little girl running along the bank towards her over the grass. A little girl in a white dress, with long, black hair. She reaches out a hand to her, to the little girl who is smiling, her face lit up with the sunshine, and then she pushes her head into the willow trunk, her eyes filled with tears.

Why did you take her away from me? Why did you take her away from me? Why did you take her away from me?

She holds the trunk of the willow tree with both her hands and lets the tears run down her cheeks, her heart breaking for the little girl dancing in the sunlight, the little girl whose shadow is dancing behind the beating of her heart.

Across the river, beneath the oldest willow tree, Grandmother shakes her head from side to side. *I didn't*, she whispers. *I didn't, I couldn't.* Her own tears drop down onto her lap. *I did*, she whispers. *I took her away from you.* And her tears dissolve into the old, old cloth of her dress, and back into the hard, rutted skin of her face and her hands. Quietly, she fades.

Lyuda tries to breathe, calming herself. She pushes back the shadow and wipes her face and again climbs down the bank to the river. She sits on the edge of the bank and slips her feet into the water. She reaches her hands down and splashes some of the cold droplets over her face. They mingle with her tears and she wipes them away. She looks down into the flowing water, rushing by. She has a vision of herself, lying on the bottom of the river, and she feels an extraordinary calm. She pictures herself lying there, with the water moving over her in a cool, delicious flow, and her looking up and out at the world. *It would be so peaceful*, she thinks. *There would be no long years in an empty house. There would be no regret. There would be no hurt.*

She closes her eyes. The river moves over her heart and leaves traces of wild flowers. *I can't bear it*, she thinks. She opens her

154

eyes slowly and puts her hand out behind her to push herself up from the bank and down into the fast-flowing current. Then she stops, and quickly pulls her feet out of the water and stands upright.

"What are you doing?" she says aloud. "This is crazy." She scrambles up the bank and starts pulling her sandals onto her wet feet. She slaps herself across the cheek with her open palm.

"You're crazy," she says again, almost shouting. "You have everything! You have Volodiya. You have money. You have a house. You have clothes. You have everything that anyone could ever want." She pauses. "And you have Maria. Little Marychka. You have her. There. You have everything."

She shakes her head furiously and her face has become hard. She looks round at the river with cold eyes and then turns away from it, and she turns away from the willow trees and walks as fast as she can back towards the village.

Across her heart, and across the willow trees, the shadow of a girl leans forward into a perfect arabesque and then disappears.

Grandmother sits on a fallen log on the riverbank. The moon has touched the night-time willow leaves with silver. The moonlight touches her hair and seems to curve around her body, giving her a slight trembling outline. Grandmother sits, and she thinks about her daughter and about her granddaughter. As she remembers, tears start to drop from her eyes, and she catches them in cupped hands.

The tears form a little pool in the crevices of her wrinkled palms, and when she has finished crying, she stands carefully and carries her tears down the slope of starlit grass to the silver river below. She steps into the water and looks up to the sky, where clouds have gathered. She wills the clouds, and the rain starts to fall, and she holds her cupped hands out to let the silver rain descend into the tears, and her hands start to tremble, and when her palms are almost full she spreads her fingers and opens her hands away from each other and the droplets flow down into the river and disappear into the night waters.

"Lyuda," she calls out into the night sky, "It is time to come back."

24

Lyuda stands in the kitchen and looks around her. She has set out all the ingredients for the cake.

Maria should be here soon, she thinks. *I'll ask her to pick some raspberries from the garden. We can put them on the cake. It will be delicious.*

On the table is a small vase of flowers, which she has gathered that morning. Red poppies and white and yellow daisies. The kitchen window is open and there is a faint scent of lilac and summer grasses. Lyuda smiles. *It is all fine,* she thinks. *Look at how lovely everything is.* She is meeting Volodiya later to choose materials for the new house. Tiles, carpets, paints. *But first I am making this cake for Marychka. And then everything else.*

She turns to the sideboard and takes a measuring cup from the cupboard and starts gathering the ingredients into the bowl. She pours a cup of flour through the sieve, and then a cup of rough, yellowed sugar. The jar of sour cream is next to the box of ten eggs, and she takes two of the eggs and breaks them into the bowl and puts the shells to one side. She stirs the mixture with a wooden spoon.

A bird is singing outside the window. She looks up and she can see it perched on the white fence, a small brown shape with a black beak. It calls out and then hops along the pointed tops of the fence posts, from one to another. Lyuda watches it and smiles. *It is all going to be fine,* she thinks.

She hears the latch of the gate being opened and she leans forward to see Maria coming down the garden path. Her heart jumps a little when she sees her, and starts to beat faster. She glances down at the bowl of cake mixture. She had wanted it to be ready when Maria came. She will have to hurry now. As she passes the kitchen window, the girl looks up, and seeing Lyuda there, she smiles. There is something in her eyes. She comes to the open door.

"Good morning," she says, "May I come in?" She is holding something in her hand.

"Of course," says Lyuda. She pushes aside the bowl with the wooden spoon in it and tucks her hair away from her face, behind her ears.

Maria comes into the kitchen, slipping through the open door and then closing it behind her. She is dressed in the red skirt and white blouse, and her black hair is hanging loose down her back. It looks a little untidy, and Lyuda thinks that she would like to brush it, to comb it into a plait for her. She would like to hold her. She shakes her head.

"Look," she says, smiling. "I was making you a cake. But you've come early. I wanted you to pick some raspberries and we could put them in the middle with the cream and on top to decorate. It'll be ready in half an hour. You can take some home to your mother."

"Lyudmilla Hrihorivna?"

The girl is looking at her. Lyuda can't remember when she had addressed her so formally, with her patronymic. She sees that she is holding some papers in her hand.

"Yes, Marychka? What is it? Do you want to sit down?"

"Lyudmilla Hrihorivna, Mama says that I'm not allowed to come and play here any more."

She stops. Lyuda does not move. She blinks. The bird sings. The girl tilts her head just a little to the side. It looks like she might cry.

"Mama says that I'm going to stay with *Babulya* for the rest of the summer. In Khotyn. I'm going on Saturday. Mama gave me a letter for you." She pauses. "I'm only allowed to stay for five minutes. Mama didn't want to let me come."

The girl holds out her hand, showing her the folded piece of paper. Lyuda wonders if she is going to cry. She wonders if her eyes are about to fill with tears, but she thinks that she shouldn't. It wouldn't be good to cry in front of the girl. She puts her top and bottom teeth together and pushes hard. Her face tenses. It is easier.

"You must do what your mother says, Marusenka." She sees a tear trickling down the girl's face. She thinks that she won't see her again for the whole summer. And then the girl will be at school. *And then I will be in the big house, just me and Volodiya. And then, and then, and then.*

Then this is it, she thinks. *This is the end.*

She let's out a little noise. Neither of them are saying anything. The girl's hand is still stretched out holding the piece of paper.

At last, Lyuda reaches towards her and takes it, but she doesn't look at it. Then she thinks of something.

"Marusenka, stay here," she says. "I want to give you something before you leave."

She goes out of the kitchen and into the bedroom, puts down the piece of paper, and opens a drawer at the bottom of her wardrobe. She finds her jewellery box hidden in the back of the drawer, and opens it. *What can I give the girl?* She looks through the pieces she has, and then she sees it: an amber necklace with a silver clasp. It is beautiful, and simple enough for a child.

She takes an empty red jewellery box and lays the dark orange necklace carefully inside it. Then she pushes the drawer closed. She looks down at the piece of paper and sees Sveta's scrawled handwriting on it. She doesn't need to read it. Maria has already told her what it says. She goes over to the mirror and checks her calm reflection. She nods. She smooths down her hair and goes back into the kitchen.

"Marusenka. I have a gift for you. You see, I don't have a little girl of my own, and I have this beautiful necklace and nobody to wear it. I'd like to give it to you."

She opens the box and holds it out to her. Maria gasps. "Oh, it's beautiful! Really? Thank you Lyuda! Can I try it on?"

Lyuda takes the necklace out of the box and clasps it around the girl's neck. Her hair smells of soil and her neck and shoulders are warm from the sunshine. "Go and look in the mirror," she says, and Maria runs over to the mirror and stares at herself in it. The dark amber beads look natural against her skin. "Thank you Lyuda, it's beautiful! I love it!" she says. "And I brought something for you, too." She turns to the kitchen table and takes the piece of paper she had put there and hands it to Lyuda. Lyuda takes it in her hands and smiles. It is a picture of a lilac tree and a bird and a sun.

"I love it," she says, looking at the little girl. "Thank you, Marusenka." She holds out her arms and Maria skips forward into them, and she holds the child to her and strokes her warm, untidy hair. She feels as if she has never held anything so precious in her entire life. She pushes her teeth together again, and then she lets the girl go.

"Time for you to get back to your mother," she says. "Have a wonderful summer with *Babulya*. Don't forget about the garden."

"I'll never forget." Maria touches the amber beads. "I'll wear the necklace every day. It's the best present anyone's ever given me."

She looks at Lyuda and there are tears in her eyes.

She is going to leave, thinks Lyuda. *I can't do it. I can't do it.*

She forces the words from her mouth.

"Maria," she says.

Little swallow.

Little rabbit.

"Goodbye," she says.

160

She sees a loose strand of black hair and she reaches out a hand to touch it, to straighten it, to smooth it, but Maria is at the kitchen door.

"Goodbye," she says.

A girl in a red skirt and a white blouse.

Maria pushes open the kitchen door.

Lyuda stands, waiting for her to pass under the window. The girl waves as she goes by and Lyuda blows her a kiss through the open space.

And then she is gone.

For a few moments, Lyuda doesn't move. Then she turns and looks at the mixture for the cake, the congealed flour sitting in a pool of beaten, yellow egg.

She feels a pressure gathering inside her head and around her heart, a squeezing, just as when she was pushing her teeth together, but now it is happening without her pushing down. She feels dizzy. It is something heavy pressing, pressing down inside her, and then she covers her face with her hands, shaking her head from side to side. She becomes aware of the air entering and leaving her body and it is suddenly difficult to breathe.

She moves her hands away from her eyes and sees again the bowl of separated mixture, the wooden spoon, the pot of honey, the walnuts, the sour cream. She reaches out and picks up the jar of sour cream.

"What has happened to my life?" she whispers, the anger and grief rushing up inside her, and she smashes the jar onto the stone floor in front of her.

The jar crashes and shatters and pieces of glass fly across the paving stones. Cream spews out over the floor and Lyuda steps back, panting. She clenches her fists and stares down at it. Broken glass is everywhere. Her heart is beating violently. She hears her mother's voice as if from far away.

Lyuda, Lyuda, Lyuda.

She starts to cry. Her tears fall and mingle with the white cream and the broken glass of her life.

"Mama," she whispers. "I am coming."

I am moving down a tunnel. There is something pulling me forward, although it is not something I can see. It is a sensation of my heart being drawn onwards, and my mind and the centre of my body, as if there were threads leading from inside me to the place where I am going, and they are carrying me to their source. It is an urgent feeling, but at the same time a good one. I am being drawn to where I want to go, although I do not know where that is.

I feel another presence in this tunnel. It is a Nightspirit. It feels safe to move close to it, to be drawn to its peaceful energy. It is easy. I want to follow it.

The tunnel is a pale grey, which merges here and there into a bright silver. I am not sure why I even call it a tunnel. It is more like a space we are moving through, or as if we are a space moving through a space; as if we are water moving through water. Although I am not sure how we are moving through it, or how we are moving at all. I follow the Nightspirit.

And then I think, *It is not a tunnel that we are in,* and as I think this, I see that in fact there is nothing at all of what I thought was a tunnel, but that it is a great, wide field of gold that we are passing through; waving, undulating dunes of pale grey and gold. And we are passing through these waves. But I think that we could dive into them, or I could release myself into them and become a part of their soft, endless rolling.

The Nightspirit is calling me onwards, but I feel a great desire to look and see inside these golden waves, and I dive into one at random, and I feel myself becoming a part of this moving light, and then through the light I can see something forming before me and I can see figures taking shape and images and I gasp. It is myself that I can see!

And the Nightspirit is calling me and I draw myself out of this wave for a moment and then dive into another one and I see myself again, and I have such a joyful smile on my face and I call out to the Nightspirit.

"Look! Look! Here I am happy!"

And I dive further in so that the images become clearer and I see Volodiya in the garden and Angela is dancing in front of him and we are laughing, all three of us! We are together and we are laughing and I see that there is such joy on my face as if I have never known any pain at all! And I start crying with happiness to see myself like this, and I am calling out.

"Look, just look! It can be alright! Don't tell me that it can't be happy!"

And the Nightspirit is trying to pull me back, and then I feel something going into me, something stabbing into me, and I try to pull away so I don't have to see any more but it is too late. I am held by something dark, and I see the same scene, and I see the shadows of Volodiya and Angela who have gone. I see they have left me there after the happiness and I am trying to leave so I don't have to see anymore, but I cannot leave, and the Nightspirit cannot draw me out because the pull of the darkness is too strong.

And I see myself as the snow is pouring down, climbing out into the whiteness, and on my face is now a look of such despair that I think that this field of gold must break into a thousand pieces. I think that it is too much to bear, that it must end. And the tears are falling down my cheeks, here, there, and I see myself lying in the snow with the snowflakes descending onto me and I see myself moving out from behind a secret and hidden waterfall, out into the warmth of death; the thing I have longed for here, there, in all my realities. The only thing I have ever truly owned. My death.

The Nightspirit has entered the wave, and she wraps herself around me and I cannot move. I am experiencing the pouring snow and the waterfall and the call of that white, white, wonderful end, and I am weeping and I cannot move.

She takes me and she pulls me gently out of the wave and she moves her light around me and around me and around me, washing away the vision, the cold, the despair.

It is not here, she whispers. *It is not now. We have to go.* And she pulls me forward, pulls me on, and I am shaking my head and I look out again over this field of moving gold, and I wonder is there even one place here where there is no despair?

She carries me forward, and now it is she who imagines the tunnel, and it forms again around us. She creates again the waves of grey and gold, but now they are closed. I cannot move into them. We can go only forwards.

Close your eyes, the spirit says to me, and I think what a strange thing this is to say, because I had not thought that my eyes were open, or even that I had such things as eyes, here in this place. And yet, I close them, and I feel her calm blue light carrying me at an incredible speed, and I am awake but not seeing, and we are going so fast that it seems like everything in my mind is falling away, like we are moving faster than my mind and leaving it behind, memory by memory, image by image, word by word.

And at last, all that is left in my mind is an image of myself, sitting at a table before a vase of flowers. And the flowers seem to grow larger in my head and I can see their colours vividly – the dripping scarlet of the poppies, the wild gold of the dandelions – and then I feel a confusion, and I shift my gaze from the flowers to the table.

And then I glance around the kitchen and I think, *I should put some fresh water in these flowers. They have been standing for days now.*

And I stand up from the chair and I go over to the kitchen window and look out over the garden for Angela.

PART THREE

25

I remember, I say, and yet I forget.

I remember that once I was a flower, that once I was a drop of water in the river, that once I was the black soil on which I tread, that once the entire world was me, and then it fades. I forget. I forget.

This is how it must be, says the river. *This is why you have come to me. You cannot carry the memories. Throw me your past. Throw me the flowers that you have picked and I will carry them away. You will be just a girl.*

I am just a girl.

It is all you need to be.

I throw the flowers into the river, one by one. One by one they are carried away, dipping below the surface and up again, drifting downstream with the current until my hands are empty and the surface of the river is clear.

Throw me your flowers. Throw me your memories. Throw me your past. Throw me your sorrows and I will carry them away.

My hands are empty.

Your hands should always be empty. My waters are always clear. Whatever is given to me, I release. If you hold on to the memories of what you were, you will become something that you are not.

I don't know what I am.

That is even more reason to hold on to nothing.

And what are you?

I am a river. I am eternal droplets of water. I am always changing and always constant. I can dry up and disappear and then be recreated from rain and continue on my path. I move forward.

And what am I?

You are the souls of all women. You are the world itself.

I am a girl.

You are every girl who has ever lived and ever will live.

Is that why I cannot understand?

You cannot understand because you do not see what is around you. You see only memories. Your world is full of shadows.

I was not always so sad.

You will not be when you wake up.

When will that be?

When you choose to.

I think I could be happy here. But the darkness…

That is why you have come to me. Release it all to me. Imagine it. Hold it. Release it.

I close my eyes, and all the souls of all women of all time are here with me. A cloud of laughter and movement, of yellow sunlight and grey tears. *Let them be flowers*, I think, and my arms are full of blossoms of all possible kinds – lilies, sunflowers, poppies, daisies, tulips, roses, lilac – and a flood of scent is all around me. There are so many flowers, I can barely hold them. I breathe in and I am carried into a cloud of memories all at once, into a millennia of lives, a perpetuity of the repeated circles of all women, creating and loving, receiving and desiring, remembering and sharing and dying.

Release them!

I take tiny steps to the edge of the river, bent down under the weight of the blossoms, and I lift the flowers up in my arms and throw them as far as I can into the water. They touch the surface of the river and spread out, covering the clearness with their bright colours. I feel an incredible desire to throw myself into the river after them, to disappear with them, but the river stops me.

This is not your path.

Let me go! I want to disappear! I want to be another voice among their voices! I want to disappear into the oblivion of all their memories.

Your voice is the only one now. You can open your eyes. You have seen what all the others are. You are alone.

I stand where I was, on the very edge of the river, my feet ready to lift me up and take me into the water.

It would be over, I say. It would be over. What a joy! There would be no need to go back, no need to return to a darkness that I did not create.

But you did create it, the river replies. *It is your own darkness that awaits you. That is why you have to go back.*

How can I do that? Why me, here, now? I could float away with the others. A single red flower.

I will not take you, says the river. *You cannot go to the place where they are going. You have not lived your life.*

I am a girl. I have lived.

Everything is ahead of you. You have an entire world to create.

I forget it.

I will remind you.

How?

Every time you come here, I will be waiting for you. Your mother will be here. Everything will remind you.

And when I have finished?

Then you can leave.

You give me your word?

I will take you there myself. When you have finished, I will take you anywhere you desire. I will take you to the others.

I would like that.

You can wake up now.

Yes, but first, wait. Let me forget. I am forgetting.

26

The night is clear above the white river and the moon, as always incomplete and always radiant, pours down her tears into the moving water. The river, always tears and always moonlight, accepts, moves, transforms. She is a white snake, coiling herself sensually across the black fields, waiting for her time.

This land is my body. In my hair are woven stars. This is my time, second after second. These are the moments of my childhood measured in tears of moonlight. In every way I know who I am, always a child and always here, the water of the river flowing through me and carrying everything that I am on, on, on.

Grandmother above pours down the light of the stars onto her daughter, whom she thinks she has failed. Lyuda, dreaming, sees before her a tunnel of silver leading out from the invisible walls of her sorrow. She struggles to stay in the darkness but her soul drifts easily into the passage and she moves in flowing starlight towards an opening ahead. As she steps out of the tunnel, her mother is there, arms open to receive her. Lyuda moves into her embrace. She is naked without her shadows; vulnerable, unsure, childlike. Grandmother wraps her green branches around her.

"I did not mean to fail you," she says, stroking her daughter's head. A star falls from Lyuda's hair and dissolves into the darkness around them. "I thought that you could find the way on your own."

Lyuda smiles. "It is a dream," she says. "A beautiful dream. Mother is here. I am so light, the air is so light."

She wakes up.

A soft kiss on my forehead. Mother's lips. Her hair hangs forward as she leans over me, and when I open my eyes I am in a cave of her falling hair, lit on each side by the sunshine coming through the window; a cavern of gold all around my face. I feel a rush of happiness, safety, love.

"Angela, little one," Mother says. She is bending over me. Her pale brown eyes are looking into mine. She reaches down and kisses me gently on each cheek and then on the forehead. With her lips, and then with her warm fingers, she is wiping tears from my face.

"My little swallow," she says. "Time to wake up."

The cavern of gold shimmers around me and then Mother straightens up from over my bed and the cavern is gone. The sunshine from the window streams into my eyes and I feel again a rush of happiness.

"Mama!" I say. "I had a beautiful dream."

"I know you were dreaming," she says. Her voice is soft. "You were crying. That's why I came to you. I woke you when you started crying."

"But it was beautiful."

"Sometimes it is like that."

"I've forgotten what I was dreaming."

"It's gone now, little one. And it's a lovely morning. Come and put some crumbs out for the bird. And come and have breakfast. I'm making a picnic lunch so we can go to the woods. Or wherever you want."

She walks to the bedroom door and from the doorframe she stops and looks back at me and smiles. Then she turns and goes into the kitchen.

The room is full of her love. It is such a warm, safe feeling that I don't want to move. I lie with Mama's kisses on my face and the golden trail of her hair where it touched my skin and the smell of her clean dress and I cannot imagine anything more lovely than how I am feeling now. I can hear Mama moving about in the kitchen, opening drawers and cupboards. I hear her pouring milk into a saucepan for the *kasha*, the porridge. I know that I could call to her right now and she would answer me. I could call out "Mamochka!" and she would come back into the doorway and smile at me again. Mamochka!

"It is time to get up," I say to myself. I slide my legs to the edge of the bed and touch the floor with my toes. I stand up. The room is filled with flowers.

Grandmother sees me dancing along the riverbank towards her in the early sunshine, out of the glade of silver birch trees. I wave at her and then turn a pirouette, my white dress twirling around my body. I have picked a twig of silver birch covered in bright green leaves and I wave it in front of me as if I am bringing in the morning. The leaves catch the first pale rays of sunlight and hold them.

My body catches the first pale rays of sunlight and holds that light.

"Grandmother! Mama has come back!" I call across the river.

"She was drawn back by the rope," she replies. "Her love for you wove into new strands and carried her here."

A doubt comes to me.

"Has the rope grown back again?"

"The old strands are starting to come together," Grandmother says. "But it has changed. There is hope. Your mother has seen there are different paths. She has understood the happiness that you bring. If she fights, then she can weave that happiness into the rope."

"What can I do to help her?"

"Show her your world. Right now she is open to all the choices. Show her your world and perhaps she will understand it."

"Yes, Grandmother, yes! I will try."

Grandmother reaches out to her granddaughter, and she touches her head with the dry twigs of her fingers.

"Little swallow," she says. "Beloved child."

In the kitchen, Mother is stirring semolina in a room filled with sunshine. She turns off the stove and puts the wooden spoon down next to the pan. She picks up a jar of sour cream standing near the window, holds it up to the sunlight, and then pours it into the semolina.

The light catches the bright leaves of my birch twig and catches the white cream falling from the jar into the saucepan. Mother looks out of the morning window and remembers a little girl dancing in a summer dress and remembers herself with a red tulip and a mother weeping.

She smiles.

"Not any more," she says, and she picks up her wooden spoon and stirs the cream.

Blink! My black eyes blink. The smell has changed again. The air is thick again. Heavy, not growing. Summer. I blink. I glance around over the edge of my nest. The same. Leaves, light, twigs, insects flying. Below, red flowers; around me, white flowers. Only the air has changed. It is better. It is like it used to be.

I hop up onto the edge of the nest. I glance back, turn my head around. Yes. *My* nest. I open my wings and concentrate, to sense where my flock is. They are here – I feel them all. They are close. It is time to find a mate. My nest is here. I am ready for a mate. I stretch out my wings as far as they will go and call out in a high, trilling song. A bird answers me – she is willing. I lift up from among the white flowers and I fly towards her call, through the familiar, insect-filled air to where she is waiting.

27

Lyuda finishes washing the dishes and hangs up the drying cloth on the small peg above the stove. She has cleaned the kitchen and the wooden chairs are balanced upside down on the table, next to a pile of clothes to be mended and a painted sewing box. The wet floor shines from mopping. Along the back wall is a row of plastic bowls and buckets, filled with water drawn from the well. She wipes her hands on her clean apron and looks critically around the kitchen. She nods.

"It hasn't been this clean since Mama was alive," she says to herself.

She goes out onto the kitchen step and looks down into her garden. The lilac is still in bloom, but fading now into cones of pale brown. A bed of sky-blue periwinkle flowers has sprung up near the gate. The grasses need to be cut down.

Over the fence, she sees Kolya bent over, digging next to his shed at the bottom of the garden. He glances up and raises his hand in salute.

Taking the garden fork to the potato patch, Lyuda digs for the new potatoes, wriggling the prongs until she can feel the roots catching. She gathers a pile of the black, oval shapes and then scoops them into her apron.

At the top of the garden, Kolya is waiting for her by the fence.

"Lyudmilla Hrihorivna."

"Kolya."

"You're looking very pretty today."

Lyuda looks down at her apron full of potatoes. She waves the fork at him. "Kolya, I'm busy."

"I brought you something."

"I don't need anything."

"I didn't say you needed something." Kolya coughs, and runs his fingers through his hair. He bends down and brings a long, dead rabbit up from behind the fence, clasping it by its feet with his red-knuckled hands. He holds it up for her to see.

"Look!" he says. "It's the biggest one I've got. I killed it this morning. It's a present."

Lyuda looks at the rabbit dangling from his hands. It has become a joke between them, over the years; Kolya offering her rabbits and words of advice and help with the house and garden. And all she has taken has been the bottles of *samohon*.

She thinks of all the other things that have been offered to her. The times when Sveta tried to come and talk. The friends of her mother's from the village. Her friends from school. She refused everything. It was easier to say no than to tell them about the place she was in; the fog of darkness that was pulling her always down, down, down. The fact that she had to struggle to take every breath, so that the darkness would not carry her into itself. The fact that every day just waking and cooking and making sure that Angela was alive was the most appalling struggle. She hadn't been able to accept any of their help.

But now, something is different. She sees the kindness in Kolya's eyes. He has brought her this rabbit. It is a gift.

She looks at him, the rabbit in his hands. His sunburned, lined face. The silver bristles.

"You were a friend of my mother?" she asks.

Kolya nods towards the garden.

"I used to play under that tree with your mother," he says, "when we were your little girl's age. She was my friend. Zorya. Your grandfather didn't like me much, though." He chuckles, showing gold teeth. He holds out the rabbit again.

"Take it, Lyudichka. Take it. It's only a rabbit."

Lyuda feels something pulling inside her. She resists it. She looks at the rabbit. She struggles for a moment, and then sets her face. She nods.

"Yes," she says. "It would be perfect for Angela. I can cook it tonight."

Kolya passes the rabbit over the fence and she grasps it in the middle. She lays it on top of the potatoes and strokes the grey fur with one finger. Her hand is shaking.

"Your mother used to keep rabbits, you know?" says Kolya. He coughs again. "I could repair those old cages of yours." He nods towards the pile of rusted hutches stacked against the side of the outhouse. "It would only take an afternoon. I'd have them ready for you. Help you get started with the rabbits. Your girl would like it."

Lyuda turns to the hutches. "I remember. I could keep them again. It would be easy, wouldn't it?"

"Of course it would."

"And you could help me repair the hutches? They might need new wire."

"If I can't, I'll build you some new ones. Give you my word on it. Next thing, you'll be keeping chickens and a goat. Find a new man while you're at it." He turns his head to the side, draws phlegm into his mouth and spits onto the ground.

Lyuda looks again at the rabbit in her apron. She shakes her head.

"Kolya, thank you. I'm going to go and marinate it."

She turns towards the kitchen.

"I'll leave some *samohon* for you later," Kolya calls after her. He scratches his chin with one hand and watches as she goes into the house, and then he turns and starts walking back down the garden to his shed and his spade.

In the kitchen, Lyuda lays the rabbit down on the table and tips the potatoes from her apron into a plastic bowl. She lifts a water container onto the sideboard and washes the potatoes, scrubbing them with a small brush and checking each one as she plucks it out, white and fresh from the water. When she has finished, she tosses them into a clean saucepan and rinses her fingers in the water.

She hears a small noise and looks towards the window. A bird is perched on the sill, eating the crumbs that Angela has sprinkled. It pecks its head downwards and then throws it back, pauses, and pecks down once again. Lyuda glances over to the kitchen table and sees the rabbit there. She runs through what she will need for the marinade and for a sauce. Herbs, vinegar, water, sour cream. She closes her eyes for a moment while she is thinking, and the sunshine drifts through the morning window over her and over the bird, and something changes in her body, something touches her skin, and her mouth turns upwards with the smallest movement, and now, without thinking, with nothing moving around her but the air and the sunshine and a distant song, she is smiling.

I am in the silver birch glade, looking for the last of the birch sap. The sun is higher now and I know that just beyond this glade Grandmother is waiting, and at home in the kitchen Mama is cooking. I don't need to know anything else. I am safe.

The sap finishes at the end of the snow, before the new leaves come in spring, but sometimes there is a little left in the trees at this time of year.

I check the jars at the base of two slender trunks, but they are empty, and I carefully pull the metal funnels out from the bark. I kneel down beside the last tree and see that the container is half-filled with cloudy liquid. It is the last sap of the year. I pull the piece of metal out and take a sip from the jar. It is sweet; both tangy and musty at the same time.

I set the jar down in between some of the tree roots and then I stand and put my hand against the tree trunk. It seems that I can hear the rounded green leaves above me whispering and chattering to one another. A bird flies up from somewhere in the glade, and then another, and I stretch back my neck, squinting upwards, and I see the gathering of twigs at the meeting of two branches and the sun shining down and I see that it is their nest.

I put my other hand on the trunk and I lay my cheek against it, the silver bark cool and smooth, almost like cloth, and through my skin, I sense the birds high up in these branches and the shape of their nest. I know the leaves moving and willing to move, and the wind guiding them. I feel the strength of the soil flowing up through the trunk and pouring out into every branch, twig, every budding leaf. I feel the pull of water rising up through the roots, and I know the simple being of this tree here, on this springtime day; here, in this sunshine; here, in this rich black earth.

I sense the glade all around me – the laughter of every tree and the light in every dancing leaf – and I say, "Thank you! Thank you for the sap, for your silver juice!" And the glade laughs, and it says, *Angela, you are welcome*! And I turn my head to the tree and I kiss the bark and do a little dancing skip around the trunk, and then I stroke the bark with my hand. I bend to pick up the jar of sap and I walk out of the glade.

And I know that for the rest of today I will be carrying this laughter inside me; this thanks, these dancing leaves. I am safe.

Mother is leaning over a cooking pot and in front of her are piles of chopped herbs in different shades of green – sorrel, parsley, dill, spring onions. She picks up a handful of sorrel and drops it into the pot of steaming borsch.

"Mama, come into the garden!" I call to her. I enter the kitchen and take her hand and pull her and she says, "Wait, Angela. Wait!" while she turns down the flame and slides a lid over the soup. She glances across to the deep saucepan where the skinned rabbit is marinating.

I lead her out of the door and down the garden path to the bottom of the garden. There it is – a flowerbed full of late lily of the valley. A blanket of dazzling white and green spread out over the earth. A thousand tiny bells and the sweetest scent imaginable all around them.

We stand before it, and Mama looks down at the flowers and then she looks at me with a smile I have never seen before on her face, and she reaches out to me and I slip my hand into hers, and it feels so small and so protected beneath her fingers.

"Little swallow. *Yak ya tebe kohayu.* How I love you so."

I hear the birds singing in the lilac tree nearby and I close my eyes on this late spring morning and my hand is in Mama's hand and I feel something light flowing from her hand to mine and I think, *what if she could?*

I whisper to her to close her eyes and I know when she has closed them because I feel another rush of lightness from her hand to mine and I whisper again – "Mama, fly!" – and suddenly Mama and I are great white storks flying through the clear blue air and the wind is rushing cold and bright against us and against our feathers, and we are pushing the air down with powerful wide strokes and Mama's wide, strong wings are beating next to mine and my smaller wings are beating down, down beside her and I feel her powerful love protecting me with each beat, beat, beat. We are flying over the rooftops of our village – some thatched, some red-tiled – with the long strips of gardens trailing out from tiny houses and the spring-lit trees below us and I can feel Mama's joy absorbing the completeness of every movement, every barb of every feather creating each stroke of her wings and carrying her beside me through this bright, rushing air. The lightness, the power, the wind. We fly and fly towards a huge nest at the top of a tree and I feel a pull towards it and Mama comes to land in a cave of twigs and I land behind her and she turns and wraps her wide wings around me, little bird disappearing into softness.

From the most wonderful place in the world, I breathe in, and I think that I could stay in this long, white moment forever and never leave it, never breathe out, never release this happiness back into the flow of time.

Mama, Mamochka, Mamusya, Matenka moiya!

"How I love you so," she murmurs again.

Grandmother steps down the grassy bank to the river. In the reflection, she can see her daughter and granddaughter standing before a blanket of white flowers, hands clasped and smiling. She steps into the water with bare feet, and it is cold in the late spring morning, with a slow current pulling her forwards. Grandmother faces towards the flow of the current so that the river is curving around her body, and she looks downstream. She sees two birds flying in the distance over the thatched village rooftops. A great white stork with wide wings beating and a smaller stork beside it.

"My daughter has returned," she says to the river, and the water acknowledges her words, flowing around her body and sharing her joy.

Grandmother watches the reflection of the birds until the two white shapes merge into one, and then she closes her eyes.

"It is possible," she says. "Angela is showing her the way."

Lyuda opens her eyes and blinks several times, the dazzle of the bright flowers filling her gaze. She looks down at Angela beside her – the little soft hand in her own – and she feels an overwhelming desire not to move. She breathes in deeply and closes her eyes again and feels the sunshine on her hair, and the warmth of Angela's fingers. She smells the sweetness of the lily of the valley and the nearby river and the fading lilac and sees a flash of white wings and she thinks, *I could stay in this moment forever.*

She holds the air deep inside her, and feels a pressure; not just in her lungs, but in her head. She feels a familiar pull, a warm insistent pull, and a voice speaking to her. The voice knows her.

There is no light, the voice says. *There is no light here for you. This is not where you belong.* She knows that what the voice says is true. She knows that when she breathes out, when she releases the breath, then she will be releasing herself to this truth. She knows that this is not her light. She knows where she belongs.

At last, she cannot hold it any longer. She exhales, and as she does so, her face folds down and the darkness surges up within her. It is the most natural feeling in the world. She has failed again. She closes her eyes.

Angela is pulling her hand away, laughing. She spreads her arms out on each side of her and waves them up and down. "Look, Mama," she laughs. "I am a bird! Mama, can you do it, too? We can play at being birds!"

Lyuda shudders, and shakes her head. She looks at Angela and sees another flash of white wings, and at the same time she hears the voice in her head, repeating the words.

There is no light here for you.

For a moment, she stands frozen, unable to understand what she can do, but her eyes are resting on Angela, and she has the thought, *I can try. Perhaps it is not where I belong. But I can try.*

She takes a breath and slowly raises her arms on each side of her, and then rises on her toes.

"Yes," she says. "Yes! Look! I can do it!"

She waves her arms up and down, the voice in her head repeating, repeating, and then she turns around and the skirt of her dress swirls around her body.

Angela watches her and also turns on her tiptoes and then she runs to her mother and wraps her arms around her waist, and Lyuda wraps her arms around her daughter, and the sunshine falls quietly down onto their spring garden.

28

Lyuda lies half-waking in the bed for a few moments before pushing back the sheet and sitting up. She rubs her eyes and smooths her hair back from her face, and then she smiles and stretches her arms above her head as far as they will go, spreading her fingers out wide. Her body tenses in pleasure, and then relaxes.

She turns to look at Angela, who is just emerging from sleep. *What a lovely dream*, she thinks. *Flying. And I was so strong. My wings were so strong. I could go anywhere.* She closes her eyes and extends her fingers again, as wide as she can, and she starts to laugh. Angela half-opens her eyes.

"Mamochka," she says.

Lyuda slips out of the bed and Angela moves aside to let her sit down, and she strokes her daughter's soft hair, untangling it with her fingers.

"Mamochka," Angela says again, and Lyuda feels an overpowering desire to wrap this tiny girl inside her great white wings, and hold her there forever.

"My dearest," she says, and then something dark moves across her heart. She can feel the voice ready to start pulling her back and she rejects it with a shake of her head. She leans down and puts her arms around the little girl and lays her cheek against her soft cheek, and for a moment they are flying again, and she feels that rushing air so cold against her feathers, the power of her wings, the lift and fall as she moved them. *Beat, beat, beat.*

"Mama, Mamochka!" Angela wriggles beneath her and Lyuda pulls herself up, laughing.

"Sorry!" she says. "I was daydreaming!"

Angela sits up in bed and giggles, then pushes the hair back over her shoulders. She rubs her eyes with the palms of her hands.

"Mama, play with me in the garden today. Will you? After breakfast? And then I'll help you make the soup."

"Yes," says Lyuda. "Yes, my love, I will."

She reaches out and strokes Angela's hair again, and then she gets up from the bed and thinks, *I feel so light!* She goes through the door into the kitchen in her nightgown and when Angela cannot see, she rises up on her tiptoes and turns a quick pirouette, her white nightdress swirling around her, and she laughs.

The Nightspirit watches Lyuda and sees the strings of darkness weaving around her heart. She sees the laughter pushing them away and then watches them creeping silently back. She sees Lyuda turn a pirouette on the kitchen floor and the shower of bright light flung out on all sides of her, and the kitchen lit up in a swirl of white and gold. She sees Angela plaiting her hair in a half-dream; her long, brown arms stretched out behind her back like feathered wings.

Zoryana, the time is running out, she calls to Grandmother, showing her the darkness winding around her daughter.

"She is trying," says Grandmother. "We must let her find her way."

Soon, the girl will not be able to hold off the darkness. It will be woven too deep into the rope. It will change her path and her decisions.

185

Grandmother sighs, and draws the green light of the willows around herself. She watches Lyuda in the kitchen, struggling to stay within the morning sunshine, struggling to hold on to a white-feather dream, the shadows always ready to close around her.

She sees Angela in the bedroom, pulling a white dress over her head and rubbing her eyes with small fists, getting ready to share herself with the new day.

"There is still time," Grandmother says.

I sit with Grandmother on the willowbank. The afternoon is quiet and close, the water and trees murmuring in a deep, heavy tone. Mother's old tears flow by in the river, a pale grey under the pressing heat.

"I am trying," I say to Grandmother. "I am trying to show her, but I feel something is wrong. What if it isn't enough? What if I can't do it? What if she doesn't know how to do it?"

Grandmother reaches out and touches my head with her fingertips. I close my eyes. The afternoon heat is pushing down on me and I do not want to cry, but something is building up; a fear, a frustration, even an anger.

Grandmother draws her hand over my hair.

"Let me show you something," she says.

Her fingers are resting on my forehead, and my eyes are closed, and with her own eyes closed, Grandmother pictures a summer garden and a child running through long grass around the trunk of a lilac tree. Bright, dark eyes and laughing in shrieks. A woman stands high up above her, looking down.

"Go there," says Grandmother softly, and I feel the increasing pressure of her fingers on my skin. "Go down, down, down. Until you are there."

186

I lay my head against the willow trunk and my energy fills the memory of the child. I am laughing and running through the long grass, pulling it up on either side of me with my fists. My hands are full of this grass and I run towards the woman, standing tall above me with this long, golden hair, and I throw the grass into the air and she laughs and catches me in her arms and lifts me up so high! So high up to her breast, to her face, and she kisses me and laughs and kisses me and twirls me around in her arms so that my legs fly out backwards and I am laughing and shrieking. And then she holds me against her skin and we walk around the garden, and she is whispering in my ear, but I cannot understand the words, they are just these whispers of love pouring into me, weaving through my hair, filling me with this colour of gold, which is all around her, and we are both surrounded by this colour and it seems to be around me and wafting out from me at the same time, and Mother is murmuring into my ear and carrying me through this wild garden and behind us is a trail of light that she is creating.

And now I can make out some of the words she is saying. "Look, look, little one, look my darling, look at this, and look at that." And everything I turn my attention to, everything I look at, turns golden.

And now, in her arms – in her warm, close arms – everything in the garden is this colour, and everything is shimmering when I look at it, even Mother's hair, touching my face. I can see the shining strands making up the single soft curl between her cheek and mine, and there is a scent of lilac and the fistful of long grass that I am holding and warm skin and hair all mixed together, and Mother's eyes are moving here and there, from me to the garden as she says, "Look, Look!" and I look, my eyes moving from her to a glistening flower, to this bright leaf, to this wide-winged butterfly, to this strand of grass, to this tiny bird flickering across the garden, its wings moving so fast that it seems as if they are not moving at all.

The scent is so delicious I want to keep my bright eyes open so that I can smell and look all at the same time, and Mother's warm, warm body holding me so close, and her light flowing into me and my light flowing back into her and she says to me, "Look!"

And I laugh, because there is no other expression of the joy that I am feeling, there is no other way to say to her with every possible part of me, *I love you! I love you! I love you!* Because she is already saying it to me with this endless profusion of light; and she and I together, in this light.

And while I am in this most wonderful moment, I hear Grandmother's voice speaking to me from far away. She is calling me back with her words. She is saying something to me and Mother is saying something to me and the two voices are confusing and I can hear neither one nor the other clearly, and then Mother's voice is fading and Grandmother's voice is growing louder and the golden light is disappearing and I start shouting, "No! No! Let me stay!" And I feel the touch of Grandmother's fingers on my forehead and I hear a voice saying, "Open your eyes, Angela."

And I open my eyes and Grandmother is looking down into my face and around her head is a pale golden light, like Mother's, as if I have carried it back to her.

And she is speaking, and I cannot speak, because the memory is so intense that I do not want to do anything that would bring me into the present moment; anything that would acknowledge, beyond a doubt, with a single word, that I am here, and not there, but Grandmother is speaking, and at last I look up into her old, blue eyes, and I see that she understands how much I want to stay there.

"You cannot stay," she says, in the softest voice. "You cannot stay. But you had to see."

I am not able to speak, and she is silent for a moment and draws her hand over my head, waiting for me to return.

"Your mother has been in the place that you know," Grandmother says. "Not in the way that you go there, but she knows that light. She knew it when you were a baby. It is like a wave for her, coming and going, but she doesn't know how to stay within the wave. She loses it, and she cannot find her way back."

I whisper. "What can I do?" The shimmering light around Grandmother's head is fading.

"Hold on to the memory I have shown you, and bring it back to her. She will remember, little one. She will remember."

I dance into the kitchen. I have picked every flower that I could find and in my hands is a wild handful of lily of the valley and riotous daisies and sky-blue periwinkle and long grasses and twigs of green silver birch from the glade.

"Mama, look!" I call out, and she turns from the stove and her face lights up when she sees the flowers, and my face behind the flowers.

"They're lovely!" she says.

I can smell the cooking rabbit, and I say, "Mama, can you give me a jar for the flowers? Can I take some of this water here? Is that alright?"

"Of course you can," she says, and she takes a clean jar from the shelf next to the windowsill and she bends down and dips it into the metal water bucket against the far wall and hands it to me, and I lower the flower stalks carefully into the water so that it won't spill onto the floor that Mama has washed, and then I hold out the jar to Mother.

"I picked them for you." I say.

She takes the jar and brings it up to her face, and the scent of the lily of the valley and the wild grasses and the periwinkle seems to spread through the room as she breathes them in.

"You could almost fly away on this scent," she says. She closes her eyes.

I giggle, and make a little hop from one leg to the other.

"Mama?" She opens her eyes and smiles. She holds out the jar to me.

"Put them on the table," she says.

"Mama? Can I help? Can I do something?"

She turns and picks up the wooden spoon, which she had put down next to the cooking pot, and she lifts up the lid and there is a rush of steam and the sharp, creamy smell of cooked rabbit pours out into the kitchen.

"It's ready," she says. "Of course you can help. Fetch the forks and glasses and sit down. I can't remember when we last ate rabbit. Do you remember?"

"I don't think I ever have," I say.

Mama spoons boiled potatoes onto our chipped plates and then she lays two pieces of rabbit onto each and pours juice over them and brings them to the table.

"It feels strange, just the two of us, eating such a good meal like this," she says. "We should be having guests. We should have invited Sveta."

"And Taras and Petro! I want to see them again!"

"We'll do that," Mama says. "We'll go and see them tomorrow. We'll invite them for dinner. We can have the rest of the rabbit and I'll fry potatoes. I can make a cake. Would you like that?"

"Yes, Mama. I'd like that."

Mama pushes her chair away from the table and stands up.

"Wait here. Eat some of that rabbit. I want to give you something."

She goes across the kitchen into the bedroom, and I notice how pretty her hair is – the curls pinned up and shining – and how her face seems to have changed and become softer in the last few days. And then she comes back into the room and she is holding a long box and she says, "Look, little one!" And she crouches down next to my chair and opens the box and inside it is a dark-orange amber necklace with a silver clasp.

"Your grandmother gave this to me. My mother, Zoryana. I think you would look beautiful in it."

She takes the necklace out of the box and fixes the clasp around my neck.

"Go and look," she says.

I go to the mirror and see the orange beads glowing against my dark skin, and I think that I must look like some exotic queen, a *tsaritsya* from far away, and I raise my chin and spread my long, black hair over my shoulders like a *tsaritsya* would, and then I gather it up and hold it with both hands on the top of my head and picture a golden crown there, set with glowing orange jewels.

"So?"

I turn away from the mirror.

"I love it!" I say, and I skip towards Mama, exotic princess from far away, and put my arms around her neck and kiss her.

"Thank you, Mamochka!"

And suddenly, I know where I am going to keep this magical necklace. As soon as Mama won't notice, I am going to take it to the bottom of the garden, to the far corner across from the lily of the valley where there is a fallen log. This is where I keep my treasures. I will hide my necklace here, safe in its box, along with the turquoise egg, which dropped out of a bird's nest last year, a thin gold ring, which was buried in the roots of the lilac tree, and a small mirror with a red velvet back.

"You look perfect in it," Mama says. She reaches out a hand and takes a strand of my hair and she curls it around her finger, as she loves to do. Then she lets it go and turns back to the table.

"Now let's finish this rabbit," she says. "And tomorrow, we'll go and see Sveta."

I sit back down in my place, opposite her, and I think that Mama has looked so happy tonight, and that it is working, that she is opening up to my world, just as Grandmother said that she might, and this thought makes me feel like running and jumping and flying! Then, I remember how Mama was able to fly today, and I wonder if she was able to do this when she was little, and I turn to her and I want to ask her, although I am not quite sure how to ask, and I see that she is not eating the rabbit and the potatoes, but has been looking at me while I have been thinking and she has such a happy expression on her face that all at once, I want to say absolutely nothing.

I am safe.

29

Lyuda pushes open the blue-painted gate with one hand, and with the other she smooths down her skirt and then her hair. Her lips are drawn in a tight line across her face. She closes the gate behind her and looks up to the window of the house. A figure is watching through a net curtain. She raises her hand and the figure turns and moves away from the window.

Lyuda walks through the garden towards the front of the house. On each side of the path there are tall sunflowers, as yet unopened, and next to the fence is a cherry tree covered in pale pink blossom. The front door opens and a woman comes out onto the wooden porch. She is wearing a faded work-shirt and a patterned headscarf, knotted at the back of her head.

"Lyuda?"

"Sveta. Svetichka."

The woman takes a step down onto the path. Her forehead wrinkles.

"*Bozhe miy!* My god, has something happened? Is Angela alright?"

"No, no. Angela's fine. Nothing's happened. I—"

"Lyuda, my god, you haven't been here for so long. It's got to be seven years since you last came. Where's Angela?"

"She's fine. She's at home."

"You know she comes here. To play with the boys."

"I know. Of course I know."

"Are you going to come in? Vasya's out somewhere. Taras is here. Petro is somewhere with his friends. Are you going to come in? I can't believe you're here. I don't have anything to give you. I could have made a cake. *Bozhe miy!* No, it doesn't matter."

Sveta stops talking and she goes over to Lyuda and puts her arms around her and holds her. She puts a hand up to the back of Lyuda's head and touches her hair.

"I can't believe it," she says. "That you're here."

She pulls away from the embrace and looks at Lyuda.

"You're not even crying," she says.

"Why would I cry?" says Lyuda, with a little smile.

"Will you come into the house?"

"I don't think so. I just came to ask. It sounds silly now. It's just that Kolya gave us a rabbit."

"Kolya next door?"

"Yes. He gave us a rabbit. And I cooked it and we were eating it. And it was so strange eating it without someone there. Without any guests."

"Of course it felt wrong. And you know I like rabbit." She pauses. "I cook it better than you as well."

Lyuda smiles. "You always cooked better than me. I never really learned, did I?"

The two women pause.

"Sveta?"

Lyuda holds out her hands and Sveta looks down and then takes them. "Sveta, it just feels like... I think I could do it. I think maybe I could do it. I came here—"

Sveta pulls Lyuda's hand towards the house. "Come on. Come in for a moment."

Lyuda shakes her head. "No. I'll come in next time."

Sveta nods. "I still can't believe you came. After all this time. I'm going to come and see you tomorrow. Can I do that? I'll bring you something. I'll make a cake."

"Kolya said he'd fix the rabbit hutches. He said it would be easy to keep rabbits again."

"Of course it would. If he can't do it, I'll get Vasya to do it. Get him to build some new ones for us while he's at it. Stop him getting drunk for an afternoon."

Lyuda looks at her.

"I'm sorry, Sveta. Are you alright? I didn't even ask."

"Don't worry. Ask me tomorrow. I won't tell you without a mouthful of cake anyway. He drinks, I eat. Look at me!"

Sveta strokes her hands over her hips and stomach and then laughs. Lyuda smiles and touches her hair.

"Look at us both," she says.

Sveta suddenly turns her head to one side.

"Lyuda, you know what I heard?" she says.

"What?"

"I heard they need someone in the post office. Tanya left to have a baby and they put a sign outside."

"So?"

"So you could do it. Why not? You could work there. Get some money. Not much, but something. Why not?"

"I hadn't thought about it."

"Well, you should think about it. I mean, why not? Angela will be in school. What are you going to do?"

"Mama would hate it."

"Not as much as she'd hate…" Sveta taps the side of her neck with two fingers, "…drinking."

Lyuda turns her head away and Sveta quickly reaches for her hands again.

"Lyudichka, I'm sorry. I didn't say a thing. God, I'm so sorry. Forget what I said. I didn't say anything."

"It's fine." Lyuda pulls her shoulders up. "It's only the truth."

"Listen, let's go there tomorrow. I'll go with you. We'll just walk down there and talk to them."

"Do you think I *can* do it?"

"Of course you can do it. I'll come to your house tomorrow at ten. Will you be ready?"

Lyuda gives a little nod and Sveta lets go of her hand and takes her in her arms.

"It wasn't your fault, you know," she whispers into Lyuda's ear. "It wasn't your fault that he left. They all do it. I sometimes wish Vasya would get the hell out, for all the use he is."

Lyuda doesn't speak, but Sveta can feel her head moving forward and back.

"I still can't believe you came," Sveta says. As she pulls away, she catches the scent of vodka on Lyuda's breath. She takes a step back.

"Lyudichka. Tomorrow, when we go there, don't smell of… you know. I mean, don't drink before we go."

Lyuda's cheeks redden and she struggles to hold Sveta's eye. She shakes her head.

"I won't. I'll be ready."

"Angela, come and help me get the water."

Mama is standing on the kitchen step, holding the water pail.

I skip towards her through the garden, and I feel my plait coming undone and reach behind me to twist the loose ends together.

Mama goes ahead and waits for me by the gate. I run up to her and stand on tiptoe to unlatch it. Mama strokes her hand over the splintered wood.

"We need to fix this," she says. "I'll ask someone to come and mend it. Maybe Kolya could do it." She glances over her shoulder to Kolya's garden, but he isn't there.

We leave the gate unlatched behind us and climb the little slope to the village street.

"Mama, what happened to the gate? Who broke it?"

Mother stops and looks down at me. She seems to be thinking, and then she turns her head to one side.

"How do you know someone broke it?"

"Well then, how is it broken?"

She looks at me for a few moments more and then she starts walking again. I see her looking around at the village street, which is lined with cherry trees, the bottom of their trunks freshly painted in limewash white. Our shadows are falling across the dusty road, all the way to the other side. Above us, on the tops of the telegraph poles, are the wide twig baskets of storks' nests. I see that Mama is smiling.

"Angela, sometimes things just break. They just break. Sometimes nobody has to break them."

We have come to the well, and she stops and puts down the bucket. I can't seem to understand what she is saying.

"But can we fix it?"

Mama starts to laugh and I stare at her because it is the strangest sound. I don't think I have ever heard her laugh like this before. It sounds like a gurgling, or a deep birdcall, or water trying to squeeze through a blocked tap.

"Sometimes," she says, still laughing, and I still can't understand her.

"Mama?"

"Yes?"

She stops laughing and opens the green-painted lid of the well and lifts the bucket off its hook. She starts to turn the metal handle. She winds it easily with one hand, down and down until the bucket hits the bottom and the chain tightens as it fills with water.

"Mama?"

She smiles, and then turns and looks at me. Her eyes seem far away.

"Can I help you pull it?"

"Yes. Yes, my love," she says, and I put my hand over hers and together we wind up the heavy bucket and I can hear the slipslop noise of the water tipping over the edge of the bucket and the echoes as it splashes back down to the bottom of the well. We wind the pail right to the top and then Mama lifts it out and pours it into our own bucket. The water is silver inside, with a glistening, mirrored surface. Mama hangs the well bucket back onto its hook and closes the green roof.

"May I?" I ask, and she nods her head and I reach down and scoop some of the water into my cupped hands, and I bend my head down to drink it from my palms. Cold, cold, cold! I shiver, then giggle, and I reach down and take another mouthful.

"Mama, it's the most delicious thing in the world!" I say, and I look at her, and her face changes and she is laughing again and she dips her hands into the bucket and brings them to her mouth, dripping, and bends over to drink, and when she drops her hands I see that her eyes are shining.

We carry the bucket back to the house, my hand in hers, and she puts it down on the kitchen step and I cover it with the chipped plate.

"Mama, may I go and pick some more flowers for the kitchen?" I ask her, and she reaches out and touches my head.

"Pick any that you like," she says, and I think that I will go and find her the most beautiful flowers in the entire world, because I suddenly feel that if there is anything I can do to make Mama happy, anything at all, then right now, I have to do it.

30

There is a tap at the door. Lyuda looks at herself in the mirror one last time and pats the back of her head, where a neat bun is secured with metal hairpins. She is wearing a tight, grey skirt and a white blouse with lace panels. Her lips are dark purple.

She walks across the kitchen and opens the door. Sveta is standing on the doorstep, holding a cake. Lyuda smiles nervously at her.

"I can't believe you're here," she says.

"I can't believe I'm here," says Sveta. She steps into the house and pushes off her shoes. She looks around for a pair of slippers, but there aren't any, and she stands in her bare feet on the stone floor.

"What kind of cake is it?" asks Lyuda.

"Prune and walnut," says Sveta. "It's all I had. I'd have made honey cake but I didn't have that black honey."

"I like it with prunes. I can't remember when I last tasted it. Let's eat it when we get back."

"I'll put it over here."

Sveta lays the brown cake in the middle of the kitchen table and looks around for something to cover it with. Lyuda opens a drawer, takes out a clean dishcloth and hands it to her.

"Keep the flies off," she says.

"Are you ready to go?"

"Do I look ready?"

Sveta runs her eyes up and down her friend's figure. "You look great. You look really good. I'd forgotten how blond your hair is. I thought it'd gone darker."

Lyuda touches her hair and Sveta glances around the kitchen.

"It doesn't look so different here," she says. "Where's that wicker chair your *tato* used to sit in? It was in that corner wasn't it? He used to sit there all the time."

"I threw it out," says Lyuda. They both look into the empty corner. "After *Tato* died, Mama started to sit there. And then she died and—"

"Of course you threw it out," says Sveta. "Good thing, too."

"It felt like they were all sitting there. Watching me. Watching my life."

Sveta turns around, taking in the familiar room.

"It looks just the same," she says. She walks over to the window and peers out through the net curtains at the lilac tree and the high grasses and the bench.

"Lyuda," she says, turning round, "these curtains are filthy. They'd look much better if you washed them. I could wash them for you. Or get new ones. They're torn, too."

She reaches out a hand and pulls at the material, where there is a fraying hole in the grey net. A spray of dust rises up around her fingers.

Lyuda hears her words, and she feels a pressure pushing inside her head, and a dizziness. She reaches for the back of a chair to hold onto, and closes her eyes. She can hear herself breathing through her mouth. In and out.

"Lyuda, are you alright?"

Lyuda opens her eyes. Sveta has let go of the curtains and is staring at her. Lyuda touches her forehead.

"Everything's dirty," she says at last, breathing heavily. "Everything's got holes. It's all filthy. Really. Go and look. See the bedroom, full of dust, filthy. Go and look!"

"*Bozhe*, Lyuda. I'm sorry." Sveta shakes her head. She crosses the kitchen to Lyuda and puts her arms around her. "I'm sorry. I'm really sorry. I'm so sorry."

Lyuda takes a long breath and the dizziness passes. She lets go of the chair.

"It's fine," she says. "It doesn't matter. Let's go."

She walks around Sveta to the doorway and pushes her feet into a pair of black high-heeled shoes, which are laid out by the entrance. She waits for Sveta to go into the garden and then pulls the front door shut behind her and walks down the path, balancing unsteadily in the shoes. At the bottom of the slope, she pauses, and Sveta starts to laugh.

"Come on, take my hand," she says, and she reaches out to Lyuda and pulls her up the slope to the dusty street.

"I can't believe you've forgotten how to walk in those shoes," she says. "Do you remember when…"

She stops, and sees that Lyuda is distracted.

"Come on. It's going to be fine. It's not like they don't know you."

She takes Lyuda's hand and they walk together down the road. Lyuda glances around her to the windows of the passing houses, to see if the neighbours are watching, but she doesn't see any faces behind the curtains.

At the end of the street they turn a corner to where the post office and a food shop stand back from the road in a little paved courtyard. Above the post office is a yellow sign with *Poshta* written on it in large, black letters. Sveta squeezes Lyuda's hand.

"Don't be nervous," she says. "They know who you are. You pick up your payments here every month."

Lyuda gives a little smile. "I suppose so."

"Either they've got a job or they don't. But anyway, you look great. You look really good *dorohenka*."

Sveta pushes open the door, and a bell rings as they enter a small, dark room.

I push open the kitchen door and I immediately notice the plate on the table, covered with a cloth, next to the jar of white and blue flowers I picked for Mama. I lift the cloth and look at the wide cake, covered with ground walnut crumbs and sunken in the middle. It looks delicious. I carefully pick a crumb from the top and lean my head back and drop it into my mouth from my fingertips as if I was a bird catching a tiny fly in mid-air. *Snap!* The crumb is gone. I select another and snap this one, too.

I lay the cloth back over the cake and, since I am alone in the kitchen, I imagine that the whole room is filled with flying birds. I stretch out my arms and my fingers and they become strong, brown feathers. I lift up, and perch on the back of a chair and the sparrows and swallows and chaffinches and blue tits are darting around the room with quick, flapping wings. I fly up from the chair to the window and then from the window to the top of the cupboard. My feathers brush against the tip of a swallow's wing and then I fly out of the open window and up over the garden and into this wide, wide blue sky, and I can fly in any direction, for as long as I want, in this wonderful, endless clear air.

And then I think, *I will be the sky, I will be the ether*, and I tumble out of the bird and I dissolve myself into the surrounding air, and all at once I no longer have these beating, soaring wings, but I have become this incredible expanse of blue. I am as perfect and complete as the entire world, and I stretch onwards forever! I am everything! I am wind and cloud, I am the life of plants, the breath of every living creature, I am the transforming power in everything.

I! I! I!

And I myself am breathing in and breathing out with this immense power, expanding and contracting, giving myself to every living thing and then taking back what is given in return.

The air feels my spirit within itself and it smiles, and it speaks to me. *Welcome little daughter!* And I do not speak, but I breathe in with all the plants and all the living things of the world, and I breathe out again.

At the post office, the bell rings, and an old woman emerges from the back door and approaches the counter. The room is divided into three sections, with signs printed on yellow paper announcing *Post, Bills* and *Stationery*. At the far end of the room is a rusty-looking till. The woman's face is swollen, with a wide nose and a mass of wrinkles beneath a brown headscarf. Her bright blue eyes look strangely young, staring out from the creased, bloated face.

"Nataliya Stepanivna," says Sveta, in a respectful voice. The old woman is looking at Lyuda.

"Lyudmilla Hrihorivna," she says slowly. Her voice is cracked and strangely high-pitched.

"Nataliya Stepanivna," replies Lyuda, looking back at the woman. Her hands are clasped in front of her and she rubs her thumbs over the skin of her palms.

The old woman gives a little chuckle. "I thought you were dead," she says. "I heard there was a funeral."

Lyuda takes half a step back, her head suddenly pounding. She feels dizzy again. "What are you talking about?" she says. "It was my mother who died. You know my mother. Zoryana Ivanivna."

"I know," says the woman, smiling. Her blue eyes are fixed on Lyuda, who reaches out to grasp Sveta's arm. "But I heard it was you. I heard it was *you* who died. I heard it was *your* funeral." She leans forward over the counter. "Now, why would I have heard that?"

Sveta steps forward.

"Nataliya Stepanivna," she says. "I don't know what you heard. You know that Lyuda comes here for her payments. You have all the books. I don't know what you heard."

The woman looks at Sveta as if for the first time. She runs her eyes up and down her figure.

"Svitlana Petrivna," she says. "That's about what I would have expected from you."

"Nataliya Stepanivna," says Sveta again. Her face has gone red. "We're interested in a job here. I know that Tanya has left to have her baby and you're looking for someone. There was a notice. Lyuda is interested in the job."

The woman chuckles again and flattens her hands onto the counter. Her fingers are short and swollen and it looks as if the joints have set into painful curves.

"There's a job," she says. "Now who's interested in it?"

Lyuda takes half a step forward. She feels another rush of dizziness going through her but she shakes her head.

"I am."

She leans forward to rest her hands on the counter and she notices that her fingernails are dirty. She closes them into her fists and looks up at the old woman. "I am," she says again. "I need some work."

The woman looks from Lyuda to Sveta and then back again. Her eyes narrow to slits, and without their bright, youthful blue softening the old face, her skin becomes a sea of brown creases, the narrow lips barely distinguishable. Lyuda notices a dark mole on her cheek, with three black hairs growing out of it. The woman speaks, and her voice is filled with malice.

"There's no job here for you," she says. And then she pauses, watching Lyuda's reaction through her narrowed eyes. She sees that Lyuda's hands have started to shake.

"Your mother would be ashamed of you," she says. "Look at you. Everyone knows what you do."

She leans her head to the side and taps her neck with two fingers, just as Sveta had done the day before.

"Look at yourself," she says. "There's no job here. Not for you. Your mother would be ashamed. I knew her. Your father too. *Piyak!*" she spits. "Drunkard. I can smell it on you."

She sniffs and nods her head, her eyes still fixed on Lyuda.

Sveta takes a step back and reaches for Lyuda's arm and pulls her towards the door.

"You're a miserable old woman," she hisses. "You're an old witch. You shouldn't be working here."

She pushes open the door and the bell rings and she shoves Lyuda through it and out into the courtyard.

"Let me know when there's a funeral," the woman calls out after them, and Sveta slams the door and turns and puts her arms around Lyuda.

"Oh my god. *Bozhe miy!* Lyudichka, I don't know what happened. Oh my god. Lyuda, are you alright?"

She pulls back and she sees that Lyuda's eyes are closed, but that two streams of tears are running down her face and dripping onto the lace of her blouse. Without opening her eyes, Lyuda reaches up into her hair and starts pulling the hairpins out of her bun.

"Lyuda, stop it! She's an old witch. Lyuda, *dorohenka!* You don't understand what things are like, any more. Things are different. She probably lost everything herself. She's probably got her husband at home knocking her head in every night. She probably drinks herself. For god's sake, Lyuda, it's not about you. I'm sorry, but it's not about you."

Lyuda opens her eyes and lets the tears fall out. In her hands are the metal hairpins. Her hair has tumbled down in curls around her shoulders. She suddenly looks very young.

"I'm tired," she says, and she reaches up and wipes the tears off her cheeks. "I want to go home."

Lyuda closes her front door and stands on the other side, listening to Sveta's footsteps moving away. She glances at the cake lying on the table, covered with the dishcloth. She hears the gate open and the sound of the broken latch being fastened.

It's alright, she whispers to herself. *It's going to be alright. This is one day. I can fight this.*

She wipes her face, waits a minute, and then opens the door again. She steps outside and goes over to the fence and looks down into the neighbouring garden.

"Kolya?"

She hears the squeak of a door being opened and Kolya comes out of his house, rubbing his hands on his trousers. He nods at her.

"You've come for another rabbit?" he asks, and winks.

Lyuda gives him a small smile. "Kolya," she says, "I want to buy some…"

Kolya nods and coughs onto the back of his hand. He is wearing a thick tweed suit and black rubber boots pulled up to his knees. He jerks his head to the side.

"Come round," he says. "I've got it here."

Lyuda turns away from the fence and walks up the garden path and through the gate, and then the few steps over to Kolya's. His front garden is marked out with neat lines of green potato plants. He is waiting for her on the front step.

"Want to take a look?" he asks, and motions his head towards the kitchen door.

Lyuda moves past him and leans around to look inside the kitchen. On the stove, a huge red pot is set over a low flame. A thin metal tube is protruding from its lid and threaded into another pot, set on a high chair next to the stove. The room smells of sugar, beetroot and alcohol.

"I never saw that before," she says, coming out of the kitchen. "You'll have to teach me one day." She smiles at him.

"No, Lyudichka," says Kolya. "Man's work. Not for pretty girls like you." He runs his eyes over her tight skirt and her breasts under the lace blouse.

"You're looking very lovely, Lyudichka. Someone coming round tonight?"

"Sure, of course," says Lyuda. "You know me. Someone every night."

Kolya sniffs, and points to the shed at the bottom of the garden. "It's down there. Let's go and get it."

He waits for Lyuda to go first, and then he walks after her down the path, watching her hips and backside moving in the skirt and the high-heeled shoes. At the bottom of the garden, Lyuda stops and waits while Kolya pushes his shoulder against the door to open it. He goes in, and then holds the door open for her.

She can see that the floor of the shed is stacked with garden equipment. Plastic and glass bottles, filled with clear liquid, are lined up on wooden shelves. She takes a step into the enclosed space, and Kolya reaches up to a shelf and takes down two bottles.

"How many, sweetheart?" he asks.

"Two or three," she says, and then he turns, holding the bottles, and leans into her and kisses her on the mouth, making a growling noise.

"You're so…" he says.

Lyuda pushes him away. His hot breath is all over her face, tasting of vodka and garlic.

"Kolya, get off me! What are you doing?"

Kolya slides the bottles back onto a shelf and then reaches round and pulls her hard against his crotch. Lyuda struggles to shove him away but he holds her with both hands and kisses her again, his bristles and tongue scratching her skin. Lyuda frees an arm and pushes his mouth away and then she reaches up and

207

hits him across the face as hard as she can. Kolya grunts and releases her and she backs out of the shed, panting.

"You dirty old goat! You're disgusting. I'm not that desperate!"

She twists round and stumbles up the path, the tight skirt and heels hindering every step. Halfway up the garden, she trips on a tree root and falls forward, but then catches herself on the edge of the fence. Her whole body is shaking, and her breath is jerking in and out. She can taste him in her mouth – the garlic, the alcohol, his tongue – and she screws up her face, wiping her mouth with the back of her hand. The buttons of her blouse have come undone, but her hands are trembling too much to fasten them up.

Kolya has come out of the shed, his face twisted in anger. He is holding a hand up to his cheek.

"Little bitch! That's why you can't keep a man. Chase them all off, don't you? I heard you screaming all those times. I heard everything you said to him."

Lyuda puts her hands over her ears and hurries past the kitchen door and out of the gate, running the few steps down the path to her own house. She opens the front door and then slams it behind her and slides the bolt across. She collapses at the kitchen table, panting, and tries to calm her breathing. Pushing off the high-heeled shoes, she picks them up and throws them as hard as she can at the door. They make a dull thud and fall to the ground. She rips open the blouse she is wearing and pulls it off and throws it onto the floor, and then gets up and pulls off her skirt and walks into the bedroom in her underwear. She grabs her housedress from the back of the chair and pulls it over her body.

She wipes her mouth again and gathers a glob of phlegm into her throat, and then she unbolts the front door and opens it and she spits it out into the garden. Turning back, she catches a glimpse of Kolya coming up the path, a bottle of *samohon* in each hand. His face looks sunken and old.

"Lyudichka!" he calls out. "I'm…"

Lyuda slams the front door before she can hear a word, and pushes the bolt back again. She looks around her kitchen and sees the cake on the table, and the memory of the post office comes back to her and she shakes her head. She waits a few moments, just breathing in and out, and then she swallows, wipes her mouth with the back of her hand, and goes over to the door and puts on her house shoes. She pushes the black high-heels into the corner with her foot, and then goes to the stove and reaches for a saucepan filled with green borsch, and she starts to heat the soup.

It is evening and Angela is sleeping.

At the kitchen table, Lyuda sits, holding a glossy blue headscarf. She is running it through her hands, back and forth. Outside the front door, on the step, is a dead rabbit and three plastic bottles full of vodka.

There is a knock at the door and someone tries the handle, but the door is bolted.

"Lyuda?"

It is Sveta's voice, and it comes to Lyuda across the room slowly, as if it is not a real sound, but fragments of other noises that have come together at this moment to make up the strange sound of her name. *Ly-u-da.*

She doesn't look up. Her face doesn't move. She pulls the headscarf back and forth between her hands and winds it around her fingers.

"Lyuda?"

There is more knocking at the door.

"Are you alright? Open the door. I know you're in there, Lyuda. There's a rabbit on the doorstep and some bottles. Come and bring them in."

209

She knocks again. The noise of the wood resonates through the kitchen.

"Lyuda, open the door."

Sveta goes to the window, but she can't see in through the dirty glass and the curtains. She knocks on the window and Lyuda thinks of the bird pecking there.

Peck, peck, peck.

Knock, knock, knock.

"I'm coming back tomorrow morning," Sveta says. "I've got to get back to the children. It's going to be fine, Lyuda. Eat the cake. I made it for you. I'll see you tomorrow."

There is a pause and Lyuda thinks that she must have left. Then another knock; faster, harder.

"*Bozhe!* Lyuda, you're not the only one with problems, you know. I'm sorry it was a rough day but you can't spend your whole life hiding. Just pull yourself together. No one has it easy. You think I have it easy?"

Lyuda can hear the heavy breathing outside the window. She weaves the headscarf between her fingers.

"I'm taking the rabbit. Otherwise a fox will get it."

She hears Sveta returning to the front door and the sound of her bending downwards and lifting something from the step. She hears the gate latch being lifted and dropped.

Lyuda stands up. It feels as if everything around her is growing and shrinking in great breaths of confusion; as if everything is growing unbearably large and open, and then shrinking down until she is so cramped that she has no room even to draw in air. And it is as if this is happening at the same time – the opening and the closing, the awful expansion and the shrinking – and she sees that her hands are shaking and she puts the glossy headscarf down onto the kitchen table and she goes into the bedroom where Angela is sleeping. She stands above her daughter, watching her for a few moments, and then she reaches down and touches her cheek with her fingertips. She runs them over the skin and she touches the edge of her ear and strokes a single hair away from her face. She kneels down next to the bed and then she bends her head down and pushes it into the mattress. She closes her eyes and breathes in deeply, trying to stop any thoughts from entering her mind, pushing out everything except for the sound and the smell of her sleeping daughter.

At last, she lifts herself up from the bed and goes across the room to a wooden chest. She opens it and rummages down beneath piles of dusty blankets and jumpers until she finds a length of yellow material, patterned with small flowers, and she pulls it out and shakes it open over the floor.

She closes the chest and carries the cloth into the kitchen where she drapes it over the back of a chair. She looks at the window where she wants to hang it, to cover the flaking paint. She looks at the grey net curtains drawn across and the frayed hole that Sveta found that morning. *They must have been white once*, she thinks. She tries to remember back to her childhood, to find a colour in her memory, but she cannot. There is only the white paint of the window, and the smell of the paint, and something red.

This will change the room, she thinks. *These curtains will make it brighter. I'll throw the others out. Yellow cloth. Sunshine.*

She takes a pair of scissors out of a drawer to cut down the old net and she steps out of her slippers and clambers onto the sideboard, hitching up the skirt of her housedress.

Close up, the windowpanes are filthy, streaked with dust and grime. She wipes one of them with her finger, and as she touches the cool glass, something passes through her. Her eyes narrow and she feels a pressure in the back of her head. She looks at the line her finger has drawn across the dirt, and then she runs all of her fingertips down the glass, drawing five lines down to the bottom of the pane. She shivers. She is on her knees on the sideboard and outside, the evening is just starting to fade into darkness. *It was here*, she thinks.

Through this window I watched him walk away from me.

Through this window I looked for him to come back.

I waited for something to happen. I waited for something that would explain what was happening in my life. I waited for something to take away everything that was crushing me.

I waited for Mother. I waited for Volodiya. I waited for a lover. I waited for anything, anything, anything.

And now I see. There was nothing to wait for.

She thinks of Kolya. She thinks of the post office. She thinks of the vodka sitting outside on her step, in plastic bottles. A feeling slips through her that is almost unbearably sweet.

Vova, she thinks. *Vova, where are you now? I can't believe that you are somewhere. How could it be possible that you are still alive and real and living somewhere now?*

And is it possible that you could come back?

She pushes her forehead against the windowpane and breathes in the dust and stares out at the path and the gate.

The garden looks beautiful in the falling light. It is the end of the lilac and the flowers have faded into long brown cones and the grasses and the wild daisies are high.

And he could walk through the gate right now. He could just open it. He could just walk up this path and open the door and take me in his arms and then what would any of this mean? Anything at all?

She feels the pressure pushing harder against her head and pushing against her chest. She is breathing heavily.

What if I could make it happen? What if there was something I could do that would make him walk down that path, over the lilac flowers? And he would walk back into this room and put his arms around me. What would I do?

She pictures him for a moment, his dark hair and his brown eyes and the love in them when he had looked at her. She pictures him walking towards the house, glancing up at the window, seeing her there.

I would tell him to go to hell. I would spit in his face. I wouldn't let him back into the house.

She lets out a low, strangled moan.

And yet.

Lyuda looks up at the curtains again. She puts down the scissors. She climbs off the sideboard and in her bare feet she walks to the front door and she slides back the bolt and opens it. She picks up the three plastic containers of vodka from the step and puts two of them down on the table and she unscrews the lid of the third one and she takes a long swig straight from the bottle. The anger rises in her body and meets with an equal sadness, and together they flow through her. Grey, warm, safe. Lyuda pushes the breath slowly out from between her lips.

Outside, the snow is falling steadily. Down, down, down.

"At last," she whispers. "It is over."

31

Everything is moving very slowly. Mama is standing by the window, gazing out into the garden, but I think that she is not seeing anything at all. Her eyes are clear and full of light, as if they have been washed with bright tears, and now she is seeing everything dull and murky, through those tears.

Now she is turning towards me. She comes over to me and kisses me on the forehead and her warm lips touch my skin for a long time. Like a goodbye. As if her touch is a goodbye; as if every movement of her arm, her head, her shoulder is a gradual movement away from me.

She looks down at me and her gaze covers me with a waterfall of those bright, grey tears. I try to reach out through them, but she turns, and I see that they are falling everywhere, all over the kitchen and outside, over the entire garden, like a glistening rain with the sunshine behind it. Everywhere she turns these tears are falling.

I dance through the garden in a white dress.

Mother blinks. The waterfall shatters into sunlight.

"I cannot do it," she says.

I run to the willowbank.

"Show me more," I call to Grandmother. "Mother is going to leave. You must show me more. I can bring the memory back to her."

I climb up the riverbank. I am breathing heavily. Grandmother looks tired.

"I want more," I say. "I want to see other times, other memories. If Mama and I were like that once, then we can be like that again. I can bring her back. I can remind her of what we were. I can remind her of what she did."

I stand before Grandmother, impatient, breathless. She sighs. She looks very old here, alone on her riverbank.

"It is not so simple," she says. "I can take you back, but it might not be the same."

"What do you mean?"

"I mean that if she changes, then the memory changes. It cannot be fixed. You can only go where she has left a path to follow back."

Grandmother sighs again. She does not know all the rules. She feels Lyuda's darkness, close and heavy. It is difficult to see anything clearly.

"Little one," she says. "I do not know. I can try. Come and sit."

I sit on the grass and I lie back, resting my head in Grandmother's lap. She strokes my hair, her dry hands scratching over my damp skin. I close my eyes.

"I want to see Mother," I say. "You have to show me. You have to take me back."

"Shhhhh," she says. "Shhhhh. We will go there."

Grandmother pictures Lyuda, and I push my head deeper into the branches of her lap and her green fingers are touching my forehead and I am waiting for the sunshine to come; the garden and the golden light.

Suddenly, I shiver. Snow is falling. I am cold. I open my eyes. There is a warmth around me but something in my centre is cold. Above me, white snowflakes are pouring from the sky;

sparkling, soft shapes, which get bigger as they fall towards me. One lands on my cheek. It is cold. Its wetness spreads over my skin. Another lands and touches my hand. My body is shifted and the heat shifts. I look to the side, around me, and I see on one side Mother's skin, covered in tiny bumps, a flap of her dress, a small blue button; and on the other side the white, white garden.

I am in Mother's arms. I am cold but I do not want to cry.

Something is happening with Mother. She is whispering to herself, or to me. I sense she is scared. She wants to do something. I am also scared. And very cold. My blanket is open. I want to cry, but something inside me tells me not to cry, that if I do, then I will draw all the cold into my throat, take it into my body, and I may die. I shiver again. Mother pulls me closer to her. I try to hear what she is whispering.

"Angela, Angela," she is saying. She bends over me and I can see her face, drawn out and full of despair. There are silvery streaks on her skin, shining with ice. Her pale brown eyes are the saddest things I have ever seen.

On the riverbank, tears run down my cheeks. I am shivering. Mother's lips touch my forehead.

"My god, you are so cold," she says. She starts to cry again and the despair flows out of her and into my body. "My god, Angela. What am I going to do? My little one, what am I going to do?"

She stands there in the snow, her baby open to the cold, with tears flowing down her cheeks, her arms and her hands trembling. She shakes her head from side to side. "It cannot be like this," she says. "It is not possible to bear. This is not how it can be."

Something inside me is breaking. Something inside me that will never be able to heal is being torn from end to end. I know this feeling. I am remembering. Grandmother wipes away my tears with her fingertips. "You have to know," she says. She feels the heaviness of my wound pushing down on her shoulders and her body sinks wearily beneath it.

In Mother's arms, the snow falls onto my face and onto the edges of my blanket and onto my body inside the blanket. I think I am going to die, here in her arms, here in the whiteness. I prepare myself to leave. I know the way. Mother will come with me. She is shaking her head and crying and I do not know how she is holding me when she is shivering so much, and her tears drop down onto my face and they are warm, and then she looks down and sees, as if for the first time, this child in her arms, this little face bathed in snow and tears, and she gasps. A jolt of panic goes through her. I feel her shaking hands pulling the blanket around me and then she is pushing open the kitchen door and there is a great rush of warmth from the hot room and Mother slams the door and she carries me to the bed and gets into it and pulls the covers up over me, holding me against her body.

"My darling," she is saying. "My darling, my darling. What was I thinking, my little one, my love, I will live for you. Angela, darling, my little one, I will live for you. I will live for you, I will hold on for you. Angela, Angela, Angela."

The words cover me like warm water, like her warm tears. My body is still cold on the inside but Mother is pressing the blankets around me and she is kissing my face where the tears have fallen and where the snow has melted, and her mouth is warm and on the riverbank my body is shaking and I am moving my head from side to side and my tears are flowing like another grey river.

"Angela," Grandmother is calling to me. "Angela. The sun is shining. Come back."

Out of Mother's despair I am drawn back to a spring afternoon. I open my eyes and sit up from Grandmother's lap. I am dizzy from crying. I look at Grandmother through blurred eyes and she puts a finger to her lips. "Shhhhh," she says. "Breathe, don't talk, breathe."

I breathe, and I am calmer. The river flows past. Grey, slow, heavy.

"This is what she did for you," she says at last. "She lived for you. This is how she loved you."

"I wanted sunshine," I whisper.

Breathe. Breathe. Breathe.

"There is sunshine," she says. "But you wanted to see her love. You have to understand. This was what she gave you."

"Tears?"

"Life."

"Her life?"

She does not answer. I leave her and I swim to the other side, the cold water calming my body and my face. I feel different now I have seen this. I feel changed. Older, lighter, heavier, sadder, deeper. I have a great urge to go home to Mother. I start to run. I am running between the willow trees and they are waving after me. *Go,* they say. They know the love that Mother has for me. They know the love I am longing for. They know what Grandmother carries in her old, tired bark.

I run.

Something is changing. The crows are moving like a black shadow in the distance. There is a wind gathering and we are calling to one another in the flock to leave, to shelter, to hide. It is a wind that we do not know. I fly fast around the garden trying to see what is different. I will not leave. There are eggs in my nest. My partner. We will shelter. I hear a howling from far away, from the distant woods. A wolf. I cannot see anything different. The sky is blue. Sunshine. Only the crows in a slow movement. *Caw, caw, caw.* My wings are tingling. The flock is unsettled but we will stay. I fly up to my nest and feel calmer.

There are white flowers around the nest, fading to brown. Our eggs are hatching soon. We will wait.

The sky calls to me. *Daughter, come and fly!*

I turn my gaze upwards, and the clear blue expanse darkens. I see granite clouds drawing towards me from the distant horizon; I feel their looming shadow ready to cover me.

I swing my legs. The air is growing colder. My skin rises in tiny peaks, answering the wind.

I rub my arms with my hands, which are still warm.

I swing my legs.

Come, says the sky. *Come and be what you will.*

I look up into the darkening clouds.

I lift into the air and I dissolve myself into them.

The sky darkens.

I call out to everything around me.

"Come!" I cry. "The whole world must be turned into tears and pass away."

I draw the clouds to me, seeking the water from the sky and keeping it close; gathering the thoughts into form, one after another, cloud upon cloud, closer and closer into the darkest place. And I call to the sky that there is no need here for light, and the sky closes as I cover it with my anger, and when at last everything is dark and everything is brought into a tight, furious centre, then I whisper to the clouds around me, "It is time," and I release a scream into the universe and the clouds let out a deafening roll of thunder that goes on and on and on, and lightning flashes down repeatedly onto the garden and the village and the river and over everything that I know, and when the thunder and my scream are finished, then I pull my arms from around my chest and I hold them out and I let the rains pour down onto the earth.

Down and down we pour, in a great rushing flow of our very selves, flooding the earth with that which is us; with the water, the rain, the sadness, the guilt, with everything that we hold and that holds us. We are a dark torrent, pouring into the river and over the garden and into the cups of the browning lilac and into the water bucket, and we fill the black earth with our black tears and I pour myself down onto the form of Grandmother, mixing my grief with her green leaves and her branches and she doesn't move, but she lets it fall through her and she turns the colour of the rain, her hair transforms to ashen grey, and water flows through the crevices of her face and down into the roots of the willow trees and onto the silver birches, pushing the delicate leaves down, down, down so that they cannot spring up again, dancing, and I call again for the lightning and I hurl it across the sky with another howl, and when everything is black and everything is covered in my pain, then I feel a whisper of calm coming to me, amidst my storm; a voice which is so soft that I do not know if it is I speaking or another, and the voice says to me, *It is all well, daughter. It is all right, Angela. Everything is light.*

And when I hear this voice, then my pain does not go away; but, as if from a far, far distance, I know that it will be well. I know that I will be all right; that I can rest.

32

I fall asleep in a state of deep peace, and while I sleep, my Nightspirit pours herself down into me in clear, healing waves of light, without memory, without knowledge, without pain. I dream that I am lying in a great, wide nest with Mother's wings around me. It is the safest, warmest place in the world.

I come out of my dream and I open my eyes to a dark room. I look over to Mother's bed and I see that she isn't in it. I get out of my bed and I go into the unlit kitchen in my bare feet and my white nightdress, which is torn above the knee. Mama is sitting at the table with her head buried in her arms. Beside her is an empty plastic bottle.

My heart cracks. I remember everything. She is going to leave me. She will not choose to stay. I stand at the doorway and I start to cry. She will never choose me. I will never be enough. I stand, crying, my heart hurting so much I think it might shatter into a thousand pieces.

Mother lies beneath the surface of the water and smiles at the flowers above her and the reflections of the green willows. The water flows. My tears fall.

"I am coming," says Mother.

I inhale with a gasp and Mother's head jerks up and she turns around. The smile on her face moves into eyes of panic and she stumbles up from the table.

"Darling," she half-chokes, and she runs across the night-time room towards me and takes me in her arms. My heart is lying all over the kitchen floor. My neck is wet with tears. She opens her wings and spreads them wide and covers me with them. But it isn't enough. It will never be enough. She cannot comfort me now because she has made her choice. I wasn't enough. She cannot pick up my heart, because her desire not to break it wasn't strong enough. There is nothing that can comfort me.

I curl my body up into a ball and transform myself into nothing. I disappear. Where there were tears and wetness and pieces of my heart, now there is nothing. Not even air. Not even water. Not even a dream.

❧

It is morning.

After the storm, the village is resting; pausing before the day's work begins, repairing tiled roofs, checking livestock and gathering broken branches.

Mother brings me a glass of water mixed with honey and I sit in bed drinking it. She is trying to lift my spirits and stay here with me, but I know she wants to leave. I sip the pale yellow water but it tastes empty. It does not taste of her love. I get up from the bed and I go over to the window and I pour the rest of the water out into the garden.

I go into the kitchen holding the empty glass. Mother is standing over the stove, stirring a saucepan of *kasha*, grey porridge. There is a dish of strawberries on the table and a sunken brown cake. I cannot eat any food that she has cooked.

"Mama. I want to go to the river. I want to see how high it is after the storm. Can I go?"

She pauses, and seems to struggle, her face crumpling and then straightening.

"Yes," she says at last. "But not for long. Come back quickly."

When I have gone, she stands in the kitchen. She doesn't stir the *kasha* and it begins to burn on the bottom of the pan. She tries to focus, but her mind is drawn to the river.

"Angela. Angela, I am staying," she says.

She imagines the river, and the water full of flowers. It would be so easy. One foot and then the other foot, and she would lie down. She can feel the current moving over her, pulling her gently where she wants to go.

"I would not struggle," she says to the empty room. She turns off the stove and goes out of the front door. She passes through the garden and up the slope to the village street. She walks along it, her unbrushed hair loose down her back, her housedress and apron streaked with dirt. She comes to the turning for the silver birch copse and goes down the path. Broken branches are hanging from the trees after the storm, but she doesn't look up at them.

Mother passes through the glade to the river. It is starting to get hot. I am sitting huddled beneath a willow tree, my long brown knees pulled up under my chin. Grandmother is sitting opposite, on the other side, watching me.

Mother cannot see either of us. She pauses on the riverbank and then bends down and takes off her sandals. She reaches around behind her and fumbles with the strings of her stained apron, pulling the bow loose, and then she lifts the apron over her head and lets it drop onto the grass. She climbs down the bank and steps into the river. The water is up to her waist and her housedress floats out before her in the current. She smiles, and flowers drift into the water around her, white daisies and scarlet poppies. She stretches out her hand and touches them as they float by, drawing her fingers over the petals. A light rain of lilac blossoms falls into the river. A farewell. I close my eyes and I disappear into nothing.

From the bottom of the river, Mother watches everything. She sees the birds overhead, swallows darting across the sky to their nests and back, insects touching the surface of the water, the shadow of flowers floating above.

She sees me, lying with my head on Grandmother's green lap. Long willow branches are hanging around us and Grandmother's gnarled hands are laid on my forehead. She sees a rope of black thread, like a thin snake, winding itself around her mother and her daughter, weaving and winding, and she reaches out a hand to grasp it, to pull it away from us; but as her hand stretches out, she sees that the black threads are coming from her own outstretched fingers. Tiny black threads of silk.

A scarlet flower drifts onto the surface of the water, and floats away.

Mother stands in the kitchen, holding the wooden spoon. The *kasha* has started to burn and she shakes her head to bring her back to the present, and stirs the thick mixture round in the pan. She wipes her hands on her apron and reaches back to tuck her long hair into her dress, to keep it away from the stove.

"Angela," she calls out to me, and I come in from the garden, hoping, hoping to feel something different, to see Mother smiling, to see some light around her. I smell the burning *kasha* and I see the struggle in her eyes.

"Angela," she says to me. "Angela, run outside and pick some flowers. The breakfast is nearly ready. We'll need to fetch more water as well. Will you help me?"

"Yes, Mama. Yes, yes, yes, yes, yes!" I say, and I run outside on bare feet. I jump over the water pail on the step and run down into the garden, the black soil soft and dry, and the sound of a bird singing.

Mother watches me from the window. I turn round and catch sight of her face, and I pick the nearest flower, a red tulip, and I run up to the window, and I hold it out to her.

33

In the wind, Mother and I are carried far and high, a silver rope binding us to each other in the rushing ether.

"A silver rope," cries Mother. "And what is that?"

"A rope of memories and dreams," I say.

She catches my words, one by one, out of the air. I am in front of her, creating sky all around us through which to fly.

"Bring them all!" I call to her, over the wind. "Your hopes and regrets, your memories and dreams. Leave nothing behind."

The skies Mother is creating are filled with stormy, angry, dark clouds.

"Mother," I shout. "The darkness. Let it go, let all of it go!"

Mother releases the strands of the silver rope and they tumble from her into the sky. The memories, the dreams, the wishes, the regrets, the desires and hopes; all of them are released and they fall, with the silver rope, out into the dark clouds.

I look for the air to clear, for the storm to fade, but Mother is panicking.

"What am I, then?" she cries out. "What am I without them? I am going to disappear!"

She lets out a terrible, wolf-like howl and dives down out of the path of the wind which is carrying me, grasping in the air to the left and right, grasping for all the things she has let go; here a wish, here a regret, here a memory of me, dancing in a sunlit garden.

"You are air!" I call to her. "You are the wind itself. Look, Mother! Look at me!" And I dissolve into the ether and fly fast and free and madly and I split into a million bright blue pieces and surround her with myself.

"Look, Mother, look!"

And she looks and she sees and she reaches out and touches the blue around her, but she feels me separate from what she has known. She feels me around her, but she cannot feel the girl, her daughter, dancing in that garden, and without this, she cannot accept that any of it is real.

"It is all real!" I say, still moving around her, still rushing madly through the skies that I am creating before us. "It is all real, the memory is real, the regrets are real, I am real, the dancing girl is real! Mother, it is all real! But it is not all you!"

She fades, with both hands clasping this one single memory; this one solitary prism through which, right now, she can understand anything at all. Her hands close around it, crushing it into nothing.

I, sunlit in a summer garden, bend; crushed beneath her great hands.

"It is not even you!" I try to say. But she misunderstands me, the memory. I try to say to her, "The memory, it is not you. It is me, dancing in the garden. It is *me* you are crushing."

"But it was *my* eyes that saw it," she says. "And nobody else's eyes. And if I hadn't seen it, then there would be no memory. And if I don't hold on to it, then what will happen to it? What will happen to me, seeing it? What will happen to any of it? To the garden, to the sunlight, to the place where you were dancing?"

"Mother..." I try to say.

The skies are calm.

In a sunlit garden, a memory has been crushed.

I can breathe deeply, in and out, in and out. But it has changed. I am no longer the dancing girl in the springtime sunlight.

I am a shadow of fear. A brief dark streak of reality twisted into something that never was.

Mother watches from the window, and sees that it has gone. That no girl is dancing in the garden under a rain of lilac blossoms.

She breathes in and out. In and out.

"And now what?" she says.

Grandmother, from the willowbank, sees that her daughter is breaking into pieces. She can see the long, deep cracks appearing across her fragile reality; she can see her reaching out for shadows, which disappear as soon as she focuses on them. She sees her lifting the bottle of clear liquid, which is her last defence against what she can only understand to be a hell closing in on her, and on everything she knows.

"Lyuda!" she cries. "It is not too late."

While I am sleeping, Mother is pouring *samohon* into her mouth like cool, fresh well water. In my sleep, I hold the pillow against my damp cheek and I dream of Mother, a nest, a flock of flying white birds.

A strong breeze springs up and I suddenly cannot control the beating of my wings. I have lost sight of Mother in the flock; the air is circling us and I cannot see properly. The breeze turns to wind and the wind turns to hail and from hail into a thick, driving snow. The snow beats and blinds me, and I rip open the pillow against my cheek and release a flood of tiny white feathers. They swirl madly around me until I cannot see; the snow and the feathers are pounding into my flying body. I try in vain to beat my wings through this white blindness, to escape it. But I am choking on the feathers, and gradually I begin to fade out of the dream and I realise that I am asleep and that I am a girl, in her bed, with wings fading to arms and hope fading into whiteness and a mother, blinded by her own suffocating dream, unable to hold onto a single last shred of reality.

A white stork flies over the roof of the house, beating its serene wings. It flies towards its nest, moving the dark air with every downward beat. As it passes into a beam of clear moonlight, Grandmother looks up into the pale sky, and she shudders.

Mother takes another sip of vodka and she breathes out a long, slow darkness, which winds its way through the rooms of the house, gathering strength. It rises, approaching me. I struggle to breathe through the white feathers and I fight with my hands against them and, choking, I try to find a single point of light that could guide me out of this awful dream, which could guide me home.

"Grandmother!" I call out. "I need your help. I cannot find my way through."

"I cannot leave the willowbank," cries Grandmother, trying not to add her own panic to mine. "Your Nightspirit will come. She will guide you."

"I cannot bear it," I say. "I cannot see Mother like this."

I fade into my dream, knowing that my Nightspirit will come, and Grandmother turns her face to the river, and to the stars.

"Show me what I can do," she asks them. "Everything else has failed."

My Nightspirit guides me to the willowbank, filling me again with her clear, healing light. She passes me to Grandmother, who takes my hands in hers, and she does not touch my forehead but she looks into my eyes and I look back into her ancient blue eyes and find myself in a kind of tunnel that we are creating with our gaze, and a wave of calm washes over me as I enter.

I have a tingling feeling, as if this tunnel has always been here, an invisible strand of silver between Grandmother and me; and at the same time, it seems to be appearing anew beneath every step I take.

As I move, I hear a faint tinkling at my feet. I look down and see that tiny pieces of glass – like clear, hardened tears – are falling off my body and onto the floor of the tunnel. As they fall, the pain I have been feeling is lifting away, shadow by shadow, and the most delicious relief comes to me as I step out of this darkness and into the simplest happiness, and it is at once overwhelming, uplifting!

I brush my skirt, my legs, my arms, and the remainder of the tears drop in jagged shards to the ground. I move forward – so light! – and I look ahead through the grey tunnel, and to one side I see some sort of an opening; a moving green colour, which is drawing me towards it, a shimmering of gold and green. And I step into this opening and see that I am in a garden.

Immediately, I think this is the same garden as the one in the first memory – the long grass and those sensual smells and the sound of the birdsong – and I gaze around me and see the arms of a woman and I see a child lying, and I smell those warm, comforting scents of skin and hair and river. I am full of anticipation to experience again this sensuous memory, and I shift to see if I can move in these arms where she will show me the wonders around us, and I take a step forward, and I cannot understand – how could I take a step? – and then I feel that there is a great warmth close to me and I suddenly see that it is not I who am lying in these arms; it is my arms holding this warmth!

I am holding a child and I am moving around the garden, and I take a step forwards and I remember what I must say, and I say, "Look!"

And I point to a sunshine-dusted butterfly, which is settling onto a wild daisy, and then I say, "Look!"

And I point to a bird above us, which is rising from its nest in the lilac tree, and then I say, "Look!"

And I turn my body around so that all of the garden becomes a blur of summer gold, and I hear a trill of laughter like a morning swallow and I turn faster and faster and I feel the love of the child in my arms flowing through me and creating a wind around me and I turn and turn and turn until the wind has taken on a momentum of its own, and then the child and I gradually slow until we are standing still and the golden garden has become nothing but a swirl of light all around us, and in the midst of this golden light, I bend my head down to brush the child's face with my lips.

The joy I am feeling with this warm spirit in my arms, and my lips touching her sun-brushed cheek, is something I have never experienced before. The overwhelming joy of knowing another person is in this world, and knowing that my love for them will fill every one of my waking moments while my heart continues to beat; the joy of knowing that from this time, there is a love that will lift me up, that will flow stronger than any other thing I have known.

And in this moment, I understand the rope, and I understand why Grandmother has come back: to help her daughter. And I understand why Mother has tried so hard to stay, and tried to keep her sadness away from me. And I look down at this promise – this light in my arms, this love which is my future – and there is nothing, nothing I have ever wanted more than for this to be true. Not in all my times of transformation, in my freedom of flight, in my moments of the early morning. This is what I want. The river. The garden. This child in my arms. The light flowing through her, and through me. And my mother.

As this understanding comes over me, the garden starts to fade, and I look for the opening of the tunnel, suddenly desperate to get back to Grandmother, and to Mother. I don't know if there is still time. I don't know if I can. Because something is changing.

With this vision of myself and my child, with this new desire to be a part of the world that Mama lives in, I feel something is closing. I feel that my choice to step into this world means leaving behind the part of myself that is open to the flow of spirit around me; accepting a new dream, the singularity of my path. And to teach that dream, in time, to my own daughter.

I feel this – the changes, the choice before me – but with all of my heart, this is what I choose. This is my last wish. Before my doors close, before I can no longer decide who and how to create myself in each of my waking moments. This is what I choose.

I am back in the tunnel, and now I am running, and I can feel Grandmother at the end of the tunnel, and somehow I tumble out onto the riverbank, and Grandmother can see that something has changed, and her face lights up with a bright blue hope and she says, "Go, Angela! Go, as fast as you can!" And I am swimming across the river to find Mother, and Grandmother turns her face to the stars, and to the waters, and she says, "Thank you, thank you. My heart is yours, you have granted my request. I thank you."

34

Lyuda washes herself under the shower head in the garden, her skin rising and falling against the flow of cool water. She reaches for a threadbare towel and slowly rubs each of her limbs dry. The garden is dawn-grey and Volodiya is asleep in their bed. The surface of her body feels alive against the air and the towel. *It is like he is everywhere,* she thinks. *It is like Volodiya is touching me through each drop of water, through the air, through every stroke of cloth over my skin.* She thinks of his arms around her and she shivers. *There is nothing I wouldn't do for his touch.*

She wraps the towel under her arms and walks back to the house through the dawn grass and a shadowy garden. The kitchen floor is cold under her feet and she passes quickly through to the bedroom and to Volodiya. Around his body she senses a warmth into which she can sink; a warm energy in which her own body can disappear, a space in which somehow, somehow, she no longer has to exist.

She shivers. She unwraps the towel from around her chest and she moves herself into the bed. Volodiya shifts under the covers and encloses her in his arms; a woman, skin touched by water and hair touched by morning grey. He encloses the woman in his sleeping arms and she disappears into him, somehow, somehow. *It is perfect,* says Lyuda, from far away. *At last, it is perfect.*

Lyuda takes the spoon from the jar of sour cream. She pulls it out slowly, letting the white mass gather around the head as she lifts it and brings it to her mouth. She places the tip of the spoon between her lips and holds it there, her tongue licking off the cream, savouring the last moments. She closes her eyes, and she knows what is going to happen. She puts down the spoon and she twists the lid back on the jar and she goes into the bedroom. She takes the hairpins out of her hair so that it tumbles down her back; brown curls, golden curls. She breathes in and out and she lies down on her bed. She empties her mind and lets it drift her to the willowbank, a sunny afternoon, and a bottle of *samohon*.

I run.

The *samohon* is weaving its way through her body like a slow river.

On the willowbank, the afternoon sun speckles through the filter of dancing willow leaves, golden and warm on Lyuda's long hair and over her quiet face.

She squints through the sunshine to the other side of the river, to the line of willow trees standing wide and calm. Her eyes narrow them into a faint blur, so they are just a streak of green against the black fields beyond, like the single stroke of a paintbrush across a black canvas. She raises her hand in the air and starts to paint the landscape; a new yellow sun above the fields, flowers falling in the water, and –

"A single red tulip," she says out loud. "A red tulip and a dancing girl."

She paints them in. Falling flowers and a falling red tulip.

She tips back the clear glass bottle and drinks. A long sip. Another long sip. She shivers and savours the sweet, lingering seconds – one, two, three – as the *samohon* winds down into her body.

I run.

She takes off her sandals, one by one, and throws them, one by one, into the river. They float away, dipping and rising on the surface of the water. She walks down the slope to the edge of the river. The grass beneath her feet is springy; the sunshine touches her hair. Her eyes are dry, drained of tears; tunnels of light focused only on a single, green death.

With her paintbrush, she paints the river before her, fast and deep, an inexorable current; a powerful pull, strong enough to take her, hold her, embrace her, and release her into her deepest desire.

It is flowing. She paints herself into it, stepping carefully. A leg into the deep water, another leg. It is higher than her waist and she has to use all of her resistance not to get swept away before she has reached the middle of the water. She paints a last single object – a red tulip – and pushes it behind her ear. She throws the brush far out into the water and it floats away. Imagination, memory, desire. Gone, and a rush of emptiness.

I enter the house.

Mother stands in the river, the water curved around her body. She is ready. Her eyes follow the streak of red disappearing into the distance, and she remembers the words of the river.

I will take you where you want to go.

"Now it is time," she says.

I do not kick off my shoes, and from the corner of my eye I see a jar of sour cream on the sideboard below the window and I see that the kitchen is neat and that Mother is not in it and I run straight through to the bedroom, calling, "Mama! Mama! Mama!"

There is the trace of a sound in the back of Lyuda's head, and she tries to let the hiss of the river flow over it, but she finds it is getting louder, and repeating, like a drum beat, summoning her. She fights against the sound, but it is drawing her away. There is a struggle, as she tries to stay with the river, with the soothing, hissing rush, with the cold emptiness that is ready to embrace her. But the drum is getting louder, and now there is a high song to it, and the song is calling to something within her, and she has no choice but to respond.

Mama, Mamochka, Mamusya, Matenka moiya!

"No," she says. "No, Angela. I can't, I can't!" But I am calling – "Mama! Mama! Mama!" – and I am pulling her hand and she is trying with all of her strength not to open her eyes, not to see me, not to be drawn away from the place where she is, but I will not let go! I am pulling her hand for myself and for the child I have felt in my arms. And I remember the feeling once again, and I shout, "Mama! Come back!"

Around Lyuda, the river is fading, the flow of the current, the dancing green of the willows, the smooth stones beneath her feet. She struggles to hold on to them, but the sounds in her head are growing clearer and louder, and one by one the images disappear, until at last, all that remains is the sight of a small girl before her, with long, tangled hair and a white dress.

Mama opens her eyes, and she is with me.

"Mama!" I say. "There is something you have to see! Come with me!"

I take her hand, and I am leading her into the garden where I was before, where Grandmother had taken me. I lead her here with my hand holding hers tightly, and as we enter, she changes, and she is older, she is a different woman, suddenly no longer the young and broken girl. She is calmer, and her face is lined and there is colour in her cheeks, and her hair is woven into a dark golden plait and wound around her head. She no longer seems scared. She no longer seems like a small girl.

"Mama, look!" I say, and she is turning around in this garden and then her eyes rest upon me, and I know that she is seeing me as the young mother that I am – my happy, tired face above a child in my arms, and the light that is all around us.

And I say, "Mama, this is what I choose. Mama, this can only be if you are with me. Mama, this can only happen if you stay with me."

And Mother says, "Come, Angela." And she is walking towards the house, and I follow her, with the child in my arms, and Mother goes to our front door and she steps inside the kitchen and looks around, and we can see that everything is clean, and that the wind is blowing the yellow curtains open, and on the table are bowls of fruit and bread and jars of jam and honey, and on the wall next to the stove there is a mirror, and Mother goes over to the mirror and she stands in front of it, and she looks at herself, as if trying to understand who this might be, the person who has come to this place, who has walked the steps of her journey, who has come through the darkness to this place of peace.

She looks into the mirror, into the calm, brown eyes, the new lines on her face, the neat, plaited hair, the colour in her cheeks from working outside in the garden. But she stares for the longest time into her eyes, seeking the pain, seeking the regret, seeking the longing.

But the veil of falling water has gone, and all that looks back at her is peace.

35

Sveta moves around her kitchen, making a list in her head of all the things she has to do that day. She takes a wet cloth and wipes the windowsill, which is covered in dust and tiny flies, and she lifts the lid of the soup and stirs it with a metal spoon. There is a sound of hammering in the garden, and through the yellow and black sunflowers she can see Vasya knocking nails into planks of wood, building a makeshift shower across from the outhouse.

She puts her hand to her head and adjusts the headscarf she is wearing, and then she unties it and reties it at the back of her neck. She glances into the bedroom at the back of the house where the beds are pushed neatly against the windows and covered up with blankets, and then she goes out into the hallway, changes from her slippers to her outdoor shoes, and stands on the front step.

She sees that the sunflowers are growing well and she looks over to her neighbour's garden and the gardens beyond it, lush with greenery, separated by wooden fences and tall trellises woven with vines and honeysuckle. She listens for a moment to the sounds of the village – dogs barking close by, the flutter of swallows' wings darting up and down, the shouting of children and the banging of the hammer onto metal nails.

She walks down the path through the open sunflowers towards Vasya, and she sees that Taras is beside him, holding the bag of nails, passing one to his father. Vasya's face is covered in sweat and he wipes his forehead with his forearm and picks up another of the planks. He fits the wood into place and then looks up at her watching him, and jerks his head towards the house.

"Bring something to drink," he says, and turns back to the wood, holding the nail between thick fingers.

Sveta watches him for a few moments, aiming the hammer, Taras following his movements, and she can hear a bird trilling and pecking nearby, and the sunshine is warm through her headscarf, and then she turns and starts walking back to the house, along a path lined with yellow sunflowers, and there is a smile on her face.

Grandmother, on the riverbank, is drawing herself into the willow for the last time.

In the early morning, with only the sounds of the river hissing and the calling of birds and the village dogs barking in the distance, she brings her spirit into the tree and releases it. Without effort, it flows into every part of the willow, into every coiled leaf, every opening bud; down, down to the roots sunk deep into the black soil. She feels the waters of the river drawn up through the roots; up, up to the wide, ridged trunk, to the branches, to the hanging tendrils. And as the water is drawn up through Grandmother's body, through each of her limbs, she uncurls her fingers, stretching them out, and the young leaves, wet with morning dew, unfurl, waking, into the grey morning.

She hears a voice calling to her. Grisha is reaching out his hand.

"It is time to come back," he says. "The path has been set. Your work is finished."

Grandmother feels the tree breathing around her, drawing in, releasing. She senses all the parts of it at once, working and transforming, the leaves growing, the roots drinking, the constant regeneration by sunshine, by water, by song. The taking and the giving.

She holds out her hand to Grisha.

"Look," she says.

She waits until his fingers are touching hers, and then she shows him what she can see from the willow. The wind moving in patterns above the river, the dance of the leaves to the singing water, the birds dipping and laughing and the intense peace of the tree itself, in its ancient constancy, and its rebirth second by second, in every green leaf, in every bud, in every breath of sunshine.

Grisha allows the gift to move through him, and he takes it all into himself.

"I had forgotten," he says, breathing in with the willow, and breathing out again. "I had forgotten why we return."

Grandmother smiles, and releases herself from the willow into his arms.

"Now it is time to rest," she says, as they fade into the morning sunlight.

I come to land at the edge of the nest and I glance around for threats. It is clear. My mate lifts up in a smooth flight and leaves to seek for food. I jerk my head down. Five eggs. Cream and pale blue. I settle onto the nest. I can feel the warmth of the eggs. My eggs. It will not be long. The garden is singing around me. My mate is flying. All of the flock are building and nesting and hatching and mating. It is a good season. Food is everywhere. Warmth is constant. The eggs will hatch and we will feed them and wait until they are strong and then they will leave to join the other fledglings, to discover for themselves the darting insects,

241

the imperative song, the call of the morning and the sweetest dew, which settles in the flower cups during the night-time hours. The distant river. They will discover all of this. But for now, they are safe, beneath me. Five smooth eggs.

I hear the beating of my mate's wings. She is returning. She has food in her mouth. I raise my wings and hop to the side of the nest. She has returned. I glance around. There are no threats.

I fly.

36

Lyuda sits down heavily beneath the lilac tree.

The spring is already fading, and she can feel the pull of the summer months, as the wild abundance of the first sunshine passes to a lusher, calmer green; the months where day after day will be spent in a dazed heat, and the river will be filled with laughing children and the market stalls will be overflowing with furred peaches and sweet black grapes.

Lyuda looks around her garden and she sees the shadows passing there. The shadow of a small girl with a long, fair plait. The shadow of her mother, feeding the rabbits and walking down the path with a bucket of cold water from the well. The shadow of her father, hammering nails into the bench that her mother never liked. And now, there are new shadows, faint ones: the shadow of a young woman with a child in her arms, and the shadow of a woman who Lyuda now wonders, wonders if one day she could be. A woman who has chosen what will be in her life. A woman who stands strong between the choices that she has made and the heartbreak that life brings with those choices. A woman who understands that the seasons pass, one after the other, and that the winter will come and bring with it a time of grief, but that beyond the winter there is something new, and that behind the seasons, beating the strokes of a more ancient time, is the love that her mother has given to her, and that she is now giving to her daughter, to the shadow, laughing now in the sunlit garden at a white-and-yellow butterfly, at a falling blossom, at a leaf caught in the summer breeze.

There is the sound of the gate opening, and then the latch falling back into its clasp.

"Lyudmilla Hrihorivna."

It is Kolya.

Lyuda turns her head round as Kolya walks down the garden path towards her.

"Kolya," she says. "You can start over there."

She points towards the narrow bench next to the fence, where the shadow of her father is hammering the nails, where the shadow of her mother sits with a sour look on her face.

"It's never been wide enough," she says, still pointing. "Mother hated it. We need an extra plank, or even two. And a coat of paint. I think yellow would look good."

Kolya walks over to the bench and sits down on it. He is holding a hammer and a handful of nails.

"I've got the wood," he says. "I'll need to cut it down to size. I'll have to fetch the saw. Should be finished by the afternoon."

He looks over to Lyuda beneath the tree.

"Then maybe we can share some of that *samohon*." He clears his throat. "Make a change from drinking it alone."

Lyuda pushes herself up from the ground and brushes the soil from her dress. She seeks Kolya's eye and holds it.

"If you finish the bench early, you can start on the rabbit hutches," she says. "And I want to build a shower. Down by the outhouse. And fix the gate. And everything needs a new coat of paint."

She turns towards the house.

"I'll bring some tea," she says. "And I'm making a honey cake later. You can have some of that."

She walks up the garden path, through the overgrown grasses and the red tulips growing wild among them, and she pauses on the doorstep, running through her head what she will need for the cake. Black honey, flour, eggs, walnuts, sour cream.

"An-ge-la," she calls.

Kolya coughs, and scratches his stubble with his fingernails. He watches her go into the house, and then he stands slowly from the bench and picks up his hammer and nails.

"One kiss," he growls. "One kiss and I have to repair her whole house."

He glances once more towards the kitchen, where he can see Lyuda's shape moving beyond the frame of the yellow curtains. The sun is lighting on her fair hair, and he can see that she is speaking, or singing, or calling to her daughter.

He nods, thinking of her mother Zoryana, who he remembers through the same window, wearing a blue dress, and of his mother and Zoryana's mother, who were friends, laughing over the fence as he and Zoryana played in the flowerbeds, and their grandmothers, bright eyed and watchful, sitting in their gardens amidst a chaos of goats and hens and geese and rabbits and flowers and vegetables and grandchildren and singing birds.

He nods again.

"That's how it is meant to be," he says to himself, and then he turns back to the bench, the hammer and the nails in his hands, and sets to work.

I come dancing into the kitchen when Mother calls me.

"Angela, I am making a cake," she says to me. "Can you run to the market? We need some more walnuts."

She is standing by the window; behind her are the yellow curtains we have put up together. Behind her is the green, green garden, and there is the banging of a hammer, and the birds are singing. Soon, the new birds will be born. Perhaps I will find another broken egg in the grass for my treasure chest.

"Yes, Mama," I say. "Yes, I'll go now."

I skip up to her and I stand on my tiptoes and I kiss her cheek, and she winds her fingers lightly around my hair, and she says, "We need to do you a new plait *zayinka*, little rabbit. This one is coming undone."

"When I get back," I say, and I skip out of the kitchen and into the garden. A bird is singing there, and I catch the thread of its song and I release myself into it. I shift the girl into a quiet background and enter the breath of music, which carries me into the bird. We are flying to the market, to find morsels of dried fruit and small nuts to carry back to the nest. The air is warm and easy and there are insects everywhere to peck, to eat, and my nest is filled with speckled blue-and-white eggs and soon there will be gasping, open mouths to feed, and we will need to make them fat and strong so that their young wings will carry them far and fast from predators, to seek food, to discover the winds and lands around this garden that is our home.

I fly, my wings flapping fast above the village, and I know I won't be able to do this forever. But for now, I move with the spirit of everything around me. I can feel it closing, the door. I can feel the pull of the single stream. The pull of one single thread of thought. The door will close, and I will be decided. I will be a girl, a single spirit, a single thread of silk in the rope. And my life will weave onwards and onwards, weaving with the choices of my mother and my grandmother, and for the daughter who will come and the granddaughter, and the flow of the river onwards, onwards, towards the dreamer, towards the place where all imagination starts, towards the place where we all began.

Below me is the village. Below me, the people, the teachers, the labourers, the lovers, the children, the wives and the husbands. The heartbroken and the enamoured. And I hope that there will be someone there for Mother. Someone to lift her up into the years ahead. Someone to walk with her through the silver birch glade and dance with her on the bank of the river, as the accordions and the violins of the village drift towards them on the summer breeze.

But for these last days, these precious last hours and moments, I will be everyone. My most beloved bird, the late-spring flowers in the garden, the breath of wind carrying the pollen to its lovers, the slender strand of grass pushing upwards, upwards from the rich black soil.

And I find that I have flown past the market, over the glade of silver birch trees, and have come to the willowbank, with the wide, sleepy river and the willows trailing their branches into its moving waters. It is quiet here, now that Grandmother has gone, but I like to fly across the river, to sit in her tree, to remember her stories, to see the wind moving in patterns above the river, the dance of the leaves to the singing water, the birds dipping and laughing, and the intense peace of the tree itself, in its ancient constancy, and its rebirth second by second, in every green leaf, in every bud, in every breath of sunshine.

And now, something is calling me. My mate in the nest, asking for food. The garden, asking for my spirit to flow through it. My mother in the kitchen, looking for me to run laughing through the kitchen doorway, and into her arms.

I fly.

With heartfelt thanks to

John Uff and Diana Uff for support in every possible way, including reading, re-reading and many kind words; Katja Rusanen and Maite Valdivia for sharing the journey of becoming a writer, and the journey onwards; Timothy Gilbert for superb carpentry in the Barcelona flat and for being a great friend; Vitaly Butenko for friendship, partnership and extraordinary life experiences; Father Yuvenaly for taking me around western Ukraine and answering hours of questions; Hunter Tremayne for believing in an early draft of the novel and surviving a heart attack while giving me feedback on it; Leslie Gardner for taking a risk on a new writer; Rebecca Coles for superb advice on the title; Dan Coles for hours of dedicated reading, editing and support, and for bringing the joy which completed this novel; Valentina and Robert for being extraordinary in every way and for teaching me far more than I could ever teach you.

A special thank you to Clarissa Pinkola Estés: the wolves are in your honour.

For helping to shape this novel, thank you to Anna Green for a beautiful cover; to Andrew Lowe for thoughtful and precise editing; to Anna Hogarty for faultless proofreading; to Nicky Lovick for structural advice; to Leila Dewji and Ali Dewji for a superb service, professionalism and expertise.

And last, and always, always first, to Francesca Hector: the friend who knows the song in my heart and sings it back to me when I have forgotten the words.

Thank you.

LEONORA MERIEL

The Unity Game

Can a love born in space survive in the chaos of Earth?

A rich man is losing his sanity.

An extraterrestrial risks its life in search of love.

A dead man must unlock the secrets of an unknown dimension to bring them together and save humanity.

The Unity Game tells an epic story of redemption and rebirth in a universe more ingenious and surprising than you ever thought possible.

What begins with a New York banker's descent into terror and madness soon becomes a sprawling race through and against time itself.

Until he can piece together a hidden world, his happiness will remain, tantalizingly, just beyond his grasp.

Metaphysical thriller and interstellar mystery, *The Unity Game* is a spellbinding tale from an exciting and original new voice in fiction.

GRANITE CLOUD

CPSIA information can be obtained
at www.ICGtesting.com
Printed in the USA
BVHW031920110919
558186BV00001B/138/P